I0746060

BOOKS BY TINA FOLSOM

Ace on the Run (Code Name Stargate, Book 1)

Fox in plain Sight (Code Name Stargate, Book 2)

Yankee in the Wind (Code Name Stargate, Book 3)

Tiger on the Prowl (Code Name Stargate, Book 4)

Samson's Lovely Mortal (Scanguards Vampires, Book 1)

Amaury's Hellion (Scanguards Vampires, Book 2)

Gabriel's Mate (Scanguards Vampires, Book 3)

Yvette's Haven (Scanguards Vampires, Book 4)

Zane's Redemption (Scanguards Vampires, Book 5)

Quinn's Undying Rose (Scanguards Vampires, Book 6)

Oliver's Hunger (Scanguards Vampires, Book 7)

Thomas's Choice (Scanguards Vampires, Book 8)

Silent Bite (Scanguards Vampires, Book 8 1/2)

Cain's Identity (Scanguards Vampires, Book 9)

Luther's Return (Scanguards Vampires, Book 10)

Blake's Pursuit (Scanguards Vampires, Book 11)

Fateful Reunion (Scanguards Vampires, Book 11 1/2)

John's Yearning (Scanguards Vampires, Book 12)

Ryder's Storm (Scanguards Vampires, Book 13)

Damian's Conquest (Scanguards Vampires, Book 14)

Grayson's Challenge (Scanguards Vampires, Book 15)

Lover Uncloaked (Stealth Guardians, Book 1)

Master Unchained (Stealth Guardians, Book 2)

Warrior Unraveled (Stealth Guardians, Book 3)

Guardian Undone (Stealth Guardians, Book 4)

Immortal Unveiled (Stealth Guardians, Book 5)

Protector Unmatched (Stealth Guardians, Book 6)

Demon Unleashed (Stealth Guardians, Book 7)

A Touch of Greek (Out of Olympus, Book 1)

A Scent of Greek (Out of Olympus, Book 2)

A Taste of Greek (Out of Olympus, Book 3)

A Hush of Greek (Out of Olympus, Book 4)

Venice Vampyr (Novellas 1 – 4)

Teasing (The Hamptons Bachelor Club, Book 1)

Enticing (The Hamptons Bachelor Club, Book 2)

Beguiling (The Hamptons Bachelor Club, Book 3)

Scorching (The Hamptons Bachelor Club, Book 4)

Alluring (The Hamptons Bachelor Club, Book 5)

Sizzling (The Hamptons Bachelor Club, Book 6)

PROTECTOR UNMATCHED

STEALTH GUARDIANS #6

TINA FOLSOM

1

"You'll be murdered!"

At the words, Pearce spun around, hair dripping wet, feet bare, and nearly dropped the towel he'd been about to remove from where it covered his naked skin from waist to knees. He held the damp towel in place and stared at the intruder.

It was an unwritten rule at the compound that nobody entered a warrior's private quarters without invitation. In the many years that he'd lived in Baltimore, nobody had ever violated his privacy. Even though there were locks on the doors, nobody ever used them. What would have been the point? A Stealth Guardian could walk through walls and doors as if walking through air, thus rendering locks useless. However, the human wives of his compound comrades were another matter—they didn't possess the abilities of their preternatural husbands. Same went for the female psychic in their midst. Although she had supernatural skills, walking through walls wasn't one of them. Hence she'd simply opened the door—without invitation and, apparently, without knocking first.

"What the fuck, Winter?" he growled at her.

Brushing away the reprimand as if she didn't care, Winter

approached. "Didn't you hear me, Pearce? You're going to get stabbed!"

"Yeah, I believe it. Just as soon as Logan finds you in my quarters!"

Winter's mate, his fellow Stealth Guardian Logan, was a fiercely possessive man and skilled with his deathly dagger. If he found Winter in Pearce's rooms, wearing a bathrobe over her flimsy nightgown, with Pearce half-naked to top it all off, there'd be hell to pay. At best, Logan would beat the crap out of him; at worst, he'd use his dagger, a weapon that could kill even an immortal, to inflict real damage.

"Are you out of your fucking mind, coming here? What if Logan finds you in my rooms?"

She made a dismissive hand movement. "Don't get your knickers in a twist. He's in the shower."

"Yeah, so was I," Pearce said dryly, making a corresponding motion with his free hand, the one not currently clutching the towel. "And now, I'd like to get dressed." He pointed to the door. "Without an audience."

"You don't understand," Winter continued, her voice laden with frustration. "It's not Logan who's gonna kill you, but Daphne."

Water dripped into Pearce's eyes, and he wiped his hand over his face and brushed his wet hair, which was in need of a trim, back. "Who the fuck is Daphne?"

"The woman who killed you in my vision."

"You had a vision about me?"

She let herself fall onto the couch and sighed. "Finally, you're getting it. If you're that slow on the uptake, no wonder you're gonna get killed."

Pearce rolled his eyes. "You could have led with this."

"With what?"

"The fact that you had a vision. And with knocking first."

"Well, sorry for being concerned, but my visions are never wrong." She rose with a huff. "But if you'd rather run into danger without being prepared, be my guest." She headed for the door.

"I'm sorry, Winter. Don't go."

At the door, she hesitated, then turned slowly. "So, you believe me now?"

"I never said I didn't believe you. I just wasn't pleased about your mode of delivery. It's not every day that a man finds out he's gonna be murdered."

"Stabbed by a Stealth Guardian dagger, to be exact," she said. "By a woman!"

"A female demon," Pearce corrected her.

Winter shook her head, though the motion was hesitant. "I don't think so. I can't say for sure, but I think she was human."

"What makes you think that?"

"She had an injured arm. The wound was bleeding. Red."

"No green blood? You sure about that?" There were two ways of recognizing a demon. One was their green blood. "And her eyes? Were they green?"

"I couldn't tell the color, but they didn't glow poison-green like I've seen in other demons."

And Winter had encountered demons, more than she'd ever wanted to. Luckily, she'd survived the ordeal. If any non-Stealth Guardian could recognize a demon's green eyes, then it was Winter.

Pearce contemplated Winter's words for a moment. "She could have worn colored contact lenses."

"Could have, but that still leaves the bleeding arm."

"Hmm." The risk to be eventually killed by a demon came with the territory of being a Stealth Guardian warrior. But being killed by a human? "How do you know her name?"

"You called her Daphne, before she stabbed you in the chest. You knew her."

Pearce shook his head. "That's impossible. I don't know anybody named Daphne."

"You did in my vision."

He searched his memory, but he was certain that he knew no woman named Daphne. "What else? Where will it happen?"

Winter looked as if she was about to shrug, but then thought better of it and raised her head as if suddenly remembering something. "Actually, it was weird. It looked like a backstage area of a theater or a movie stage—you know, where they film TV shows. It looked like a set for some sort of medieval show or play."

"A film studio?"

"Yes, or a theater."

"Tell me more about the woman," Pearce demanded.

"Not sure what to tell you about her."

"Age, hair color, size, ugly or pretty, thin or fat, you know."

Winter looked into the distance as if to recall the image. "She was maybe in her thirties, but then, I find it hard to guess women's ages. Let's just say she was over twenty-five and probably under forty. Nice looking, not skinny, but muscular."

"Butch?"

Winter rolled her eyes. "Men! No, not butch; she just looked like she took care of herself, like she works out and eats right. She was pretty, too. Long black hair. Kinda cute."

"Oh great!" Pearce said with a good dose of sarcasm. "Not only will I be killed by a human woman, but by a cute one. That'll make it all right. Wouldn't wanna go to my death staring at the face of an ugly woman." He sighed. "Sorry, go on. What else do you remember?"

"She wore strange clothes."

"What?"

"Actually, more like a costume. You know, like a female superhero."

"That makes no sense."

Winter shrugged. "You weren't dressed any less strange. You wore some sort of medieval uniform. You know, as if you were both dressing up for a Halloween party."

Pearce shook his head. "I don't go to Halloween parties. Anything else you noticed?"

"One thing was really weird." She hesitated.

"What?"

"You didn't fight back."

"Excuse me?"

"When she stabbed you, you just stared at her as if you wanted her to do it." Winter let out a nervous chuckle. "Maybe I just imagined that. But your expression, the way you looked at her... It was odd. You didn't look like you were angry at her or saw her as an enemy. Almost as if you trusted her."

"That makes no sense."

"Maybe it does," Winter said. "She could be some sort of Mata Hari who's putting the moves on you, seduces you, and then betrays you."

"Oh, please! As if I'm stupid enough not to recognize when a woman tries to use me. I'd never fall for that. Besides, I don't even know anybody named Daphne."

"Which is a good thing, because it means you can still change the future."

He nodded. "You're right. I have to eliminate the threat."

Winter swallowed hard. "Eliminate? That's not why I told you about the vision. I don't mean for anybody to get hurt."

"Winter, you should have learned by now that somebody is always gonna get hurt." And a threat had to be eliminated before it was too late. "Better my would-be killer than me."

"So what are you gonna do?"

"I need to figure out who she is." And he had an idea how to accomplish that task. "Would you recognize her if you saw a photo of her?"

Winter furrowed her forehead. "But you just said you don't know anybody named Daphne. And now you have photos?"

"I don't, but the DMV does."

"There must be thousands of Daphnes in all the DMV databases in the U.S."

"We'll start with Maryland. There can't be that many. It's not a very popular name. And we have parameters to limit the search: a female with black hair aged between twenty-five and forty."

"I wouldn't limit the search to black hair only. What if she dyed her hair?"

"Good point. Still, there can't be that many women named Daphne. Meet me in the command center once Logan has left for his assignment. I'll run the search in the meantime, and then we'll go through the photos."

Winter nodded. "Fine."

As she turned to the door, Pearce said, "And Winter..."

She looked over her shoulder. "Yes?"

"Not a word to the others about your vision. Not even to Logan. I don't want anybody to know before I can figure out what we're dealing with here. Agreed?"

"For now, fine. But once we know who she is and why she wants to kill you, we need to talk to the others."

"One step at a time," he said, and watched Winter leave his quarters.

Once he knew who this woman was, he'd do what needed to be done.

2

———

It was midmorning when Winter finally entered the command center, where Pearce sat in front of a bank of computers.

"What took you so long?" He didn't want to sound accusatory, but he was impatient. It didn't happen every day that he found out he was going to get murdered. He looked over his shoulder.

"Sorry," Winter said, lowering her lashes as she approached.

Pearce stared at the golden shimmer that covered her face. In fact, even her neck and every part of skin that was exposed exhibited the same sheen. In disbelief, he shook his head. "You've got to be kidding me."

Winter sat down in the chair next to him, but didn't look at him directly. "What?"

"Oh, please."

Finally, she met his gaze. "What was I supposed to do? Logan got a call that his meeting was delayed a couple of hours. So, he was free."

"Sure he was," Pearce said dryly. Free to make love to his wife the Stealth Guardian way, pouring his *virta*, his life force, into her to heighten her arousal, giving her an orgasm every time he touched her. And as long as his virta coursed through her veins, she would shimmer golden. With four of the warriors at his compound now bonded,

Pearce thought he'd gotten used to seeing their women walk around with the telltale golden shimmer every so often. But for some reason, it still jolted him. After leaving his parents' home and moving into a compound, surrounded by single men and one Stealth Guardian female, he didn't have to deal much with that particular sight.

"If I'd said no, Logan would have known that something was up."

Pearce rolled his eyes. "Yeah, sure, that was the reason you let him drag you back to bed." He sighed. "That man of yours is insatiable."

Winter smiled. "He is."

Clearly, his admonishment went right over her head. Lost cause!

"Well, you're here now." He pulled up a window he'd been working on earlier and directed Winter's gaze to it. "I've already narrowed the search down."

"Wait. What did you do?"

"I went into the census. Since 1880, more than thirty thousand girls were named Daphne in the United States. The name was most popular in 1962." He glanced at Winter. "There were over eleven hundred babies named Daphne that year. But any Daphne born back then would be too old now. You said she was maybe in her late twenties, early thirties?"

"Yes, but I'm horrible at guessing another woman's age, so you'd better do a wider search. Maybe from twenty to forty, just to be safe."

"Okay, no problem." He switched to another window that showed the MVA—the Maryland Department of Transportation Motor Vehicle Administration—database. He'd hacked into it earlier and left himself a backdoor to easily get back in. He started typing in his search criteria. "Let's see: female, age twenty to forty, first name Daphne." He hit the enter button and watched a little wheel spinning.

"There shouldn't be too many, right?" Winter asked. "Even if there were a thousand Daphnes born each year for twenty years across the U.S., they can't all live in Maryland. I mean, it's a small state."

"True. But we can't be certain that she's from Maryland, or that she has a driver's license here. If there are no viable hits here, we'll have to go through the neighboring states' DMV databases. But let's cross that bridge when we get to it." There was no need worrying about something that might not be an issue.

Ding!

The computer chime indicated that the search was done.

"Fifty-four records," Pearce read. "You said she had black hair. We could narrow the search further." He was about to type something when Winter stopped him.

"I wouldn't do that. It could be dyed, and her DMV record could show a different color."

"Good point. Then let's go through the records." He turned the screen a little so that Winter had a better view of it. "Can you see?"

"Yes. Let's do it."

Slowly, Pearce pulled up the driver's licenses of the women in the search results. The first woman was black.

"Eliminate all black women," Winter said immediately. "She was definitely white."

"Okay."

The next photo showed a white woman. Winter leaned in closer. "No, she was way prettier. And her face wasn't round. Next."

With every photo, she made other comments that eliminated woman after woman. The possibilities dwindled fast.

"Wait," Winter suddenly said, and pointed to a photo. "This one looks a little like her, but her hair is all wrong. Can you save that one and we look at her again?"

Pearce nodded and pasted the woman's record into a separate folder. "Done."

Five records further and Winter stopped him again. "She looks familiar. But the hair is too short. It makes her face look so different. But if her hair were longer, it could be her."

"Okay, I'll put her in the saved pile."

They had only ten more records to go through. Several of those belonged to African American women, one to an Asian woman, and one to a woman who had a kiwi-sized birthmark on one cheek.

"Nope," Winter said.

The rest looked nothing like the woman Winter had seen in her vision.

"Okay, back to the two we saved," Pearce suggested, and opened the file, then placed the two driver's licenses side by side.

"Hmm." Winter tilted her head. "Both have some of the same features as the woman in my vision. Shape of the face, nose, chin—all of it looks very familiar. Of course, they both look a little younger, too. And the hair is tripping me up. Neither one has the same hair as the Daphne I saw. And it's so hard to imagine what they would look like with long black hair. It could be either one of them. Sorry."

Pearce nodded. "No worries. The photos were probably taken about ten years ago. We'll just have to go and visit them both to see what they look like now." He checked the driver's licenses again. "Let me run a couple of additional searches on these two to see where they work and whether they still live at the address on the license. Then we'll head out."

"We?"

He turned his head to meet Winter's surprised look. "Of course *we*. You're the only one who's seen the woman. You're the only one who can identify her."

"Can't you just go and take a picture of the two and then come back and show me?"

"It'll be easier to identify the woman if you see her up close. A picture can distort things. It's not as reliable. And we need to be sure." Because if this woman really wanted to kill him, then he might have to take drastic steps and eliminate her before she could do him any harm.

"But Logan doesn't like it when I leave the compound," she said.

"He's never gonna find out."

"Famous last words."

Pearce shrugged. "You'll be invisible the entire time." And not just because in her current state—shimmering golden—she couldn't be seen in public. The demons were still after her for her psychic gift. If Winter ever fell into their hands, they would have a tool with which to destroy the Stealth Guardians.

"Come on," he said, "don't tell me you don't get cabin fever, being cooped up here day in day out."

"Fine. I'll go with you."

It took only a few minutes to research the two Daphnes and find out where they worked. It took another twenty minutes to leave the compound invisibly and make their way to the workplace of the first Daphne. It was a preschool.

Pearce felt his heart pound harder when they entered the small building in which the preschool was located. Would he meet his would-be killer here, where wee toddlers and kids up to five years of age were playing without worry, without a care in the world? Was the woman who was going to kill him masquerading as a preschool teacher?

Pearce held Winter's arm and led her down the short corridor, reading the signs next to the doors. Though nobody was in the corridor, he didn't speak and instead pointed to one of the doors, directing Winter there. On a sign it said, *Miss Daphne Atherton's class.* A window in the door allowed them to look into the room.

He saw movement behind the door and several kids running around a woman who was handing out sugary treats. He stepped aside to give Winter sufficient space to look into the room, while he watched the corridor to make sure that nobody surprised them.

It took less than thirty seconds for Winter to turn away from the window in the door and shake her head, mouthing, "No."

He understood and nodded. Silently they left the building. Outside, still invisible, he asked, "Are you sure?"

"One hundred percent."

"Okay, let's check out the other Daphne."

3

———

A latte in one hand, a large messenger bag slung across her body, Daphne fished out her ID card from her jacket pocket. To her dismay, the lanyard got tangled up with her cell phone, which she'd haphazardly stuffed into the same pocket, and pulled it out. It dropped on the stone floor before she could catch it.

"Crap," she cursed, while she heard the security guard snicker. She tossed him an annoyed look and picked up the phone, careful not to spill the hot beverage. Inspecting the screen, she was pleased to see that the shatterproof casing had done its job. Nevertheless, she couldn't resist reacting to the security guard's snickering. "This wouldn't happen if you didn't make me show my ID every day. For God's sake, Gus, you know who I am!"

Gus stood next to his desk and shoved his beer belly in her direction. "Company policy. You know it. No exceptions. Not even for you, Daphne."

"I really don't know why that's necessary. I've been working here for six months."

"True, but what if you got fired from one day to the next, and I don't get the memo right away? Can't let anybody unauthorized enter.

Cyber security starts at home." He pointed to the card reader next to him.

Grumbling a curse underneath her breath, she tapped her card. A green light blinked.

"See," Gus said smugly, "now I know you haven't gotten fired yet. Was that so hard?"

"You have a nice day, too," she said, infusing her tone with a good dose of sarcasm. She dropped her messenger bag into a tray and shoved it through the scanner, where a second security guard inspected the contents via a computer screen.

"Try not to get fired today," Gus called after her as she marched through the metal detector. "I would miss our little chats in the mornings."

Behind the scanner, Daphne grabbed her bag again, then waited in front of the elevator doors until they opened with a ding. She cast a look back at Gus, but he wasn't looking in her direction. She liked the clean-shaven fifty-something man, but she didn't like rules. However, suddenly working in the corporate world meant she had to play by them now, whether she felt stifled by them or not.

In a way, she'd been lucky. Had her criminal defense attorney not struck a deal with Cyberhack, an international cyber security company, who regularly employed ex-hackers as a means to combat cybercrime, she would have done time in prison for hacking. To her surprise, the judge in her case had been lenient, and she'd gotten away with probation only. Part of the plea agreement had been a three-year employment contract with Cyberhack. And she had to keep her nose clean. The only hacking she was allowed to perform was in the service of the company to test their own software.

It was a good job, it paid decently—better than the laundry shop in prison, anyway—and she had relatively flexible hours. As long as she performed the tasks her boss assigned every day, she could set her own hours. But, of course, there were rules. She wasn't allowed to consort with any of the other ex-hackers the company employed. She followed that edict, not because it was a company rule, but because she wasn't interested in hanging out with them anyway.

She was done with that part of her life. She'd spent enough years in crappy apartments smelling of cold pizza and flat soft drinks, shacked up with like-minded hackers wanting to disrupt government, to change the world, to wake up people to the problems the world was facing. And where had it gotten her? Into court. And nearly into prison. She was out. Done. From now on, she would be on the straight and narrow. Follow the rules. Operate within the law.

The elevator doors opened on the fifth floor. Daphne got out and took a quick gulp of her latte, then walked down the corridor to her cubicle. Over half the cubicles were occupied with other cyber security specialists typing away feverishly. Others would arrive whenever they rolled out of bed. Daphne preferred not to arrive past ten o'clock, since she liked having her evenings to herself rather than stay late. However, this morning she'd overslept.

The neighborhood the office was located in wasn't exactly the best, and once night fell, questionable characters loitered in the dark alleys around the building. She made a point of leaving work while the sidewalks were still teeming with other workers. No need taking a chance with her life. Even though she was a criminal, she'd never committed a violent crime, and she certainly didn't want to be a victim of one. Since she was on probation, she carried no weapon to defend herself against the hoodlums that crawled out of their hiding places at night.

Daphne set her latte on the desk in her cramped cubicle, met the glances of several of her colleagues with a quick nod, then dropped her bag on the floor, plopped into her chair, and switched on the computer. While the machine powered up, she dug into her bag and pulled her noise-cancelling headphones from her messenger bag. At least she could listen to music during work, which helped her concentrate.

Once she was logged in, she quickly reviewed the work assignment her boss had sent to her screen. She shrugged to herself. If her boss knew that the tasks he gave her to work on would barely take her half a day, he would surely double her workload. But she never let on that she was capable of so much more. After all, why should she be punished for working faster and more efficiently than the other employees?

Daphne was about to put her headphones on when her cell phone vibrated in her pocket. She quickly lifted herself a few inches out of her chair to be able to see her boss's glass-enclosed office. He frowned on employees taking calls on their cell phones, but luckily, he was engrossed in a conversation with another employee. Letting herself fall back in her chair, she reached for her phone and looked at the display.

"Fuck," she cursed under her breath. Seeing her brother's name show up on the display was giving her instant heartburn. She contemplated ignoring the call, but she knew he would keep calling and texting until she replied.

"What do you want?" she answered in a hushed voice, using her hand to shield her mouth so her voice wouldn't carry across the office.

"Listen carefully."

The command jolted her involuntarily. The voice wasn't her brother's. And it sounded muffled, as if somebody was speaking through a layer of clothing.

"Who the fuck are you?"

"My name isn't important."

"So you stole his phone, asshole." It didn't surprise her. After all, the kind of people her brother hung around with had a disregard for other people's property.

"Borrowed it," the man snapped. "But you listen to me now—"

"Put my brother on!"

"He can't talk right now. He's a little tied up." Daphne could make out a chuckle in the background.

Great! So her brother had gotten drunk, and his idiot friends were playing a prank. She had no time for their games.

"You know what? Tell my brother to grow up!" She stabbed the end call button and tossed her phone on a stack of papers. "Jerks!"

Her cubicle neighbor, Neil, a geek with John Lennon glasses and a goatee, popped his head over the cubicle wall. "Problem?"

She tossed him a glance and rolled her eyes. "Family."

He grimaced. "Yep, best to ignore them. That's what I do."

"My plan exactly," she agreed, and watched him dip down again. A moment later, she heard him tapping away on his keyboard.

Ready to work, Daphne opened a new window on her screen, but before the program could even fully load, a chime on her phone alerted her to a text message. She reached for it and looked at the display. A message from her brother. Big surprise. Clearly, he was pissed that she hadn't played along with his little game. Reluctantly, she read the message.

Don't dare ignore me or your brother dies.

The message jolted her for a second. Was the guy serious? While she was still contemplating how to react and whether to respond, another message arrived.

Watch the video.

What video?

Ding! Another message, this time a video attachment.

"I'm gonna kill you myself, Tim, if you're sending me porn," she murmured to herself. Okay, she would watch the damn video, and then she'd read him the riot act. But just to be on the safe side, she slipped on her headphones and plugged the jack into her phone so nobody in the office could overhear her.

With a sigh, she tapped on the video to play it back.

At first, she wasn't sure what she was looking at. It was dark, a basement of some sort. Then a light beam was redirected to a spot in the middle of the video, and then she saw him: Tim, her twenty-seven-year-old brother. She almost didn't recognize him. His hair was disheveled, his shirt ripped, and bloodstains were visible both on his chest and around his nose and mouth. One eye looked swollen. His arms appeared to be tied behind his back.

Daphne suppressed a gasp. Oh God, what was going on?

Suddenly, Tim stared right into the camera.

"Daphne, you've gotta help me. I'm in trouble. I owe them a lot of money. Please, help me. Or they're gonna hurt me."

By the looks of it, they'd already done so.

The video suddenly ended. Horrified, she sat there frozen in place. She couldn't even blink. She'd always known about her brother's gambling problem and his inability to handle money responsibly, but she hadn't known that he'd gotten in that deep.

Shit!

The phone chimed again. Another message.

Ready to talk now?

She had no choice but to reply.

Yes.

A second later, the phone vibrated. She was receiving another call from her brother's number. She accepted the call, kept the headphone on, and spoke into the attached microphone, keeping her voice as low as possible so her cubicle neighbor couldn't hear her.

"If you hurt him—"

"Shut up!" the man interrupted her. "I'm the one talking now. Glad we were able to get your attention. Next time, don't hang up on me, or you might just piss me off." He grunted something unintelligible.

"Who are you?"

"You can call me Guido." He chuckled to himself.

Daphne didn't find it funny. "What do you want?"

"Your brother owes us money. Lots of it. He begged us not to hurt him and claims you'll help him pay off his debt to us."

"I don't have any money." Her brother knew she was living from paycheck to paycheck.

"We're aware of that. That's why you can do us a favor."

"A favor?" She couldn't imagine what kind of favor she could possibly do for this thug to get her brother out of trouble. But she didn't dare voice her skepticism.

"He says you have skills."

She swallowed hard. She didn't have to be a genius to know what he was referring to. It figured that her brother had started singing like a bird at the slightest bit of physical pain.

"I don't know what you're talking about," she lied.

"Now, now, Daphne. You don't mind if I call you Daphne, do you?" He didn't wait for an answer. "We know all about your past. The hacking, the arrest."

She cursed under her breath.

"Don't worry. Your secret is safe with us."

"It's not a secret."

But Guido, or whatever his name was, continued undeterred. "So you're gonna do a little job for us. Get us around a little security system, retrieve something, you know, that kind of job. And once we've got what we want, your brother's debt to us is wiped out, and he's free to leave."

Fuck, they wanted her to help them rob a place? A bank, most likely? "No way." If she got involved in anything like that and something went wrong, the plea deal was off, and she'd be going to jail for a very long time.

"You've got no choice."

No, she couldn't do it. It would ruin her life. There had to be another way.

"Do it, or we'll start sending you body parts in the mail."

They were bluffing. Tim couldn't have gotten involved with the kind of people who really made good on threats like that. During her time as a hacker, she'd seen enough bluffs and called them out. She'd rarely been wrong.

"You're not gonna do it," she said. "Because if you do, neither my brother nor I will ever pay you what he owes."

"You think I'm bluffing?"

Her heart beat into her throat. "Let him go. Now. He'll pay you back. We'll work something out."

"That's not how this works."

"Let him go," she demanded again.

"You don't give the orders here, lady." Then his voice became more distant, and she realized he wasn't talking to her anymore. "Looks like your sister doesn't wanna play ball. What finger should we start with?" Suddenly, loud screams she recognized as her brother's sounded in the background. Then the call was disconnected.

Her heart beating like a jackhammer, Daphne stared at her phone. What now? She had to call him back, try to reason with him. Seconds ticked by. Maybe she could pretend to go along with the plan, then speak to her probation officer and explain the situation. Then the police could set up a sting and they could save her brother from these mafiosos. Yes, that was what she would do.

With trembling fingers, she navigated to her brother's number, but before she could call, another message arrived.

A photo.

She dreaded having to look at it, but she knew she had to.

The photo depicted a bloody finger. A finger that had been severed from a hand.

Her stomach churned, and she nearly lost the little breakfast she'd had this morning. Guido had made his point. He was serious.

Her fingers trembling worse than before, she typed a short message and sent it: *I'll do it.*

Guido's message came almost immediately. *We'll be in touch with details soon. We'll be watching you. So don't be stupid. For your brother's sake.*

She knew what that meant. She couldn't involve the police.

                                4
                            ____

"Stay as close to me as possible when we're inside," Pearce urged Winter while they were approaching the building he'd identified as the workplace of Daphne Butler, the second Daphne on their short list of possible would-be killers.

Winter nodded. She knew the drill. To be on the safe side, Pearce now took her by the arm so that even if he lost his mental concentration, his touch would assure that Winter remained invisible. Because if anything happened to her on this extracurricular excursion, Logan would have his hide.

At the glass entrance door, which was closed, they had to wait a few moments until somebody opened it and entered and they could slip inside behind that person. Had Pearce been alone, he could have walked through the glass, but for Winter it was impossible. Only Stealth Guardians had the ability to dematerialize their bodies in order to pass through solid objects.

Inside the large lobby, a security guard sat behind his desk. He rose to greet the visitor, a delivery guy with an envelope. While the security guard signed for it, Pearce ushered Winter past the desk. He spotted the elevators and took two more steps, then he suddenly realized where he was. But it was too late now.

He and Winter were already passing through the metal detector. Warning bells dinged, and red lights flashed above their heads, most likely set off by the ancient dagger Pearce kept hidden in one of his boots. Quickly Pearce pulled Winter along and steered her to the side, because the security guard who was sitting next to an airport-style hand luggage scanner was already jumping up.

"What the fuck?" he cursed, and ran toward the metal detector. "What's wrong with that damn thing now?"

The security guard who'd finished signing for the delivery stared at him. "Don't ask me. You're the tech guy."

While the two security guards tried to figure out why the alarm had sounded and how to reset the machine, Pearce pressed the button to call the elevator. While they waited, he perused the company directory on the wall next to the elevator. He found what he was looking for quickly.

When the elevator doors opened, he made sure the cab was empty, then nodded for Winter to enter. From the corner of his eye, he noticed one of the guards looking toward him.

"Why's the elevator suddenly opening?" the guard asked his colleague, tapping him on the shoulder.

Pearce entered and pressed the button for the fifth floor. Slowly, the doors began to close.

"We should call maintenance," he heard the second security guy suggest, before the doors closed fully and silence surrounded them.

"That was close," Winter said.

"No biggie." Nevertheless, he felt like a fool not having thought that his dagger, and probably also his cell phone, would set off the metal detector. He blamed his rude awakening this morning for his lapse in judgment. Surely, a man who'd just found out that a woman would kill him in the near future was allowed a mistake or two.

"So, all we're gonna do is get as close to her as we can. As soon as you get a good look at her and are sure it's the woman you saw in your vision, you'll give me the thumbs-up, and we're outta there. Got it?"

"Got it. Just don't rush me. I need to be sure it's her." She hesitated. "Are you gonna have to eliminate her?"

He drew in a breath. He hadn't expected Winter's blunt question.

"Well, are you?"

"If you're sure that she stabbed me with a Stealth Guardian dagger, then I have no choice." When a sad look passed over Winter's face, he added, "But not today. Not until we're one hundred percent sure. I promise I'll find a way to make it quick and painless."

The elevator doors opened on the fifth floor before Winter could answer.

Most of this floor appeared to be a large open-plan office with cubicle after cubicle. Several glass-enclosed offices lined one side, and a kitchenette as well as some office machinery and supply closets occupied another. It would have been hard to find the cubicle that Daphne Butler occupied had the entrances to each little office pod not been identified with nametags.

Daphne's cubicle was empty—however, it appeared that she couldn't be far. The computer was switched on—the monitor locked —and personal items were strewn on the desk. A coffee cup sat next to the telephone and a jacket hung over the chair. Pearce glanced around. Daphne's cubicle neighbor, a geeky guy with small, round glasses and facial hair, pecked away on his keyboard, oblivious to the world around him. Employees in the other cubicles did the same. Everybody kept their head down.

Winter tugged at the sleeve of his jacket, and Pearce turned his head to Winter. She mouthed, "There," and pointed to the door of the ladies' room that was just being closed by a young woman. A column prevented Pearce from getting a good look at her face, but he didn't have to wait long until she approached the cubicle where Pearce and Winter were hovering.

Her head was down, and she was wiping at a stain on her sweater, cursing something unintelligible. It appeared she'd spilled something on it, because the spot was wet. Her hair was totally different from how Winter had described it: it was short and black, but not like that of a tomboy. Rather, it looked like a haircut a French woman would sport. A pixie haircut. Trendy, light, sexy. Her figure was partially obscured by the baggy sweater she wore. However, her tight jeans couldn't disguise that she had long and slender legs, so Pearce assumed that her torso was similarly appealing.

When she reached her cubicle, the geek in the cubicle next to hers said, "Got it out?"

Startled, she lifted her head, for the first time affording both him and Winter a good look at her face.

"Think so," she said to her colleague.

Pearce froze and could only stare at her as she walked past him and entered the empty cubicle with the nametag *Daphne Butler* on the outside. Winter tugged at his sleeve again. She made a sign, pointing at Daphne, then nodding. It was her. This was the woman from Winter's vision, the woman who would kill him at some point in the future. He made a motion to Winter that he understood.

Swallowing hard, he looked at Daphne again. Winter had neglected to say that his would-be killer was a stunning beauty with startling green eyes. Not the kind of green a demon's eyes were, but the kind of green that was soothing and comforting, the kind that promised sensuality and passion. Together with her black pixie haircut and her flawless skin, she looked like a woman who should be on a movie poster, not toiling away in a software company. Or killing a Stealth Guardian.

Yes, he had to remind himself again that she would kill him one day. If Winter had seen it, it would happen. When? Nobody really knew. But Winter's visions had never been wrong.

He took a step closer, entering the cubicle when Daphne suddenly turned her head toward him as if she'd heard something, even though he'd been silent. That was when he saw it. Her eyes had a slight redness to them, and the skin around them looked puffy. That was why she'd been in the ladies' room: she'd cried.

When Daphne turned back to her computer and unlocked the screen, he turned around to Winter and took her arm. They had to leave. There was nothing he could do here, even if he wanted to eliminate her right now. And suddenly he wasn't so sure anymore that he wanted to. How could he snuff out the life of a woman who seemed so vulnerable? How could he be sure that she was even capable of killing him? The residue of her tears pointed to a woman with deep emotions, with compassion, with love. How could he simply take that away from the world?

On the way out, Pearce circumvented the metal detector, not wanting to cause the two baffled security guards any more problems. When he and Winter were in a deserted alley a few blocks away, he stopped.

"Are you sure she was the woman from your vision? The woman that will kill me?"

"I'm sure. Even though her hair is different, it's her face. Everything fits. Maybe she's letting her hair grow out, and what I've seen won't happen for a while. Or maybe she wore a wig in my vision. After all, she was dressed up as if she was going to a costume party. Now what?"

"I don't know yet." He shoved a hand through his hair, contemplating his options.

"We could call a meeting, speak to the others. I'm sure they'll help you figure out how to proceed," she suggested.

"No." He resented the implication that he needed help. "I'll handle this myself." How, he wasn't sure yet. "I'll take you back. But you have to promise me to say nothing to the others, nothing about the vision, and nothing about our little excursion. Not even to Logan."

"I can't promise that. Not until you tell me what you're planning." She braced her hands at her hips. He'd always known that redheads had the reputation of being stubborn, and it appeared that this redhead had a double dose of it.

"Stay out of my business, Winter."

"It's my business too." She stabbed her finger into his chest. "My vision, my responsibility."

"I absolve you of that responsibility."

"Pff!" She made an unladylike gesture. "Fuck that."

"You kiss Logan with that mouth?"

"Don't change the subject. You're gonna tell me right here and right now what you're planning." She narrowed her eyes.

He huffed. "You wanna know what I'm planning? I have no fucking clue. Okay?" He pointed in the direction where Daphne's office building was located. "You're telling me you saw this woman stab me to death. With a Stealth Guardian dagger. If I tell the others, they're gonna expect me to eliminate her, and if I don't do it, they will. Is that what you want? Do you want me to kill her so she won't kill me? Or do you want me to try to save her life?"

There was a long pause during which neither of them spoke. Then Winter put her hand on his forearm. "I'm sorry. I was only thinking of your safety. You're my family now. You and all the others at the compound. If something happened to you, and I didn't prevent it even though I could, I would never forgive myself." She sighed. "But killing a human... I know that's a hard decision. That's why I think it's best if you talk to the others."

"There has to be another way. The future isn't written yet." When he met Winter's eyes, he remembered something. "You remember the visions you had of your dying at the hands of the demons?"

She nodded.

"They never came to pass, because you changed the future when you met Logan. He saved you from your fate. Maybe I can do the same."

"But how?"

"By getting to know Daphne. By finding out what her reason for killing me could be."

Winter shook her head. "That's crazy. What if by getting to know her you're putting the event into motion? My vision was supposed to warn you so that you'd never meet her. And if you don't meet her and don't get to know her, she won't kill you. You just have to stay away from her. Maybe it's as simple as that."

"Your visions are rarely simple," he said. "And you know that they can change. They did when you met Logan. When he fell in love with you and risked his own life to save you from the demons, your future changed despite the vision. Please give me that same chance. To change the future."

Winter let out a long breath. "You know that Logan is gonna kill me when he finds out about the vision and that I didn't tell him or the others."

"Let Logan be my problem. Besides, he loves you too much to be mad at you for more than a minute."

"What you're trying to do is risky," she warned him. "And there's no guarantee that I'll have a second vision to apprise you of whether what you're doing will work and indeed change the future."

"Everything a Stealth Guardian does is risky. That's what we signed up for."

"As long as you know what you're doing."

Did he? It was best not to tell Winter about his doubts, or she would turn around and talk to Logan and his brethren. And he had doubts. Changing a future foretold by a vision was a monumental task. And he didn't even know where to start.

"Do you?" Winter suddenly asked.

"Do I what?"

"Know what you're doing."

"Of course," he said with a confidence he didn't possess.

5

The day seemed to have dragged on forever. When Daphne finally finished the tasks on her list and signed off the computer, it was already dark outside. She snatched her things and rode down in the elevator. The security guards had changed shifts, and in a way, she was glad that Gus wasn't on duty anymore. She wouldn't have been able to joke with him on her way out.

Shock still sat deep in her bones. Recalling the sight of the severed digit still made her nauseated and reminded her that she hadn't eaten anything all day. But she knew she had to get something into her stomach, if only to keep her strength up and be ready for when Guido —clearly not his real name—contacted her again to give her the details of what she needed to do to free her brother.

Assuming that Guido's henchman was watching her, she cast a look over her shoulder every so often as she hurried to a busier area where coffeeshops, fast food places, grocery stores, and small boutiques were open late. Even though she noticed nobody following her, she felt the hairs at the back of her neck rise and shivered. Would this be her life now until her brother was safe again, always looking over her shoulder, always worrying that she was being watched?

She hated this feeling. It was bad enough that she was on

probation and had to comply with way too many rules. But now? She was violating her probation just by keeping the fact that she was being blackmailed from her probation officer and the police. If anything went wrong, not only would her probation be revoked, her brother would die a horrible death. She shuddered at that thought.

She shook her head and tried to rid herself of the negative thoughts. There was nothing she could do until not-his-real-name-Guido contacted her again. She assumed they were watching her right now to make sure she kept her mouth shut before they revealed to her what part she would play in their criminal plan.

Frustrated, she stopped on the sidewalk and looked around. She had to eat something; maybe then her mind would be clearer again. Maybe then she would come up with a plan of her own. One that kept her clean in the eyes of the law and her brother away from bodily harm.

Not in the mood to go to a restaurant, she decided to enter the supermarket on the next corner to grab something simple that she could heat up in the privacy of her own apartment, and then eat in front of the TV to distract herself from her problems.

The store was busy with office workers who had the same idea as Daphne. Some of the aisles were so packed that shoppers bumped into each other and squeezed by far too close for comfort. At the freezer section, which was always filled with ready-made microwavable meals, she perused the selection. It had been picked over, and her choices were a vegetarian pasta dish, a chicken pot pie, or an Asian stir fry. She bent over the chest freezer when she spotted another option that was half hidden beneath a bag of French fries. She tried to reach it, but her messenger bag got caught on the lip of the chest freezer.

"Crap!" she said quietly. But having seen that the fourth option was beef stroganoff, one of her favorites, she wasn't going to give up. Swiftly, she put her messenger bag next to her feet and dove back into the freezer. Her fingers closed around the ready-made meal, and she pulled. It was wedged between the French fries and the lattice dividing the freezer into different sections. With her second hand, she reached for the bag of French fries, then finally was able to wedge the beef stroganoff free.

Triumphantly, her prize in her hand, she emerged from the freezer, then she suddenly felt something brush against her shin. Startled, she spun her head to it, but there was nothing. Only her messenger bag sitting next to her feet.

"Phew!"

She began to perspire. How stupid of her to have left her bag there at her feet where anybody could have just snatched it while she had her head deep in the freezer. Luckily, it was still here. She would be smarter next time.

There were four checkouts. She chose the one marked with a *Fifteen items or less* sign. Luckily, tonight people obeyed the rule, and the three ahead of her had no more than five items each. The line moved quickly until it was her turn. The cashier scanned the item and bagged it.

"Seven eighty-five, please. Cash or card?"

Daphne, already digging into her messenger bag, replied, "Cash." She searched for her wallet. "Sorry, just a moment." She opened the flap of the bag. It took her only seconds to realize that her wallet wasn't inside. Had she left it at the office? Or had somebody stolen it?

"My wallet. It was here earlier," she said to the cashier.

"You can't pay?" the cashier asked loudly, and she cringed, wanting to crawl into a hole.

Embarrassment flushed her cheeks.

"I'm sorry, but it should be here. I might have left it in the office."

"Mmm-hmm."

"You're holding up the line," a woman complained from farther behind her.

"I've got it," the man behind the impatient woman suddenly said. Daphne turned halfway and watched him hand the cashier a twenty and slide his own purchase toward hers. "Just put it on the same tab as mine."

"But you can't just—"

"It's no problem. I forget my wallet all the time," the man said while the cashier added his pre-packed sandwich to her purchase and calculated the change.

"But—"

"It's done," the cashier said with an exasperated look, and handed the man the change.

The stranger took it, then reached for the shopping bag and motioned toward the exit. "I think we're holding up traffic."

Still shell-shocked, Daphne took a few steps to clear the checkout area and stopped. Finally, she had a chance to really look at the guy. He was handsome. That was the first thing she noticed, and for a while, it was the only thing. A few seconds passed before she could really take everything else in. He was in his mid to late thirties, tall and muscular. His hair was short and not quite as dark as hers; his face sported a five-o'clock shadow, his teeth were white, and his nose straight. But the most striking thing were his eyes. Baby-blue, an unusual color for a man with dark hair, but it suited him.

However, he was a stranger, and she hated being indebted to anybody, particularly a stranger.

"I'm gonna pay you back," she blurted.

"That's really not necessary." He gave her a big smile, which made him look even more handsome. "I'm glad I could help out. Maybe one day you can do me a favor."

His last word triggered something in her. Of course! It was the same word Guido had used only hours earlier. This was all a setup. Guido had sent this guy to watch her. Why else would he be helping her out? Perhaps it was a test. If this guy pretended to be a hero and was trying to ingratiate himself, then maybe they were testing if she would confide in him once he'd gained her trust. Clearly, whatever Guido and his crooks were planning was a big deal, or they wouldn't go to such lengths to make sure she wasn't going to sing.

Fine—she could play that game too. If this guy was indeed Guido's henchman, then she would turn the tables on him. If she could get access to his cell phone or any other electronic device he carried, he wouldn't even know what was happening. And once she knew where they kept her brother and how many people were guarding him, she could contact her probation officer so he could get the police to extract her brother from right under their noses.

She smiled back at Guido's henchman. "I'm Daphne. And considering the cashier bagged our food together, why don't I buy you a beer to go with your sandwich?"

He raised an eyebrow. "I thought you had no money." He grinned. "Or was that just a ploy to test my chivalry?"

Wow, the guy was laying it on really thick! Way to use that charm and those baby-blues!

"I've got beer in the fridge." She knew it was a risky move to invite him back to her place, but she also knew that Guido needed her to do this job. His henchman wouldn't hurt her. If he did, he would jeopardize Guido's plan. "Unless you don't go home with strange women whose food you just paid for."

His mouth gaped open.

Good, he clearly hadn't expected her to be so direct. She'd thrown him off his game. If all of Guido's associates were that easy, her brother would be home safe in no time—albeit with a missing finger. However, maybe that would be a lesson to her brother never to get involved with the likes of Guido again.

The stranger finally seemed to find his voice again. "Uh, actually, I'd love a beer with that sandwich." He stretched out his hand. "My name is Pearce."

6

———

Standing in front of his bathroom mirror, Zoltan took colored contact lenses out of the box and slid them over his green eyes. Unfortunately, even the lenses he had an optician's lab custom-make for him—under the pretense of being allergic to all lenses other than the ones made of this special compound—dissolved after about twelve hours. The secretion of a demon's eyes burned through regular lenses even faster. Those lasted only a couple of hours tops, thus revealing the telltale poison-green eyes branding their owner as a demon.

However, they were good enough for his underlings, since any demon was dispensable. He, the Great One, was not. For him, only the best would do. He'd hired a very talented—and very discreet—scientist to improve the lenses he was currently wearing, so far without success. But he wasn't giving up. His need to stay up top, in the human world, rather than in the Underworld that he ruled with an iron fist, grew with every day. Here, in the condo that he'd claimed as his own, after dispensing with its original owner, he felt more at home than in the caves that smelled of sulfur and were heated by streams of lava.

None of his demons, not even his right-hand man Vintoq, knew about his abode in the human world. This was his refuge, the place he withdrew to when he was sick of the stupidity of his underlings. The place where he sometimes wondered what life would be like if he weren't a demon. Of course, those thoughts never lasted long, because he loved being a demon, loved the power, loved the control that came with being the demons' ruler. And most of all, he loved to feed on the fear of humans when they realized that they had lost, that he would snuff out their pitiful lives. It was meant to fill a void, a void that had started growing bigger during the last few months. To fill that void, he had to feed off the lifeforce of humans more frequently than ever before. His hunger for sex had grown by the same measure. And he didn't care how he got it. Be it demon or human female, it didn't matter to him, because deep down, he knew that neither could truly fill the emptiness in him, the feeling that there was something else he needed. Something beyond feeding, fighting, and fucking.

And to top it all off, the crippling migraines he'd been suffering for a long time now showed no signs of waning. He'd tried everything: human medications, street drugs, opioids—hell, he'd even tried weed. But nothing helped. The migraines were unpredictable and often hit him out of nowhere. It was another reason he spent increasingly more time in the human world, where he could hide the attacks from his underlings. He'd had several close calls, but luckily, so far, none of his subjects had caught on to his affliction. If they ever did, his days as their leader were numbered. Nobody wanted a weakling as their leader. And that was what they would see: a man so weak that a migraine could bring him to his knees.

He invented more and more excuses so his absences wouldn't cause suspicion, but Vintoq was a smart demon, and one day, he would figure it out. And then his loyalty would be tested. Zoltan couldn't allow it to come to that. What he needed was a decisive victory over the Stealth Guardians, their archenemies, the immortals who stood between the demons and their goal of dominating humans, turning them into their slaves, feeding off their fear. If he could defeat the Stealth Guardians once and for all, his eternal reign would be cemented.

But first things first. Zoltan glanced at his watch. It was time for his meeting. From his bedroom closet, he retrieved a wad of cash, just in case he needed it tonight, then he grabbed his leather jacket and stuffed the money into the inside pocket, before putting it on. A dagger was already hidden on his body—not because he suspected to run into Stealth Guardians, but because he didn't trust the man he was meeting. Better be prepared.

Ready, he snatched his keys, shoved them into his pocket, and left the condo. As he walked to the elevator, he heard the door click shut behind him. A soft ding sounded, announcing the elevator. The doors opened seconds later, and he stepped into the empty cab. He pressed the button for the garage. The sportscar his predecessor had owned, and which now belonged to Zoltan, was parked in the darkest corner of the otherwise well-lit parking garage. Zoltan unlocked it, hopped in, and let the engine roar. Eric Vaughn, whose name Zoltan used while in the human world, had had good taste in cars. He appreciated that about the man. At least he wasn't forced to drive a pickup truck, hatchback, or—God forbid—a minivan.

The drive to the area where one warehouse bordered another was short and didn't allow him to really test the car's speed. One day, when he had more time on his hands, he'd take it out for a spin on one of the freeways that weaved in and out of the city, to find out what this engine was capable of. Maybe he'd even experience the high that racecar drivers spoke of when hitting top speeds. Perhaps the thrill would give him satisfaction.

He brushed the thoughts away and concentrated on the next step in his plan.

At a street corner a block away from the meeting point, Zoltan pulled the car into a parking spot and killed the engine. He exited the car and locked it, then walked, hands in his jacket pockets, to the next intersection and turned right. Two buildings down was a dive bar that had seen better days. He walked to the entrance when he heard a hissing sound. He looked up and saw the neon *Open* sign flicker, then burn out completely. His presence had done that. It happened whenever a demon got in close proximity to neon or fluorescent lights.

Had a Stealth Guardian been near, Zoltan's disguise would have been blown. But the humans inside the bar had no idea what had just happened and what it meant.

The man he was meeting was already sitting in a booth, a beer that he didn't drink from in front of him. He never drank during their meetings. Vasili, the dealer in stolen goods, wanted to keep his wits about him.

Zoltan slid into the booth and waved to the bartender, ordering a whiskey.

"What have you got for me?" Zoltan asked.

Vasili cast a quick look around, making sure nobody was within earshot, then said, "I think it's the motherlode." His thick accent gave away the fact that he was an Eastern European immigrant, probably Russian. He tried to make up for it with his choice of words. It didn't work.

"You said that last time, yet nothing came of it," Zoltan reminded him. Only the fact that Vasili had the best connections among the fences on the East Coast meant he'd let him live after his previous failure.

"I found it, trust me. All I need to do now is get my hands on it."

Zoltan huffed. "So, in fact, you don't have it." Not a surprise.

"I know where it is. I know who's got it. And I know how to get it."

"Which means you haven't even seen it."

"I know it matches what you're looking for."

When the bartender suddenly showed up with a glass of whiskey, Vasili fell silent. Zoltan pulled a bill from his pocket and handed it to the man.

"Thanks. No change." He didn't want the bartender to come back and interrupt them again.

Once he'd left the table, Zoltan asked Vasili, "Why don't we make this simple? You tell me where I can find it, and I get it myself."

"That's not how it works. I procure things; you buy them from me. I'd be cutting myself out of a deal if I gave up my sources."

That would have been too easy. Clearly Vasili wasn't born yesterday. He also knew how to disappear. Once, Zoltan had tried to follow him to find out more about who he talked to, but the guy was as slippery as an eel and had shaken Zoltan off like a speck of dirt on his sleeve. For now, Zoltan had to work with the guy, even though he didn't trust him.

"You'll still get paid, even if you give me the location." Zoltan had to try one last time for good measure.

"Yeah, about the money." Vasili leaned in closer and lowered his voice. "I'll need some dough upfront this time. This job involves a bit of planning. It's protected well. I have higher expenses with this job, if you get my drift."

Zoltan did, but he wasn't stupid. "You'll get paid." He took a short pause. "After I see a picture of it. Gotta make sure it's really what I'm looking for."

"But—"

"After," Zoltan insisted, and downed the glass of whiskey in one big gulp. He liked the burning sensation it left in his throat. He rose. "And this time it'd better be what I'm looking for." He glared at Vasili. "Do we understand each other?"

Vasili swallowed visibly. "Yes, sure, o-o-of course."

Seconds later, Zoltan slammed the door of the bar shut behind him and marched outside. When he reached his car, he could feel the first waves of pain bombard his head. The migraine was starting. He managed to get in the car before the blinding pain crippled him. His body convulsed with every wave that pounded his head like a battering ram. One day, his skull would explode. One day, this would kill him.

The pain was so intense that he broke down and whimpered like a babbling fool.

"Please, make it go away! Don't do this to me! Take the pain away! I'll do anything for it."

When he heard his own weak words in his ears, he knew that his days as the Great One were numbered. And that knowledge brought on a whole different kind of pain.

7

Pearce's hackles had gone up the moment Daphne invited him to her place. Something was up. No woman in her right mind invited a complete stranger to her home mere minutes after meeting him—even if he'd helped her out of an embarrassing situation. A situation he'd caused by swiping her wallet from her messenger bag while she was freezer-diving. He'd been invisible while doing so. Moments later, he'd ducked behind a display, made sure neither a camera nor a shopper saw him, and made himself visible again. His charade had worked. Too well, in fact.

While Daphne's wallet was burning a hole in the inside pocket of his jacket, he couldn't get past the fact that Daphne didn't act like a normal woman. What did she have up her sleeve? Was she some skilled assassin and therefore not afraid of inviting a stranger to her home? Well, he'd be on his guard, not giving her a chance to get the drop on him. He had things up his sleeve too: invisibility and the ability to walk through walls. Besides, he was bigger and stronger than Daphne. And he was armed, though at the moment, he wondered whether it was a good thing to carry a dagger forged in the Dark Days with him. Maybe that was how she would obtain the weapon with which to kill him in the first place, by stealing it from him.

It was too late to change it now. Daphne was already unlocking the door to her second-floor apartment.

"Sorry, it's a bit messy," she said, and flipped the light switch before entering.

Pearce hesitated for just a moment while he quickly assessed his surroundings, which he could clearly see from the door. It was a one-bedroom apartment. There were only two doors inside, one that stood open and led into a tiny bathroom, and one that was closed and presumably led into the bedroom. Slowly, he crossed the threshold. The large room he stood was a living room, kitchen, dining room, and foyer all in one. In one corner, a computer station was set up. The furniture looked worn, yet comfortable. On the wall behind the sofa hung a psychedelic print.

"Would you shut the door, please?" She looked over her shoulder and met his gaze. "Or have you changed your mind?"

He pulled himself together. "Sorry, just admiring your decorating touch." Yeah, that was smooth. He pulled the door shut and took a few steps into the apartment.

"Very funny," she commented, and pointed to the print. "If you're referring to this, that's only there because the landlord won't fix the plaster that's been peeling off the wall. Had to cover it with something. And the store downstairs had a sale." She shrugged.

"Sorry, I didn't mean it that way," Pearce said, and placed the grocery bag on the kitchen counter. "I have to confess something."

Daphne suddenly froze as if she expected bad news. The silence that hung between them seemed to charge the air in the room with electricity.

"I... uh, I'm not used to being invited into the home of a beautiful woman. Particularly not after just meeting her." It was partially true.

"Oh."

When he saw her hesitant expression, he decided to add a joke. "I mean, you're not just gonna have your way with me, are you?"

Something flashed in her eyes. "Have my way with you?"

"Yeah, you know, tear my clothes off and all that." He forced a smile, then a chuckle. "I mean, I'm just a computer geek. I don't go out on dates much." That was true. He'd worked far too much in the last few months.

Her face lit up. "You work with computers?"

"Yeah."

"Me too."

"Get out! Really?" He'd figured that much when he'd found out where she worked, though he hadn't done a thorough background check on her yet.

She nodded. "That's a coincidence."

He smiled at her. "Sure is."

"And you can feel at ease," Daphne added. "I'm not a nymphomaniac who invited you to tear your clothes off. I just wanted to thank you for helping me out in the supermarket." She opened the fridge. "So you want that beer?"

"Absolutely." He accepted the beer and winked at her. "And just so you know, it's not that I'd say no to you."

Daphne rolled her eyes, but then chuckled and took a beer for herself. "I'll make a mental note in case the urge overcomes me."

The situation was defused—however, it didn't mean he could relax now, because he knew exactly what Daphne was doing. She was spinning her web like a spider ensnaring her prey. But he could be patient too. And vigilant.

Minutes later, they both sat on the couch and chowed down on their dinner, washing it down with bottles of beer. If he didn't know that Daphne would one day kill him, he would have found the whole situation perfect: a perfect date with a woman who had similar interests, a woman whose company he enjoyed.

Pearce kept the conversation light, made a few jokes they both laughed at, and finished his sandwich. He leaned back on the sofa and looked at Daphne, who was emptying her bottle.

"Hmm, I needed that," she said, and started cleaning up.

He rose too and took his plate to the kitchen. "I suppose that's my cue to take a hike." Even though he didn't want to leave yet.

"I didn't say that," she said while placing her plate and the utensils in the sink.

There was something about Daphne. While she pretended to be unconcerned about having a stranger in her home, he'd noticed the furtive glances she cast him whenever she thought he wasn't paying attention, and the tenseness with which she held her body. Was she looking for an opportunity to strike, to execute her plan, to kill him? He tossed out that thought. Winter had said he'd be killed in a theater or a film studio, not in an apartment, and Daphne's hair had been much longer in the vision.

"Do you enjoy the theater?" he asked without thinking.

She turned her head to him. "Are you asking me out?"

She'd completely misunderstood him. He'd simply been looking for a connection between Daphne and the place where he would die. But since she was assuming... "In a roundabout way, yeah. I did mention that I'm kinda shy around beautiful women, did I not?"

"You don't come across as shy. I think you know exactly what you're doing."

He wasn't all that sure about that. If he knew what he was doing, he'd be eliminating her right here, right now, and not trying to find out why she wanted to kill him in the first place. And a fine mess he was making of the entire situation.

He met her gaze and noticed the odd look she was giving him. Was she suspecting something? Time to play the shy geek. "So, is that a yes? You'll go on a date with me?"

"Where's your phone?" she asked.

"Why?"

"Because I want to program my number in so you can call me and let me know where and when to meet."

"Oh, uh, yeah, sure. Let me get my jacket."

But she was already heading for the armchair, where he'd deposited his jacket earlier.

Shit! If she stuck her hand into the pockets, she'd find her wallet, and then the jig was up. He hurried to the chair and snatched his jacket before she could lay her hands on it. Quickly, he pulled his cell phone from his outside pocket and unlocked it.

"Here you go." He handed her the phone and grinned. "And you'd better not be typing in a wrong number in the hopes of ditching me. It won't work, 'cause I know where you live."

He saw a shiver run through her and wondered if he'd said something wrong. She turned sideways as if she didn't want him to see what she was typing, so he took a step closer and looked over her shoulder.

"Is something wrong?" he asked.

Daphne lifted her head and turned it slightly. Her face was only inches from his now. But she didn't say anything as if she'd lost her ability to speak.

"Daphne?" he whispered. "Am I coming on too strong?" As he said it, he finally realized what he'd been doing the entire evening. He'd been flirting with her, not because he wanted to know why she would one day kill him, but because he was attracted to her.

"If I kissed you right now, would you regret having invited me?" he asked.

Her lashes fluttered and then swung upward, revealing her eyes fully. Her green irises seemed to shimmer with hundreds of facets. He let a second pass, then another, giving Daphne time to step back, time to tell him that she didn't want this. She did nothing of the sort, simply locked eyes with him.

Pearce lifted his hand and slid it onto her nape, while he stroked her neck with his thumb. A heartbeat later, he slanted his lips over hers and kissed her. Gently at first, just lips touching lips. Chaste. Innocent. Tender.

HE'D WARNED HER, given her enough time to pull back, to say no, but Daphne hadn't heeded the warning. Pearce's phone still in her hands, she'd at first been too worried that he noticed that she'd tried to go into the settings to plant a trace. That was the reason why she'd turned her back to him, but he'd looked over her shoulder, and she'd been unable to execute her plan. And when he'd locked eyes with her, a new plan had formed in her head. One that was ultimately more dangerous and fraught with too many variables. And it depended upon one fundamental question: would she be willing to use her body to save her brother?

Apparently, her body was answering that particular question for itself. Because not only did she not push Pearce away, she tilted her head slightly and parted her lips to allow him access, to invite him. She could certainly blame all kinds of things for this: her love for her brother, her fear of landing in prison if she did whatever the kidnappers wanted, her attraction to Guido's henchman despite knowing what these people were capable of. For all she knew, Pearce could have been the one who'd cut off her brother's finger. Yet here she was, allowing him to kiss her.

Well, of course, she could blame the kiss itself. This man knew what he was doing. He was no shy computer geek like he pretended to be. He'd probably never seen a line of code in his entire life. Because no geek she'd ever met kissed like this. And in her time as a hacker, she'd met plenty.

No, Pearce was something else altogether. His kiss spoke of passion, of experience, of desire and lust. Of so many things she should never share with an enemy. Yet she responded to him, allowed him to explore her, to tease soft moans from her, to send erotic shivers down her spine. He tasted of maleness, of power and strength, of danger. Maybe it was the danger she responded to most. Maybe she'd missed that in the last six months after she'd been forced to give up her life as a hacker. That had to be it, because why else would she put her arms around him and press her body to his, chest to chest, groin to groin?

Her response seemed to do something to him, because he suddenly moaned too. Whatever the reason was, why he'd decided to kiss her—and she was sure it was part of Guido's plan to keep an eye on her—it didn't leave him cold. Perhaps, if she played her cards right, she could use it against him and his associates. Though right now, her brain didn't seem to function properly, because all she could think of was this kiss, this man, his hands on her.

One hand was still on her nape, but the other one he was now sliding down her back to her ass. He gripped her possessively and yanked her against him so hard that she couldn't ignore the other reaction she'd conjured in Pearce: he was as hard as a crowbar. He definitely wasn't faking this. He was attracted to her, but would it be sufficient to make him betray Guido?

Again, she couldn't find an answer to her question, because her brain kept shutting down, and her senses overloaded. Her apartment suddenly felt like a sauna. The blood in her veins was like hot lava, while her skin prickled with anticipation. She hadn't felt like this in a long time. Everything around her seemed to blend into the background. Nothing seemed real anymore.

Tired of her problems and the choices she had to make, she let herself go. A few moments of bliss, of abandon, surely couldn't hurt. Even if what she did was wrong. Even if Pearce was an enemy. An enemy with the perfect touch. A touch that awakened something in her, a need she'd not fulfilled in quite a while, the need to feel a man's hands and lips on her.

With every second their mouths were fused, the heat between them increased. As if they were two matches rubbing against each other, daring the other to ignite first.

When Pearce squeezed her ass harder while rubbing his hard-on against her, a loud moan escaped her. Suddenly, he ripped his lips from hers and loosened his grip.

"I'm sorry," he said, his baby-blues shining with lust. "I'm going too fast, aren't I?" He took his hand off her backside and let out a breath. "I didn't mean to maul you like that."

"Maul me?" Far from it. Though the word did act as a cold shower.

"Yeah, your lips are all red." He rubbed his chin. "Sorry, five o'clock shadow. Had I known, I would have shaved..."

She almost had to chuckle at that. Almost. His act was good. First, he'd played the shy but loveable geek, then the experienced kisser, and now he was the date who showed concern.

"It's okay," she said automatically, and turned her head away.

But a moment later, she felt his fingers underneath her chin, turning her face back to him. "I should probably leave."

Damn it, how was she gonna get access to his cell phone now? Or a chance to win him over to her side so he would betray Guido? "So soon?"

With a smile, he shook his head. "As tempting as this is, I can't stay. I know where it would end. And I'm not gonna take advantage of you like that." He brushed his knuckles over her cheek in a gesture so tender that it made her forget for a moment who he was. "But you haven't seen the last of me yet." He pressed a soft kiss on her lips. "Now how about that phone number so I can ask you out for a proper date?"

She looked at her hands and realized that she wasn't holding the cell phone anymore. Where was it? But before she could look around, Pearce was already reaching for something on the floor. It was his phone.

"Oh, sorry, I must have dropped it," she said.

"Not your fault," he said, and unlocked it. "Now, what's your number?"

Seeing that he wasn't handing the phone back to her but had decided to program the number himself, she had no choice but to recite it for him.

He typed it in, then added her name. Her full name. She sucked in a breath, and he looked up instantly. Their eyes met.

He looked caught. Guilty. This confirmed it more than ever before. But she was curious what excuse he would have for knowing her last name, when she'd only introduced herself by her first name.

"How did you know my last name?"

He hesitated for just a fraction of a second, then pointed over his shoulder. "Uh, the mail on your kitchen counter." He shrugged. "Sorry, didn't mean to nose around, but I notice stuff."

"Hmm." Smart. She cast a look toward the counter, where, indeed, some of her mail was piling up.

Pearce pressed a button on his phone, and a second later, her own cell phone began to ring.

"Now you have my number." He disconnected the call, and the ringing stopped. "And you can program me in under Douglas, Pearce Douglas."

"I will," she promised, and right after he was gone, she would scour the internet to find out if a Pearce Douglas existed, or whether he'd just made up the name to put her at ease.

Pearce grabbed his jacket and put it on, then shoved his phone into his pocket before looking at her again.

"Are you gonna answer when I call you?" he asked.

"Why wouldn't I?"

"Because you suddenly have that look as if you regretted letting me kiss you."

"Regretted?" She couldn't let him believe that, because there was still a chance that she could milk him for information, if not tonight, then maybe tomorrow.

She felt like a vixen when she took a step toward him, put her hand on the back of his neck, and pulled his head to her. "Does this look like regret?" she asked, and kissed him as deeply as he'd kissed her earlier.

Pearce immediately slid his arm around her waist and pulled her against him, but she was already taking her lips off his.

"Are you trying to drive me insane?" he asked, and pressed his forehead to hers, while letting out a ragged breath. "Have mercy on a shy computer geek, Daphne."

"I don't think you're as shy as you claim to be."

He laughed. "Well, I guess you're gonna find out the truth sooner or later."

Another veiled threat. He was subtle, but they both knew what game they were playing. The question was: who was better at it?

8

————

Once outside Daphne's apartment, Pearce took a deep breath. Wow! This evening hadn't gone at all how he'd expected. But he wasn't complaining. Kissing Daphne hadn't been part of his initial plan, but when it had happened and when Daphne welcomed him so openly, he'd barely been able to stop himself from ripping her clothes off and burying his rock-hard cock deep inside her until they were both sated. Only one thing had stopped him: the knowledge that Daphne was his would-be killer. He couldn't trust her. Besides, he had her wallet in his jacket pocket and a dagger in his boot. Had they gotten naked, she might have seen either item.

So he'd played the respectful man who didn't fuck a woman on the first night of meeting her, even though that was a difficult character to play. Shy computer geek had been a little easier—it came more natural, because, deep down, that's what he was. He still couldn't figure out why she'd invited him to her place, but once he was back at the compound, he'd run a full background check on her to see if it would help him understand her. But first, he had to return to Daphne's office.

Entering the locked and guarded office building at night was much easier than it had been during the day, because this time he was alone and could make use of his skill of walking through walls. He remained invisible the entire time he was inside the building, and the night security guard was none the wiser. Nevertheless, Pearce had to be careful. A few employees burned the midnight oil on the floor Daphne worked on.

As quietly as possible, Pearce made his way to her cubicle and looked for a good spot where to leave Daphne's wallet. It couldn't be in plain sight, or she'd never believe she'd forgotten it in the office. The solution came in the form of a half-eaten bag of chips. He placed the wallet underneath it, only allowing a small corner to peek from it. Tomorrow, when Daphne returned to the office and wanted to snack on the salty treats, she would discover her wallet.

His work done, he left the building the same way he'd entered it.

When he entered the compound kitchen around midnight to grab another drink, he was surprised to see that he wasn't the only one still awake. In fact, all his fellow Stealth Guardians—Aiden, Hamish, Manus, Logan, and Enya—had congregated in the kitchen.

"What the fuck, Pearce!" Logan greeted him.

"Somebody's in a bad mood. What's going on? Did we have demon activity?" Pearce asked, and glanced at the others. To his surprise, they looked just as grumpy as Logan.

"Where the fuck were you?" Manus growled.

"We're your family, and you just let us wonder what happened to you?" Hamish added.

Fuck, the jig was up. But on the off chance that this wasn't about the death vision, he played the clueless one, another role he had trouble identifying with. "Can you guys be a little less cryptic? I'm tired. I wanna go to bed."

"You're not going anywhere before we've talked about this," Logan insisted. "You were gone for hours, without asking anybody to cover your shift, without answering your phone."

Ah, shit, Pearce had totally forgotten that he was supposed to cover the late shift in the command center. In his defense, he'd thought he'd be back earlier. "So I forgot. And my phone was probably on silent." Had he forgotten to put the ringer back on after his earlier excursion with Winter? Anyway, it didn't matter. At least all his friends were pissed about was that he'd skipped a shift and hadn't answered his phone. "Sorry, guys, but you're really taking this all too seriously. Do you have any idea how many shifts I've had to cover for you guys? So, I miss one tiny little shift, and you give me crap. That blows."

He marched toward the refrigerator to get a drink.

"You think this is about a fucking shift?"

Logan's incredulous tone made Pearce look over his shoulder.

"This is about Winter's vision."

"Shit," Pearce cursed under his breath, but they all heard him. It was time to go on the offensive. "If your wife could keep a secret for longer than two seconds—"

Logan already had him by the collar of his shirt. "Don't you say one bad thing about Winter, or else! You should be grateful that she warned you! And that she was worried about you when you didn't show up for your shift and didn't answer her calls. So worried, in fact, that she confessed that she'd seen you die in her vision. But instead of heeding her warning, what do you do? You go out and chase after your killer! Have you lost your fucking mind?"

Pearce had heard enough. He pushed Logan off him and narrowed his eyes. "It's none of your fucking business what I do. Yes, Winter warned me. But she also promised to keep the vision to herself. I thought she was on board after we identified the woman from her vision together and—"

"You did what?" Logan glared at him. "Are you saying you took Winter out of the compound to identify your killer for you?"

Pearce raised an eyebrow. Apparently Winter had conveniently left that part of the story out in order not to get into more hot water with her overprotective mate. Pearce hadn't meant to rat her out; he'd simply assumed that Logan already knew.

"Oops." When Logan growled, Pearce said, "Don't blame her. I talked her into it. Besides, she was invisible the entire time. There was no danger of a demon spotting her. You can trust me on that. I'd never put your mate in danger." He looked at Hamish, Aiden, and Manus. "Nor yours."

"You'd better not," Aiden grumbled, while Hamish only nodded.

Manus tilted his chin up. "You should have called a meeting to discuss how to proceed."

"What part of it's my business did you not get?" Pearce asked.

"Well, apparently none of us got that part," Hamish said. "So, why don't you explain it to us?" He folded his arms across his chest and widened his stance.

"There's nothing to explain. I'm gonna deal with it."

"Without a Second? Out of the question," Hamish said. "You can't go out to eliminate her without backup."

Pearce felt his heart miss a beat. A shaky breath left his chest, and he suddenly felt an icy shiver slither down his spine. "Eliminate? You thought I'd gone out tonight to eliminate her?"

Hamish furrowed his brow. The others also looked perplexed. They had no idea about his plan. Apparently, Winter had been rather stingy with facts when telling her mate about the situation. It appeared that she could keep a secret after all. Not that it would do him much good now. He had to come clean before his brethren took matters into their own hands and eliminated the threat to Pearce's life.

"Well," Hamish said. "Did you?"

Pearce shook his head.

"So all you did was reconnaissance?" Manus asked. "You made no contact with the subject? Just figured out what the best way will be?"

Pearce tilted his head a little to the side. "In a manner of speaking."

"What's that supposed to mean?" Logan asked, still sounding infuriated.

"What I said!" Pearce shoved a hand through his hair. "I'm going to deal with it. With her. I need to find out why she wants to kill me. And then I'll make sure it won't happen."

Logan looked at him suspiciously. "How?"

"You know what, Logan? I've had enough of your pissy attitude for one night. It's my business how I make sure Daphne doesn't kill me, okay?" He stabbed his index finger into Logan's shoulder. "It's my fucking business!"

"It's compound business," Logan replied, his anger barely leashed.

"Oh yeah? Was it also compound business when you decided to change the outcome of Winter's own death vision? Huh? I seem to remember that you asked us to butt out too. So excuse me if I do the same. My life, my death, my choice. Do you get it?"

Logan blanched with fury. "Are you saying that you're mad enough to try and change Winter's vision by befriending your killer?"

Befriending was perhaps not the most accurate description, not after the passionate kiss that Pearce had shared with Daphne tonight, but that was none of Logan's business.

"It worked for you. You think I'm not capable of changing whatever turns Daphne into a killer?"

"Have you checked out her background? Her history?" Enya asked.

"Who says she's not a killer already?" Aiden added.

Pearce glared at him. "She's not!" Why he was so sure about that, he didn't really know. But the woman he'd held in his arms tonight had never killed anybody. And he'd do anything to make sure she never would. For both their sakes.

Hamish gave him an odd look. "Where exactly were you tonight? And what were you doing?"

"I told Logan it's none of his business, and the same goes for you. For all of you. I'm handling it my way."

Manus shook his head in disbelief. "Oh my God, you slept with her. You slept with your killer."

Shocked gasps echoed in the kitchen.

Heat shot through Pearce's core, and he clenched his fists. Manus's assumption came a little too close to the truth. He took a breath, and then, as calmly as he could, he said, "Don't be ridiculous. I don't use my dick to solve problems. I use my brain." Then he made a motion toward the door. "So, if you'll all excuse me, I've gotta run a background check." He turned his back on his friends.

"You're crazy if you think you can change the vision," Logan called after him.

"Don't do this, Pearce," Aiden warned him. "Let's think this through first."

"I believe he's thinking with his little brain," Manus added.

At the door, Pearce lifted his right hand and, without looking over his shoulder, extended his middle finger, telling his comrades what exactly he thought of their comments. And to underscore it, he made the effort of opening the door instead of walking through it, just so he could slam it shut with a loud thud.

9

———

Checking into Daphne's background was child's play—and more than just a little surprising. Pearce read through the information he'd gathered—illegally—from various government sites and—legally —from public records. In fact, he was so engrossed in the details that he realized too late that he was no longer alone in the command center.

"She's a convicted criminal?"

Pearce spun around to stare at Enya. "What do you want?"

Enya shrugged and pulled an office chair closer to sit down. "Just wanted you to know that I have your back."

Surprised, Pearce kept looking at her. "And why's that?"

"'Cause the others all seem to have amnesia when it comes to all the rules they broke when it came to their mates."

"Daphne isn't my mate."

"Not yet. But the way you defended your actions just now shows me that you care about her."

"I only care about the fact that I can't just eliminate an innocent woman because of a vision Winter had."

"Innocent?" Enya chuckled and pointed to the monitor. "Hardly. Looks like she has a bit of a rap sheet."

"One single conviction," he corrected her, and lifted his index finger to emphasize it. "For hacking. Which isn't any worse than what I do on a daily basis."

"True, but you do it to save the world."

"We don't know what Daphne's motivation might have been, but it surely wasn't monetary. She has no savings to speak of, and she lives in a run-down apartment and covers the peeling paint with a poster."

"You were in her apartment?"

Shit! He'd said too much. "Just doing my due diligence," he said curtly, and turned back to the computer.

There was a short pause, then Enya shook her head. "You were in her place when she was there. Did you spy on her? Watch her get undressed?"

Clenching his jaw, he glared at his fellow Stealth Guardian. "I'm not some pervert!"

Enya leaned back and lifted her hands. "I didn't say that. Now, if we were talking about Manus... But you, I don't see you doing that. So, why were you blushing when I asked you?"

"I wasn't blushing!"

"Pearce, I'm not blind. I can tell when somebody's blushing."

He was saved from answering Enya's embarrassing observation when a window suddenly popped open on his screen.

Alert. Searches for Pearce Douglas performed during the last 120 minutes: nineteen. More details.

"What's that?" Enya asked.

"The program that captures every search that somebody runs on anybody here in the compound."

"Oh, I forgot about that. Who would search for you nineteen times in two hours?"

"Somebody who wants to know who I really am." It wasn't hard to guess who it was.

"Daphne?" Enya murmured.

He nodded.

"But why tonight? And how does she know your full name?"

"I gave it to her."

"So you did speak to her."

"I never said I didn't."

"You let the others believe that you hadn't made contact with her."

He gave her a sideways look. "Are you gonna run to them to tell them?"

"That depends."

"On what?"

"On how this plays out." She pointed to the monitor. "Go on, then—what did she try to find out about you?"

Pearce dug into the file and quickly perused it. All searches came from the same IP address. "Let's see if that's Daphne's." He typed in a few commands, and less than a minute later, he found the location of the IP address. "China."

"So, it's not her?"

"I'm not saying that. She's a hacker who got caught. That means as part of her plea agreement, she's not allowed to do any more hacking, or the agreement is voided. She probably covered herself. Let me see." He opened another program, then pasted the IP address into it and let it run. "We'll know in a minute or two."

And they did. Pearce pointed to a map that popped up, and to a dot that now blinked. "That's her apartment. She rerouted her IP address via several countries, piggybacking on a corporate server. Clever." He looked at the timestamps. "She started googling me the moment I left."

"Maybe if you told me what happened while you were there, I could tell you from a woman's perspective what she was looking for," Enya suggested.

"Nice try." He started typing again. "First, she googled to get at all the public info. She hit the LinkedIn and Facebook pages that I set up as cover. But that clearly wasn't enough. She hacked into the MVA and the Social Security Administration."

"Is she good?"

"Pretty talented hacker. But I'm better."

He could almost hear Enya rolling her eyes. "Oh, please. What did she find at the MVA and Social Security? Any problems there?"

"Nope. All my documents are current. Nothing looks out of the ordinary there." After all, he was the one to make sure that the cover documentation for all Stealth Guardians of the Baltimore compound was kept up to date so, in case they ever got into a traffic stop or something similar, they had valid IDs. "Everything's clean."

Daphne had hacked into a few more government servers, including the FBI, the local police department, and the sex offender register. Enya pointed to those alerts and grinned. "She checked to see if you have a record. Looks to me like the kind of woman who checks to see if her date is legit."

"It wasn't a date!"

"Wow, touchy."

"It proves something totally different."

"Enlighten me."

Pearce swiveled in his chair and faced Enya. "The fact that she had to do a full search on me, and that up until now she didn't know me at all, means that whatever event is the reason she'll kill me hasn't happened yet."

Slowly, Enya let out a breath. "Have you considered that by meeting her, by talking to her, you might have just triggered this event?"

"The thought crossed my mind."

"What are you gonna do now?"

"Follow through with my plan."

"Which is?"

"Change Winter's vision so I won't die."

"Need help with that?"

"Not right now."

"You know where to find me."

"I appreciate it."

She rose and hesitated for a moment. "And Pearce, don't play with her feelings. Scorned women are dangerous."

"I wasn't—"

But Enya was already passing through the door, leaving him alone with his decision.

~

SINCE IT WAS FRIDAY, Pearce figured that Daphne might finish work earlier than the previous day, and therefore installed himself in a small bistro across the street from her office just after four o'clock. While he nursed his drink and ate a pastry, he watched the entrance to Cyberhack like a hawk. He could have called Daphne for a date, of course, but after checking her background and seeing what lengths she was going through to figure out who he was, he decided to let caution reign for now. There was no rush. It was better to watch her tonight, learn her routine, and discover those things that no background check could reveal. If he got bored of that, he could always call her for a date later.

When it was close to sunset, more and more people streamed out of the office building, until he finally saw Daphne's black pixie haircut stand out from the masses. She was casually dressed, just like the day before. Her messenger bag was slung diagonally across her torso. He had to admit, despite the fact that she seemed to have no interest in fashion, she looked good. The style suited her. It went well with her short hair and her heart-shaped face, those green eyes... He noticed that, just like the night before, she wore little to no makeup. Well, she didn't need it. Her skin was perfect. Damn, he had to rip his gaze from her before he started reliving the kiss from the night before.

Not wanting to lose sight of Daphne, Pearce quickly tossed money on the table, waved goodbye to the waitress, and went outside. Unfortunately, he'd made one miscalculation: he was visible, and since he was in plain sight of several people, and there was no alley he could dip into to make himself invisible without anybody noticing, he had to remain visible. Daphne was waiting for the lights to change in order to cross the street together with several other people. She was heading his way, though she hadn't spotted him yet.

What now? Something colorful caught his eye from his left. There, on one of the outside tables, which were all empty, stood a small vase with a tiny bunch of wildflowers. Perfect. He glanced through the windows inside. The waitress was nowhere to be seen. Quickly, he snatched the bunch of flowers out of the vase and turned back toward the intersection, expecting Daphne to be almost upon him. But she wasn't. Where had she gone?

He glanced back to Daphne's office, but she hadn't turned back there. Then he looked to his right and saw her disappear around the corner of the next building, a bank. He marched in the same direction, walking faster in order to catch up with her. When he caught sight of her again, he realized that she held her phone to her ear and had slowed down. A moment later, she stopped at the entrance of a building, but she didn't go inside. Rather, she stood there to carry on her conversation.

"Yes, I got the plans," he heard her say when he was only a few yards away from her, her face turned away from him. She sounded stressed. Had she had a hard day at work? Or perhaps she hadn't gotten enough sleep last night, since she'd scoured the internet for information on him. He knew how the lack of sleep could make people cranky. He didn't hold it against her.

Pearce was about to make Daphne aware that he was behind her when she added, "No, the security system is no problem. I can get past it."

Security system? Something was up. And he had to find out what it was.

When the door to the building suddenly opened and a businessman exited, Daphne stepped aside, father away from Pearce and still looking in the other direction. This was his chance. Pearce snatched the door before it could snap in and walked into the foyer, which turned out to be an office building. He was in luck: though there was a desk where a doorman should sit, it was empty.

Nobody saw him when he turned himself invisible, then marched through the closed door back outside, where Daphne was just finishing her conversation.

"Yes, tonight." Another pause. "No police. Yeah, I'm not stupid. And you'd better not be stupid either. If you hurt him—"

She suddenly pulled the cell phone away from her ear. "Asshole."

Clearly, whoever she'd spoken to wasn't her favorite person. And it was also clear that something illegal was going down. He had to find out what it was. And if it had anything to do with Winter's death vision, he had to stop it.

Whatever was happening tonight could be the triggering event, as Enya had called it. The event that set Daphne on her path to killing him.

He had to be on his guard.

10

———

Daphne unlocked the door to her apartment and rushed inside, flicking the light switch on the way in. She didn't have much time. Guido had been very specific about what he wanted her to do and when. As if a job like this didn't need any preparation on her side. As if she were a miracle worker. And Guido and his gang wouldn't even be there to help. They'd decided that she could do it all on her own. She was the only one who was risking something, while Guido sat back and watched. And of that she was sure: he, or somebody associated with him, watched her to make sure she didn't go to the police at the last minute.

As if she could go to the police! Her brother's life was at stake, and since she hadn't been able to get any actionable information from Pearce the night before, she had to follow Guido's orders. Tracing her brother's cell phone hadn't been successful either. It had been switched off until the moment Guido had called her from it.

It took her less than two minutes to change into black pants, a black turtleneck sweater, and black tennis shoes. Gloves completed her cat burglar look. She emptied her messenger bag and placed the few tools she needed inside: an assortment of screwdrivers, steel-cutting pliers, clamps, cables, a small flashlight, and her computer. During an unguarded moment at work, she'd printed the instructions Guido had emailed her from Tim's email account. She folded those, stuffed them in her pants pocket, and snatched her darkest jacket from her closet. With her messenger bag slung across her body, she left the apartment less than ten minutes after she'd entered it.

She'd memorized the address Guido had given her. It was in a good part of town—in fact, in a very good part. Knowing she couldn't leave any trace of where she was going, an Uber was out of the question. Instead, she took the bus as far as she could, then got off and walked the rest of the way. A few times, she looked over her shoulder, unable to shake the feeling that somebody was following her. But she saw nobody. It appeared that Guido's people were skilled at shadowing their victims.

The address turned out to be a fancy two-story house with a pristine front yard and iron fences surrounding it. One outside light illuminated the driveway, but otherwise the property was dark. Daphne looked at her watch. She was right on time, and just like Guido had said, nobody was home. And it was too early for people to be in bed already.

Daphne walked to the other side of the property, the tradesmen entrance, which was used mainly to move trashcans from the house to the street. Two of said trashcans stood at the curb, and a third one stood just inside the gate. The light shining on the driveway didn't reach here. The path was dark, and one of the streetlights that should have illuminated the tradesmen entrance had burned out, though she suspected that this was no accident.

After looking up and down the street, Daphne pulled one of the trashcans closer to the gate. Then she lifted herself up onto it, glad that the can was filled to the top, so the plastic lid supported her weight without caving in. With her gloved hands, she held on to the iron spikes of the gate, then climbed over it. Still holding on to the spikes, she swung to the side, so her feet touched the trashcan on the other side of the gate. Slowly, she lowered herself onto it. It was empty, which was probably why it had been left inside the property. The lid started giving way, but she managed to jump off and land on the ground before breaking it.

"Phew."

Before getting up, she looked over her shoulder, making sure nobody had seen her acrobatics. She wasn't used to this kind of exercise anymore. True, as a hacker there'd been a few incidents where she and her fellow computer geeks had had to vacate a place rather abruptly, often in the middle of the night, but she'd always had to leave a property, not break into one. This was different, even for her.

After verifying that she was still alone, Daphne stalked toward the house. She walked along the narrow path that led around the left of it and turned when she reached the corner of the house. She peered around it. The backyard was large and just as meticulously kept as the front yard. It bordered a similar property behind it, though the fence between the two properties was older and lower than in the front and on the sides. The large deck, which took up at least a third of the backyard, was furnished with a table and chairs as well as a supersized BBQ that looked like it cost more than the average American car.

On the back wall of the house, she found what she was looking for: a control panel. Several cables encased in steel tubes led into the panel, making it virtually impossible to cut the cables from there. The steel panel itself was locked. She could see it clearly, because the moon was just coming out from behind a cloud, providing sufficient light to make out the lock. It wasn't hard to open it. Her steel-cutting pliers and a little elbow grease took care of the lock. Her heart was already beating faster. Shit, she'd just graduated from hacker to burglar. Even a lenient judge wouldn't look past that.

In for a penny, in for a pound. It was real now. She was committing a crime. A crime that could get her five to eight in a state prison. Her brother had better be grateful for the rest of his life, considering what she was risking for him.

She wiped the perspiration off her brow, placed the pliers back in the messenger bag, pulled out her flashlight, and inspected the interior of the panel closely. Guido's instructions had been vague about what she would find there, but he'd given her the name of the security system the house was protected with. It helped. The control panel had the right connectors inside to hook up a computer.

Knowing how to proceed, Daphne pulled out her laptop and booted it up. Once logged in, she opened a program. With a firewire, she connected her computer to the control panel, waited for her computer to recognize the connection, then started typing commands.

Several lines of code appeared. She read them, knew what they meant, then reacted with code of her own. A flood of lines filled the window, falling like green raindrops on the dark background. The program was trying millions of different combinations to disable the security system.

"Come on, come on," she whispered to herself. Patience had never been her forte.

Finally, the lines of codes stopped. A last line with only one word appeared: *Disabled*.

Bingo!

She still had it. Still had the skills that she'd nearly gone to prison for. And that could land her there even now if she wasn't careful. But she couldn't think about that now. She had to finish the job before the residents returned.

Entering the property was the easiest of her tasks: one of the windows looking out over the deck had been left unlocked. How Guido had known that, she wasn't sure, but she suspected that somehow he had access to the house. Which raised the question why he wasn't doing the job himself.

Daphne slid the sash window up and crawled through the opening. When she got up and looked around, she noted that she was in the living room. The elegantly furnished room confirmed that the people here had money, and whatever was in that safe she was supposed to clean out—and Guido was very specific about taking everything out of it, no matter what it was—had to be valuable.

Orienting herself, she left the living room and headed into the hallway. There were several doors, and again she followed the instructions Guido had given her and found the study. It was masculine, furnished with lots of black leather and modern rugs and lamps. And an abstract painting, behind which she would find the safe.

More sweat collected on her nape and forehead. She wasn't made for this. At any point, the homeowners could return and find her with her hand in the cookie jar. And then it would be over. Her plea deal would be voided, her brother would be hurt further, most likely killed, and she would go to prison.

With shaking hands, she pulled the painting to the side and noticed it was mounted on a hinge, so it could be pulled away from the wall to grant access to the safe. The safe had a keypad. She pulled out the sheet of information on which Guido had listed several combinations. They all looked similar and were only a few digits off, which made her suspect that he'd stood behind the person who'd entered the code, but hadn't seen the exact combination. Those were his best guesses, and there were over thirty of them. Well, wasn't that just great?

Wiping the sweat off her forehead once more with her gloved hand, she entered the first six-number combination. The keypad flashed, and a beep sounded. *Incorrect code,* the display advised. She fared no better with the second combination. She shined her light on the piece of paper to try the third combination, then heard a sound from behind her.

Panicked, she spun around. Shock paralyzed her. There, on the other side of the large desk, stood a dark figure. A man.

A gasp escaped her. Fight or flight? Flight!

Her legs were already moving, but the man was faster. He cut off her escape route and grabbed her by her arm, yanking her back.

"Let go!" she screamed, but instantly his hand landed on her mouth, silencing her.

"Shhh!" he said. "What the fuck are you doing, breaking in here?"

She knew that voice. Recognized it immediately. Which didn't dampen the shock at all. "Pearce?" she mumbled against his hand.

"No time to chat now. The police are coming," he whispered. "Not a word, or they'll find us."

His face was close enough for her to see now. She nodded, and he lifted his hand off her mouth. She took a deep breath, but Pearce was already dragging her back toward the living room. That was when she heard them too: police sirens.

Shit!

Panic made her heart thunder into her throat. Why were the police coming? She had disabled the security system. She was sure of it.

"But I cut the alarm."

Already at the French doors in the living room, Pearce glanced at her. "Not the secondary one."

"They have two alarm systems? But why didn't you and Guido tell—"

"Me?" he interrupted, then shook his head. "I had no idea breaking into houses is your pastime." He unlocked the French doors. "Now let's go, or we're stuck here."

Confused about his comment, she tried to ask something, but as soon as she stepped on the deck, she could hear the sirens blaring. The police were already at the front gate. Their blue lights were reflected in the windows of the neighbor's house.

Pearce put a finger on his lips and pointed to the fence that separated this property from the one behind it. They ran to it, Pearce now holding her hand as if to make sure that she wasn't running in the opposite direction. At the fence, he easily lifted her over it. By the time she looked over her shoulder, he was already standing behind her. How had he managed to jump over the fence so quickly? He had to be extremely agile.

The neighbor's backyard was dark, helping them escape prying eyes. They reached the street moments later. There, Daphne stopped and took a much-needed breath. She was panting, both as a result of the exercise and her fear.

"What now?" she asked, turning to Pearce.

He was staring at something on his phone, then he looked up and pointed to the right. "This way. It's a mile. Can you run that far?"

She nodded. She wasn't exactly an accomplished sprinter, but she jogged regularly, and a mile was easily within her capabilities, even with the messenger bag that was still slung across her torso. Thank God she'd never taken it off, because in the panic she'd been in, she could have easily left it behind.

While they ran along the sidewalk, making turns and crossing intersections, Daphne had plenty of time to formulate the questions she had. Why had Pearce followed her? Why had Guido not warned her about the secondary alarm, when his henchman had known about it? Was Pearce taking her back to the place where they kept her brother? What would they do to her now? And why the hell was she going with him? Oh yeah, because the police were after her! Because that fuckwit Guido hadn't done his homework and let her run into a trap.

By the time they reached a small apartment complex, Daphne was fuming. It took all her mental strength and control to keep her anger under the hood until they reached an apartment on the second floor and Pearce unlocked the door.

Time to tell him what she thought of his and Guido's stupid plan.

11

———

Pearce pushed the door open and ushered Daphne inside, then closed the door behind them.

"Where are we?" she asked, her tone as suspicious as the look she cast around.

"My apartment," he lied. This was one of the safehouses the Stealth Guardians operated in many cities. He'd been lucky that it was empty and not far from where they'd been.

"Really?" Daphne looked around the room that was furnished with only the bare necessities.

Pearce peeled out of his jacket and tossed it on one of the kitchen chairs. The apartment was a two-bedroom unit with an eat-in kitchen and a good-sized living room. The neighbors kept to themselves, and the rent was paid via a shell company. The lock fit a universal key, which worked for every single safehouse in the city. The safehouses were used mostly in emergencies, though on occasion they'd housed vulnerable humans who needed to hide out from the demons for an extended time. A small crew of human staff serviced the apartments and stocked them with the essentials: there was always food in the freezer and beverages in the fridge to last for a couple of days.

"I just moved in," Pearce said quickly, not wanting to arouse suspicion. Then he changed the subject. "But enough about my apartment. What the fuck were you thinking, breaking into that mansion?"

She tossed him an outraged look. "Excuse me? What kind of question is that? Your boss ordered it!" She huffed angrily and braced her hands at her hips. "And while we're on the subject of your boss, why the fuck is he sending me in there without telling me there are two alarms? Did he want me to be caught? Fucking asshole!"

"Hold it, hold it!" Pearce interrupted. He had no idea what she was talking about. "My boss? I have no boss. I'm a freelancer." Well, that was a lie, of course, but his official cover said that he was a freelance programmer. And he was sticking to that. "So I don't know who you're talking about."

"Oh, freelance? Is that what they call henchmen these days?" Her cheeks were flushed, her green eyes firmly glaring at him.

"Henchmen? I'm no henchman!" The ridges in his forehead deepened.

"Oh, please! Don't play stupid with me now! Guido sent you to watch me to make sure that I follow his orders. But you had to go a step further, didn't you? You had to *help* me out in the supermarket so you had an opportunity to talk to me."

She was getting awfully close to the truth with her last statement, though he still had no idea what the deal was with Guido.

"And then you invited yourself to my place as if it was a date!"

Now he was pissed. "Invited myself? No, no, lady, it appears you have a lapse in memory. *You* invited *me*! In fact, you insisted on my joining you for dinner at your home."

"A lapse in memory? Do I also misremember that you kissed me as if I'd invited it? Huh?"

"I gave you ample chance to say no. If I recall correctly—and I do —I asked permission to kiss you. You didn't push me away. You didn't say no. Well, sorry that you're now regretting it."

"And why shouldn't I?" she yelled. "You and Guido have my

brother. You're hurting him, and you're forcing me to commit a crime for you."

Her words jolted him. "What?" He stared at her, understanding suddenly flooding through him. "You were being forced to burgle that house because some guys have kidnapped your brother?"

"Don't make it sound like you know nothing of it! I'm not stupid. Guido said he's having me watched so I won't talk to the police. And then you show up. And you warned me. You said I'll find out the truth about you one day. Guess what? I already knew the truth last night."

Pearce let out a long breath and shoved a hand through his short hair. Daphne had it all wrong.

"Daphne, there's something I have to clear up. I think you might want to sit down for this."

She crossed her arms over her chest. "I'd rather stand." Defiance shone from her eyes.

"Well, then, we'll do it standing up." He sighed. "Please hear me out to the end. Then you can ask questions, and I'll answer them." To what degree of truth, he couldn't tell yet. After all, he still had to maintain his cover.

"Talk," she said, but her eyes said that she wasn't going to believe a single word.

Nevertheless, he had to try. "I'm a freelance programmer. Last night at the checkout, I helped you out because you couldn't find your wallet. Would I have helped out an ugly guy if that person had been in the same predicament? I don't know. But I helped you because I thought you looked cute, and I figured it would give me a chance to ask you out."

Daphne's face remained impenetrable.

"I was surprised when you invited me to your house. And I thought we were hitting it off, so when it came to say goodnight, can you blame me that I wanted to kiss you and see you again?"

"Bullshit! If that were true, then why did you show up at that house tonight?"

He'd thought of an explanation for that too. It was partially true.

"I was on my way to your place to bring you flowers, but you were just leaving and looking so, I don't know, catburglarish?" That he'd followed her invisibly, he omitted. "I don't know what got into me, but I followed you, just in case you needed my help. And when I saw you breaking into that house, I knew I had to stop you from making a big mistake."

She gave him a long, assessing look. "Assuming I believe you up till here, how did you know about the second alarm?"

He smiled briefly. "I worked a lot on programming alarms. When I saw what type of alarm you disabled, I remembered that that particular company likes to upsell their clients with a secondary silent alarm. It was an educated guess, which proved to be true when the police came. That's why I had to get you out of there. I couldn't allow them to catch you. It's kind of hard to date somebody who's in prison."

Daphne suddenly dropped her arms to her side. "Oh crap." Then she let herself fall on one of the kitchen chairs, her anger visibly deflated. "You don't work for Guido?"

Pearce shook his head.

"So you're just a good guy?"

Pearce nodded. "I'd like to think so." He pulled a chair closer and sat down opposite her. "Would you now tell me what's going on? You mentioned your brother." Even though he could already piece together what was going on, he needed to get the full story from Daphne.

"I can't tell you. Guido warned me."

"Guido will never find out that you talked to me. Besides, I just helped you evade the police. Don't I deserve the truth for that, if nothing else?"

Slowly, she nodded. "You're right. I'm so grateful. I'm totally in over my head. How could I even think that I could handle something like this?"

Pearce reached for her hand and patted it. "Just breathe. And then start at the beginning. Maybe I can help you."

A shimmer of tears coated her irises. But she pulled herself together, swallowed, and nodded. "I have a younger brother, Tim. He always gets into trouble for one thing or another. The day we met in the supermarket, I'd gotten a call from a guy who called himself Guido. He said my brother owed him money, lots of money. But he'd wipe out his debt if I did a job for him. Tim must have told him that I'm a programmer." She sighed and dropped her head. "You're not gonna like this part. But I was a hacker. And I got caught." She looked up and waited for his reaction.

"Okay?" Pearce said.

"You're not shocked?"

He shrugged. "I know plenty of people in the field who've done some hacking in their time. Go on."

"Well, somehow he knew about it. Tim probably told him, stupid idiot. Anyway, Guido, or whatever his real name is, said if I broke into that house and cleaned out the safe, he'd wipe out my brother's debt and release him."

"So, he's keeping your brother locked up somewhere?" Pearce asked.

"Not only that." She met his eyes now, and a pained expression distorted her face. "They're torturing him."

"How do you know?"

"They sent me a video."

"Do you still have it?"

She nodded.

"Show me."

Daphne pulled her cell phone from her jacket pocket, then unlocked it and navigated to the video. She handed it to him.

"It's warm in here," she said, and freed herself of her messenger bag, which she set down on the floor, before taking off her jacket.

Meanwhile, Pearce tapped the video and watched it. It was short, but confirmed Daphne's statement. "They've beaten him."

"Yes. And worse." A tear stole down her cheek. She sniffled. "When I told Guido I wouldn't do it, he sent me a photo a few minutes later." She motioned to the phone. "Scroll down."

Pearce did as she asked and stared at the photo the kidnapper had sent. Then he looked up and met Daphne's eyes. "They cut off his finger."

"Yeah, because I didn't comply immediately. It's my fault." More tears streamed down her face. "Because I was worried about my own life, about my plea agreement being vacated if I got caught."

Pearce took her hand and squeezed it. "It's not your fault. Please. Don't think that."

But Daphne kept crying. His heart broke for her, but he had to tear his gaze from her, or he would pull her into his arms to comfort her, and who knew where that would lead? Instead, he looked down at the horrid photo of the severed finger again. He enlarged it and studied it in more detail. It was a pinkie. At least they hadn't severed his thumb. You could function very well without the little finger. Losing a thumb was much more devastating.

He looked at the photo again. Yeah, it was definitely a pinkie. He was about to put the phone aside when he noticed something in the bottom right corner of the picture. He zoomed in closer. It was part of a mark.

"Son of a gun!"

Daphne jerked her head up. "What?"

He pointed to the photo. "There's a copyright symbol in the lower right corner."

"Why would there be—"

Pearce chuckled. "Because this is not your brother's finger. This is a photo the kidnappers grabbed from a website that's watermarked and copyrighted its photos."

Her tears stopped flowing. "Are you sure?"

"Pretty sure, but I can check to make certain."

"How?"

"Do you mind if I email myself this photo so I can run a reverse-image search from my computer?"

"Why didn't I think of that?" She shook her head. "I should have done it when I got the photo."

As he sent the photo to himself, Pearce gave her a reassuring look.

"You were distraught when you got it. The copyright mark can really only be seen when you blow up the photo. And I'm sure you didn't really want to get a closer look at what you thought was your brother's severed finger." He placed Daphne's phone on the kitchen table and rose. "Let me just get the computer so I can run a search."

Pearce walked to the built-in closet in the living area and unlocked it. Inside were all kinds of electronics a Stealth Guardian might need if he had to remain in a safehouse for a couple of days. He snatched the computer and brought it back to the kitchen table, where he booted it up.

Daphne watched him. "So, you're really a computer programmer."

He logged on and cast her a quick smile. "Yep. Told you I'm just a shy computer geek."

"Who's not afraid to follow a burglar into a house and save her from the police."

"It was my one good deed for the day." Pearce winked at her, his fingers already flying over the keyboard, retrieving the photo from his email, and composing a search for it on the web. "This won't take long."

And it didn't. The search found the exact photo on a blog that reported on war crimes.

"There it is," Pearce said, and pointed to the photo.

Daphne nudged closer and looked at the screen. "Oh my God. It's the exact same photo." She turned her head to him. "Why? I mean, why would they use a photo from the internet?"

"They needed to make sure you'd do the job. But they weren't prepared to cut your brother's finger off."

"But they beat him up," Daphne protested. "They are bad guys."

"That may be the case. But whoever this Guido is, he doesn't seem to cross the line into mutilation. That's good for us."

"Us?"

"I'm gonna help you find where they're holding your brother."

"You'd do that?" she asked, her eyes wide. "For me? After I accused you of being Guido's goon?"

"I believe you used the word henchman." He chuckled.

"I'm so sorry. But when we met in the supermarket, all I could think of was Guido's threat. So naturally, I thought you were the one he'd sent to watch me. Honest mistake."

Suddenly something clicked in his brain. "So you really did think from the moment we met that I was a bad guy?"

She nodded.

"Then I'm curious."

"About what?"

"Why did you invite me to your house and let me kiss you when you thought I was involved in your brother's kidnapping?" It made no sense to him now. The night before, he'd thought he was just lucky and they were hitting it off, but knowing what he knew now, that couldn't have been the case.

Daphne sighed. "Because I was stupidly thinking that maybe if I could distract you and get a hold of your phone, I could program a tracer into it so I could figure out where you went and, that way, find my brother. But you didn't really give me enough time with your phone... and then you kissed me, and I figured..."

"You figured what?" Now he was really curious.

"I figured if I could seduce you, maybe you would help me and turn against Guido." She shrugged.

"Oh my God, Daphne! You were playing with fire! Imagine what could have happened if I'd really been the bad guy. I mean, how could you put yourself in that kind of danger?" He was of a mind to toss her over his lap and paddle her sweet ass. "A guy who associates with the likes of this Guido would have used you instead. Who knows what he would have done?"

"I'm sorry. I wasn't thinking straight."

He shut the computer and rose. So much for Daphne being attracted to him. She'd done it only in the misguided belief that she could help her brother. "I understand now why you're regretting what happened last night." Although he had no such feeling. He only regretted that she hadn't welcomed his kiss. "It won't happen again." He turned, ready to pack the computer away.

Daphne got up from her chair. "It's true, I did it for those reasons. But now that I know better, there's no reason for me to regret last night. In fact, now that I know you're a good guy, I'm glad that you kissed me."

He pivoted and saw her dropping her eyelids.

"I liked it," she confessed, and lifted her gaze to meet his. "A lot."

Slowly, he took a step toward her, close enough to kiss her again. "Are you saying..."

She lifted her hand to his cheek and brushed her fingers over it. "I'm so grateful for you saving me, for you giving me hope that nothing irreversible has happened to my brother, hope that everything will turn out all right despite the odds."

"So, are you saying that now you'd let me kiss you, because you're grateful?" While that wasn't exactly what he'd hoped for, he'd take it —for now.

She slowly shook her head. "No. I would like you to kiss me because we both want it."

He brought his body flush to hers, delighted about her words. "How much do you want it?"

"Really badly."

When he brought his face closer to hers, she put her hand on his chest to stop him.

"But only if you want it too. I don't want pity," she said.

Pearce grinned. "Trust me, pity is the last thing on my mind right now." Then he framed Daphne's face with his hands and kissed her.

12

———

Pearce's lips on hers felt right. Better than the night before, because now there was no deception, no misunderstanding between them. This was truly their first kiss, the one Daphne would savor. Pearce wasn't behaving like a shy computer geek. On the contrary, his kiss was that of an experienced man, a man who knew what he wanted, a man who knew he could pleasure a woman. She needed that tonight more than ever.

After the danger she'd been in tonight—and he, too, all because of her—she needed to forget her problems for a little while. Knowing that the kidnappers hadn't cut her brother's finger off after all had lifted a lot of the guilt off her shoulders. And though the danger wasn't over, she felt she'd been given a reprieve. A reprieve in Pearce's arms.

He was holding her close, pressing her to his hard body. One hand was on her nape now, caressing the soft hair and making her shiver with pleasure, while he slung his other arm around her waist and held her so close that she could barely breathe. But who needed to breathe when she could drink from Pearce's lips instead? He tasted of virility, of manliness, of strength. So different from the other computer geeks she'd dated. None of them had been so muscular. Nor so talented. Pearce knew how to tease moan after moan from her lips, turning her insides molten, her body boneless. If he severed the embrace, she would surely collapse, her knees like jelly, her head dizzy from his passionate kiss.

But it wasn't only the kiss that heated her insides. It was the way he ground his groin against her in a steady rhythm, giving her a preview of what was hidden beneath his clothes. Beneath the pants that had to be too tight by now, because the hard rod that was expanding there seemed to get bigger and harder by the second.

She felt her heart beat a frantic rhythm against her ribcage, asking to be released. Her hands were on him now, one clinging to his shoulder while she let the other slide down to his ass, gripping him there as if she had every right to do so.

A loud moan was his answer, before he mirrored her movement and possessively grabbed her backside and yanked her against him even harder. He ripped his mouth from her and drew back his head so they could look into each other's eyes. His irises seemed even more vibrant now. There was a sheen to them that she could only interpret as hunger.

"Fuck, Daphne! You're a wild one."

She chuckled at that. Nobody had ever called her wild. "Look who's talking." She rubbed her stomach against the hard ridge in his pants.

Pearce closed his eyes for a moment. "Are you trying to make me come right here?" When he opened his eyes again, there was a smile on his lips. "Or would you prefer I'd last a little longer?"

"A little longer."

"That's what I thought." Then his lips were on her mouth again, and he kissed her with even more fervor. But it wasn't all he did. He lifted his hand from her ass, and a second later, he slid it under her sweater, touching her naked skin.

Daphne sighed into his mouth and felt his lips quirk into a smile. He was definitely not a shy computer geek. Not shy at all. His hand moved higher, caressing her heated skin until he reached her breasts. There, he stopped all of a sudden and drew his head back.

"You're not wearing a bra."

She smirked. "Is that a problem?"

Apparently it wasn't, because he now cupped one breast, massaging it gently. It was just what she needed, his strong fingers playing with her nipple, his palm imprisoning her tender flesh. She let her head fall back, reveling in his touch, and felt a second hand slide under her turtleneck sweater, seeking out her other breast. Now he was kneading both at the same time. She pulled her lower lip between her teeth to stop herself from crying out at the intense thrill she experienced. Had it really been that long that a man had touched her like that? That simply having a man caress her breasts with such gusto brought her to the brink of an orgasm?

Pearce brought his lips to her ear, drawing the lobe into his mouth to suck on it. All the while, he continued to caress her nipples, to roll them between his fingers and turn them into hard little buds.

"I love those tits," he whispered into her ear.

To her surprise, she wasn't shocked at his choice of words, but turned on. He was awakening a side of her that had been dormant for too long.

"Then why don't you suck them?"

No sooner had she uttered the words than she felt cool air waft against her torso as Pearce pulled her sweater over her head and tossed it somewhere. Then his mouth was on her burning flesh, his lips capturing one nipple, sucking it deep into his mouth, while he massaged both breasts with his hands. He let the wet nipple pop from his mouth and blew against it. A shiver raced down her spine, and she felt goosebumps on her skin. Then his mouth was on her other breast, repeating the sweet torture. He squeezed her flesh harder now, kneading it more urgently, squeezing her two mounds together, before he pressed his face into them.

His breathing was more ragged now, a testament to the effect she had on him. She put her hands on his nape, caressing him, drawing him closer to her, giving him permission to take more, to be even bolder.

And she wanted to feel more, to feel his skin against hers. She lowered her arms and pulled his long-sleeved T-shirt up. He understood what she wanted and helped her rid him of it. Underneath, he was naked.

She didn't get a chance to run her hands over his bare chest, because he was already drawing her against him, crushing her breasts to his chest. Her nipples, hard and sensitive, seemed to ignite the moment they made contact with his skin. His mouth was on her again, kissing the column of her neck, then he drew back to kiss a path down her front, through the valley of her breasts. There, he licked her, long and slow, while he was cupping her breasts.

"I wanna fuck your tits," he said, and looked up.

His eyes were filled with pure lust. It was contagious.

"Then fuck them."

As soon as the words had left her lips, Pearce lifted her up and carried her toward one of the doors. He opened it and entered. It was a bedroom. He kicked the door shut behind him and lowered her onto the bed. With efficient moves, he took off his boots, then opened his pants and stepped out of them. He stood in front of her with only his boxer briefs for barely a second, before those hit the floor too.

His cock sprang free. It was even bigger than she'd imagined it, bigger than it had felt when he'd pressed it against her.

"Oh God," she murmured. He was beautiful. A perfect male specimen if there ever was one. A muscular chest, a flat stomach, strong legs, and in between them hung the most gorgeous erection she'd ever seen.

And now he was going to fuck her tits with it. She licked her lips and felt a familiar wetness in her panties. As if Pearce knew what she wanted him to do, he opened the button of her pants, lowered the zipper, and pulled them down to her knees. There, he left them, as if he didn't want her to move too much.

"Please," she murmured.

He slid one knee onto the mattress, then placed his hand between her legs and pressed against her slit. An appreciative moan issued from his throat, and he moved his hand underneath the soaked fabric. One long finger dove deeper and rubbed along her slit, making her almost lift off the bed.

"Ohh!"

But his finger was gone just as quickly as it had come.

"First your tits," he murmured, and swung himself over her as if she were the horse and he the rider. "Then your pussy."

13

____

Pearce looked down at Daphne. Her naked breasts were glorious, bigger than he'd imagined. Her thick turtleneck sweater had disguised that and given him a nice surprise when he'd rid her of it. Firm and topped with pert nipples, they'd felt like luxurious cushions when he'd pressed his face into them. They would feel even better when they cradled his cock.

Daphne stared up at him in anticipation, her lips parted, her eyes half-closed. A rosy blush colored her cheeks, and a fine sheen of perspiration blanketed her face and neck. He was pleased with how willingly she submitted to his wishes, not rejecting the idea as too kinky. Maybe she was just as caught up in the moment as he was. She'd fled the police, and while she'd been in no danger of being discovered —because he'd made her invisible from the moment he'd realized what she was doing—she didn't know that. Even now, adrenaline was pumping through her veins, and this was her outlet: agreeing to a night of pleasure and passion.

Without a word, Pearce bent down to lick the valley between her breasts to prepare her for him. He took his time with it, before raising his torso and cupping her breasts with both hands. He pressed them together then nudged forward, bringing the tip of his cock to the crease he'd created. There, he paused and sought Daphne's eyes. Her breath hitched, and she licked her lips, communicating her approval. Slowly, he pressed his cockhead forward until it slid between her breasts.

"Fuck!" he cursed. This was better than he'd imagined.

The warmth of her body combined with his saliva provided the perfect environment for his cock to slide all the way through, its tip emerging from the other end.

"Ohhh!" Daphne sighed. Her nipples turned harder and poked against his palms.

Quickly, he rocked back, pulling his cock through the warm channel between her tits once more, until only the tip of his erection was still held by her flesh. Clenching his jaw, he thrust again.

"Oh Pearce," she murmured, reaching for him.

But he couldn't allow that, not now. "Don't. If you touch me, I might spill." When she dropped her hands, he added, "You're so fucking hot, Daphne, I'm not sure I can do this for long."

A wicked smile curved her lips.

He continued thrusting back and forth, alternating the pressure with which he pressed her breasts together. But with every stroke, his control wore thinner. Breathing raggedly, he pulled back and released her breasts. With his next movement, he jumped off the bed. The cool air blowing against his hard-on helped him gain some of his control back. Hopefully enough that he could properly fuck her.

"Take off your pants," he ordered her, and realized how hoarse his voice sounded. Fuck, he had it bad.

He watched as Daphne rid herself of the remainder of her clothing and lay back on the duvet, as naked as the day she was born. There was no shyness in her when he moved his gaze over her, admiring her beautiful body, her long legs, her shapely thighs, her beautiful pussy.

"Open your legs for me," he demanded, this time less gruff.

He kneeled on the bed and watched as Daphne spread her legs wider, giving him an unobstructed view of her pussy. He reached for it and brushed his fingers along the slit.

Daphne moaned softly, and her hips rose.

"You're so wet already," he said, and looked at her face.

Their eyes met.

"Your fault," she said, tipping her chin in his direction. "You can't just fuck a girl's tits like that and expect her to remain unaffected."

"You're right," he admitted. "Maybe I should make it up to you." He scooted into the space between her spread legs.

Her eyebrows lifted, and an appreciative sound rolled over her lips. "But that's gonna make me even wetter."

"I believe that's the point." Pearce grinned and lowered his head to Daphne's pussy. He loved her lighthearted attitude. "Now, if you'll excuse me, I've got something important to do."

"Which is?"

"Making you come with my mouth."

Pearce licked over her folds and tasted the juices. The aroma sent a bolt of electricity through his body and right into his balls. They tingled with excitement, and his cock filled with more blood, ready to plunge into her and take possession of her. Her petals were soft and supple. Daphne bucked against him, and he took her movement as invitation to lick her harder, to drive his speared tongue into her slit as far as he could.

Daphne cried out, and from his peripheral vision he noticed how she gripped the duvet for dear life. Loving the effect his caresses had on her, Pearce added his hands to spread her pussy wider, before swiping his tongue upward to the little hooded organ that was waiting for him. He licked over the swollen clit and felt Daphne jolt. Perfect. Everything about her was perfect.

Holding her down with one hand, he used the other to find the entrance to her channel and slowly drove his middle finger into it. Her muscles gripped him tightly, and another loud moan came from Daphne. Gently, he started finger-fucking her, while his tongue was back on her clit, licking and sucking in a steady rhythm. Daphne rocked in rhythm with his finger, showing him how fast and how hard she liked it, demanding more friction. His mouth still on her, attending to her center of pleasure, he added a second finger to the first and stretched her wider. She would thank him for it later when she received his cock. It would take her less time to adjust to his size if he helped her stretch her channel now.

"Ohh!" she cried out, and arched her back. "Pearce, oh, yes, that's good."

For a moment, he lifted his head from her clit. "Is that so?" He thrust his two fingers deep into her to emphasize his question.

"Oh God, yes!"

"Then maybe this is even better," he said, and added a third finger. He took his time driving all three fingers into her channel, and simultaneously started licking her clit again.

On the second thrust of his three fingers, Daphne shuddered. Again, she cried out, and then he felt the spasms clamping around his fingers, imprisoning him there. He stopped thrusting, but he kept his tongue on her clit and softly caressed it while she climaxed.

When she finally stilled, he slowly pulled his fingers from her channel and lifted his head from her pussy. He looked at Daphne's chest. Her breasts were covered in perspiration, her nipples hard, her breaths ragged. Her mouth was open, her eyes closed. But she wasn't sleeping.

Pearce slowly sat up. His cock was throbbing now, demanding release. He wrapped his hand around his hard-on and began to pump, his eyes focused on Daphne, and she suddenly opened her eyes. Her gaze flew to his cock. He stopped his movements.

Daphne shook her head and crooked her finger. "I believe you said earlier you wanted to fuck my pussy."

"You looked as if you'd had enough."

"I guess I didn't mention that I'm insatiable." She sat up and took his hand, removing it from his erection. "I'm so wet now. I think you'll like that even more than fucking my tits." She brushed her lips over his mouth and kissed him. Then she withdrew her head. "And with that cock of yours, I'm sure you can get deeper than with your fingers."

He shoved her back onto the duvet and leaned over her. "Oh, I can get as deep as you want me to."

She reached for the bedside table. "Do you keep your condoms in here?"

Fuck! He hadn't thought of that. Well, he hadn't thought that following her tonight would lead to them landing in bed.

Daphne seemed to read his facial expression. "You don't have any?"

He sat back on his heels. "Sorry. I wasn't planning this at all."

She chuckled softly and shook her head. "Typical computer geek."

He shrugged and sighed. "I suppose that's the end of tonight, then."

She tilted her head a little to the side. "You know, I'm on the pill. Always have been, because of my painful periods. So..." She cast a long look over his body. "If you're healthy... I mean, if you don't have..."

"Any sexually transmitted diseases? I don't." That was the truth. As an immortal, he didn't carry any diseases. "But you have no reason to believe me. Anybody could say that."

"I know. But the fact that you point that out..." She sat up and put her hand on his nape. "I don't see you as the kind of guy who'd lie about something like that."

"So you mean..." He hesitated. "Are you sure? You know I can wait."

Again she chuckled and gave his cock a pointed look. "I don't think you can."

"Well, if you got dressed and didn't look so darn seductive, I'm sure I could wait."

"Mmm-hmm." She wrapped her hand around his hard-on.

Pearce tilted his head back and took a deep breath, fighting the urge to press Daphne onto her back and bury himself in her. "You should stop that."

"But I like touching you." She moved her hand up and down his cock. "I've never been with anybody this big."

"Now you've done it." He grabbed her and pressed her onto her back, covering her with his body. "You little tease." Before she could answer, he covered her mouth with his and silenced her the only way Daphne seemed to understand. Her tongue met his in a game as old as time.

"Pearce?"

A familiar voice suddenly interrupted his bliss. He ripped his mouth from Daphne's and whipped his head in the direction the voice had come from.

Shit!

There, at the open door, stood Enya, his compound mate, her face a mask of disapproval.

14

"Enya, what are you doing here?" Pearce yelled at the blonde who was standing in the bedroom as if the place belonged to her.

Embarrassment swept through Daphne. And then a second feeling trumped it. What if this was Pearce's girlfriend? A girlfriend who'd come home unexpectedly. One who didn't look too pleased about seeing Pearce in bed with another woman.

Daphne wiggled to get free and tried to pull on the sheet to cover herself, but Pearce was still on top of her. "Who is she?"

Pearce suddenly stared at her. "She's my..."

"Colleague," the woman said.

"...roommate," Pearce finished.

Neither answer rang true. Clearly, they were both hiding something. Ah, shit, what had she gotten herself into now?

"We work together," Pearce added. "And we share this apartment." Then he looked at the woman he'd called Enya. The woman who was way too pretty for a roommate or a colleague. "How about some privacy?"

"Fine." Enya turned on her heel, left the bedroom, and shut the door behind her.

Immediately, Daphne pushed against Pearce, and to her surprise, he lifted himself off her without complaint.

Daphne quickly rose and snatched her panties from the floor. While she hastily put them on, she cast Pearce a look. He made no attempt at getting dressed. Instead, he stared at her, a guilty look on his face.

Daphne couldn't help herself asking, "Are you sleeping with her too?"

His eyes widened. "With whom? Enya? No, of course not! Why would you think that?" He seemed truly outraged.

"Well, she seemed pissed off about finding us in bed together." She reached for her pants, but Pearce snatched her arm and pulled her to him so she had to look at him. "What?"

"Enya and I work together, and we share this place, but there's nothing else between us. She's just pissed because I was supposed to help her on a project tonight, and I stood her up, because I followed you instead. She gets mad easily, but she calms down just as quickly. You'll see. She's not a bad person if you give her a chance."

The words seemed sincere, but Daphne wasn't sure what to think. "Why did she just barge in here without knocking?"

"I'm sure she knocked, and we didn't hear her."

Daphne sighed. It was possible—after all, they had been rather engaged in their lovemaking. She hadn't heard the apartment door or the bedroom door open. So it was possible that she'd missed a knock as well. "Okay... But this is really embarrassing..."

"Trust me, I covered you with my body the entire time. Enya didn't really see anything."

Daphne rolled her eyes. "Still embarrassing. She basically watched us have sex."

A mischievous smile played around Pearce's lips. "Not quite. I wasn't even inside you yet." He pressed a soft kiss to her lips. "Unfortunately." Then he gave her a playful slap on her ass. "Let's get dressed. I'll introduce you to her properly."

He handed Daphne her pants then started getting dressed himself.

Once she'd pulled up her pants, she looked around for her sweater, then remembered where she'd left it.

"My sweater is in the living room."

"I'll get it. Wait here." His chest bare, he left the room.

She heard the murmur of low voices, but couldn't understand what they were saying. While she waited, she glanced around. Just like in the living room and kitchen, there wasn't a lot of decoration, leaving the place rather impersonal. Since Pearce had only just moved in, she could understand it.

Pearce came back, dressed in his long-sleeved T-shirt and with her turtleneck sweater in his hand. She pulled it over her head quickly, then they walked back into the living room together. Enya was leaning against the kitchen table.

"I knocked, just so you know," Enya said.

"Daphne, this is Enya. Enya, this is Daphne. We met yesterday," Pearce said.

Daphne stretched her hand out, and Enya shook it. "I'm sorry that Pearce didn't keep his appointment with you because of me."

Enya rolled her eyes. "Don't make it your fault. It's his. And he knows it." She tossed him a chiding look. Then her anger seemed to disappear. "Anyway, when he didn't show up to help me, I started looking for him. We look out for each other, you know."

Daphne smiled. Enya seemed to be a good person. A friend who cared. "I'm glad. And just so you know, he didn't stand you up for…" She motioned toward the bedroom. "He helped me out of a bad situation earlier. Without him, who knows what would have happened?"

Enya raised an eyebrow and glanced at Pearce. "Care to share?"

"That's up to Daphne," he replied.

Daphne looked at Pearce. She didn't want to involve anybody else in this mess. It was enough that Pearce knew. "I don't wanna burden anybody with this."

Pearce squeezed her arm. "Enya is in the same business as I. If we combine forces, I think we can figure out how to help your brother."

She held Pearce's gaze. "Are you sure?"

"Enya can help," Pearce insisted.

Slowly, Daphne nodded. "If you're sure about it."

"I am." He turned to Enya. "Maybe we should all sit down."

"That bad, huh?" Enya asked.

"Well, it's not good," Pearce said, then began to explain to his roommate what Daphne had gotten herself into.

He left out the fact that Daphne had a criminal record, and she was grateful for it. She didn't want to be judged by the beautiful blonde who seemed perfect in every way. It was bad enough that it was evident that Daphne was sleeping with Pearce a mere day after first meeting him. Right now, she didn't know what to think of it herself. She'd enjoyed Pearce's touch, felt wonderful when he'd made her climax, and had wanted to go further with him. Hell, she'd been more than eager to feel him inside her, without protection, without a barrier, even though he was a stranger. But in his arms, she'd felt safe. Safer than she'd ever felt.

When Pearce finished recounting the events of the night, Enya leaned back into the sofa cushions and blew out a breath. "Well, fuck me! We've gotta get those motherfuckers."

Daphne successfully suppressed a grin. Perhaps Enya wasn't that perfect after all. She cursed like a sailor and made no attempt at apologizing for it. It actually made her a bit more approachable—and likeable.

"How?" Daphne asked. "I can't trace my brother's phone. He switched off the GPS tracking I installed on it."

"You installed GPS tracking on your brother's phone?" Enya asked. "Why?"

"He always gets into trouble. I wanted to keep tabs on him."

"Smart," Pearce said. "Then we have to try to trace the kidnapper's phone instead. I suppose there was no caller ID?"

"It's the same phone," Daphne said.

"What do you mean?" Pearce asked.

"The kidnapper used Tim's phone to communicate with me."

Pearce and Enya exchanged a look. "Amateurs," they said in unison.

"If you think of tracing it, I had the same idea," Daphne said quickly, "but it's switched off. He only seems to switch it on when he's calling me. So, even if we manage to put a trace on it while he's calling, what if he doesn't stay on the phone long enough?"

"Doesn't matter," Pearce said. "We'll hack into the carrier's records, download the cell tower data, and figure out where the phone's been since your brother was taken. Right, Enya?"

Enya nodded. "You're the boss."

Daphne looked from Pearce to Enya. "But I can't let you do something illegal. If you get caught, it's on me. And then you're no better off than I." She couldn't live with the guilt of driving somebody to commit a crime to save her and her brother.

"Get caught?" Enya laughed.

Pearce joined in.

"She's funny, you know," Enya said. "I like her."

Pearce patted Daphne's hand. "We're not gonna get caught. We're good."

She sidled up to Pearce and dropped her voice. "That's what I thought too. But you know what happened."

"And that's very unlucky, but Enya and I have systems in place that make it impossible for anybody to trace the breach back to us. Trust us. Trust me. Nobody's gonna get hurt."

Daphne looked at him, then at Enya, who nodded. "Okay, what do we do?"

"Give me your phone and your passcode. I'll need to go through the calls and messages you received from your brother's phone. And then we'll start tracing it. But we can't do it from here. I need my equipment in the... uh, office."

Daphne rose to retrieve her phone. "Okay, then let's go to your office."

"You can't come," Pearce said.

"What? But this is—"

"I'm sorry, but my office is in a secure building. There's no way I can get you through security. It'll just slow us down." Pearce gave her a sad look. "I'll have to go on my own. Enya needs to stay here to set up the computer on this end so that I can get the system at the control center to feed the data directly back here."

Daphne nodded, somewhat deflated.

"When will the kidnappers contact you again to hand over the stuff you were supposed to steal tonight?"

"They said they'll call me tomorrow to arrange a place for the exchange."

"Good," Pearce said. "That gives us a little time. They won't know yet that you didn't open the safe. But there's a chance that the police report from tonight is picked up by the news. Depends on how prominent the owners are. Let's hope we can find the kidnappers before they get wind of the fact that you haven't gotten the stuff they're after."

"Yeah," Enya added. "Or we'll have a whole lot of other problems."

Daphne didn't even want to think that far ahead. "I wish I could do something."

"Just promise me you'll stay here with Enya while I go to the office to set everything up. I'll be back in a couple of hours." Then he looked at Enya. "You good with that?"

"Sure. Call me when you're there, and we can set up the connection to the computer here," Enya said.

Pearce grabbed his jacket and headed for the door. With a last look over his shoulder, he left.

Suddenly Daphne was alone with the beautiful blonde. For a few moments, there was silence. Daphne looked for something to say, but was at a loss. What was there to say? She was on edge because Pearce had left to do something illegal—for her. What if he got caught?

"You must be tired," Enya said.

Daphne turned her head to Enya. "I'm all right."

"It's late. You can crash in Pearce's room. He won't mind. There isn't much we can do right now anyway. Not until Pearce has accessed the system and can do a trace."

"I understand." She shifted from one foot to the other. "So where do you guys work that you have that kind of equipment at hand?"

"Defense contractor." Enya shrugged. "Top secret. So, not a word, okay?"

"I promise." Who was she to rat out the people who were helping her out of a terrible quagmire?

"Good. Now rest a little. I'll wait for Pearce to call."

15

With Enya's help, Pearce had been successful in establishing a secure connection between the control center computer and the laptop in the safehouse. He'd also placed a trace on Daphne's line, so that when the kidnappers called her again, Pearce would be able to find out where the call was coming from. However, not everything had gone to plan. When he entered the safehouse, Enya was waiting for him in the kitchen.

"Any alerts while I was on my way back?" he asked in a hushed voice.

She shook her head. "Nothing yet. Bad luck, huh?"

He grunted. "Why does that phone carrier have to have a server outage just when I'm trying to get in?"

"Happens," Enya said. "There's nothing you can do other than wait."

She was right. "Is Daphne sleeping?"

"Yep. She finally agreed to rest."

He glanced at the bedroom door. "Guess there's nothing either of us can do now. Might as well catch some shuteye. Why don't you go back to the compound? I can call you if I need backup."

Enya hesitated. "I think I should stay here."

"I can handle this alone."

"Yeah, I saw that earlier. You're playing with fire."

Pearce ran a hand through his hair. "She's attracted to me. I can use that."

"Attracted? You think?" Enya shook her head. "So, you really believe that by fucking the living daylights out of her you can prevent her from killing you?"

"I wasn't fucking the liv—"

Enya raised her hands. "Spare me. I'm not blind." She sighed. "Listen, I'm not begrudging you the fun, okay? But I'm concerned. She's clearly up to her eyeballs in trouble, and she's already dragged you into it. It can only end badly. Winter is never wrong."

"But she also admits that her visions can change as events change. And by helping Daphne free her brother from his kidnappers, I'm getting her out of trouble. That could be exactly what I need to do to change the outcome of Winter's vision. By helping Daphne, I'll be her friend. She'll be grateful and won't have a reason to kill me."

Enya scoffed. "Yeah, and just to get a few more Brownie points, you're fucking her. Make sure that doesn't backfire."

"What's that supposed to mean? You think I'm not a good lover?" He hated that implication. Besides, Daphne seemed to have enjoyed herself in his arms.

"Eek! Can we please not talk about that? You're like a brother to me. Trust me, I don't want to know what you do to satisfy a woman. I leave that up to you. I'm just saying that the more emotionally involved you two get, the greater the chance that those emotions will turn. I've seen it happen: we don't hate anybody more than the person we once loved and who disappointed us."

"Then I won't disappoint her."

"Yeah, good luck." Enya snatched her leather jacket and slipped it on. "Since I can't talk you out of it, I'd better leave. I'm not into watching a train wreck in progress."

"It won't be a train wreck."

"Whatever you say." She marched to the door, then looked over her shoulder. "Call me if you need me. And please, be careful. You're the only sane guy at the compound. I'd hate to lose you."

Pearce smiled. It was rare that Enya gave out compliments. "Love you too."

She left and pulled the door shut quietly behind her.

Pearce took off his jacket and hung it over the chair, then sat down at the computer and opened the window that provided him with a direct link to his computer in the command center. The server of the telephone carrier was still down. He quickly typed in a script that would notify him with a sound as soon as the server was up again.

Now all he could do was wait.

And get some sleep.

He eyed the couch. He knew it was comfortable. He'd slept here before, when protecting a charge. But tonight, the couch didn't appeal to him. Not when he knew who was sleeping in the bedroom.

He walked to his jacket and reached into the pocket. The little packet he'd gotten on the way back was there. He pulled it out and looked at it. A three-pack of condoms. Not that he'd need them tonight, or rather this morning—it was close to five a.m.—because Daphne was asleep. Nevertheless, he took them with him when he silently entered the bedroom.

His eyes adjusted to the darkness in the room. Daphne lay underneath the covers, her clothes folded on a chair nearby. Surely, after what they'd done earlier, she wouldn't mind if he slipped under the covers with her. Convinced of it, he placed the box of condoms on the bedside table and stripped down to his boxer briefs.

Pearce lifted the duvet and slid into bed. Daphne lay on her side, her back turned to him. He nudged closer and spooned her, realizing immediately that she wore nothing, not even her panties. He'd expected her to have helped herself to a T-shirt from the closet, but Daphne had opted to sleep in the nude. His body instantly reacted, his cock pumping full of blood, reminding him that he hadn't had any relief earlier. Already now, his hard-on was straining against his boxer briefs.

"Pearce?"

Daphne's sleepy voice jolted him. She stirred and turned toward him. "I didn't mean to wake you."

"Did you find something? Did you hack into the system?" she asked, all signs of sleepiness gone.

"I'm afraid I've run into a problem. The telephone company's server is down for emergency maintenance. I can't access it."

"Crap!" she cursed.

"I know. But I've got a script running right now, and as soon as the server is up, it'll ping me, and I'll be able to get to work. So, I figured I'd sleep a couple of hours." Though trying to sleep with a hard-on the size of the Empire State Building wouldn't be easy.

"So there's nothing we can do right now?" she asked.

"No, I'm sorry."

"Okay, then maybe we'll rest." On her way to lie back down, she put her hand on his nape and dragged him with her, so he was covering her with his body.

"What are you doing?" he murmured at her lips, and used his elbows to keep his weight off her.

"Are you extremely tired?"

"Why're you asking?"

She ran her hand to his waist, then slipped it underneath his boxer briefs to touch his bare skin. Then she did the same with her other hand.

"You know why I'm asking." She caressed him and shoved his boxer briefs farther down. "I can feel how hard you are."

"Can you?" He chuckled and ground his erection against her. He was enjoying the little teasing game they were playing.

"So, I was wondering what you were gonna do about it." She sounded like a naughty kitten.

"I have a few ideas."

"Such as?"

"I could take one of the condoms I brought and put it on..."

"You bought condoms? For me?"

"I figured it would make you more comfortable about sleeping with me. You know, me, a stranger."

She pulled his face to her and kissed him softly on the lips. "You're so thoughtful. Just for that, I give you free rein. So, tell me, how would you like to fuck me?"

A wave of heat shot through his center and made his heart pound in his chest. "Free rein?" He dipped his head to her neck and kissed her there, then worked his way up to her ear. "How about you lie on your side the same way you did when I got into bed? Just pretend you're asleep."

"Hmm. Promise you'll take me hard."

"If that's what you want…" He lifted himself off her and turned to the nightstand. Within seconds, he'd shed his boxer briefs, sheathed himself with the condom, and was ready.

Daphne now lay on her side, her back to him. The moment she'd given him free rein, it had been the first and only thing that had come to his mind. Sliding into bed with a naked woman and plunging into her, knowing she would welcome him the moment she awoke from his first thrust, implied an intimacy reserved only for longtime lovers. He didn't know why he craved this particular intimacy with Daphne, but he wanted this, needed this.

Silently, he slid back into bed and spooned her, lining up his groin with her ass. He stroked along her thigh, then lifted it just enough so he could align his cock with her pussy. He nudged forward a fraction, then a little more, feeling the moisture from her folds. She was ready for him. And he was ready for her.

One hand holding her hip, he drove into her, deep and fast, just like she'd demanded it. Daphne's moan broke the silence.

"Oh yes!" she cried out.

Pearce repeated his action, pulling out and sliding back into her. This time, he let go of her hip and brought his hand up to her torso, cupping one breast, squeezing it hard on the next thrust. Daphne pushed her ass back into his groin whenever he thrust forward, doubling the impact. Her hand was on his upper thigh now, holding on to him as if she wanted to force him to fuck her harder.

This was better than he'd hoped. Wilder. Harder. Faster. This was the kind of fucking he'd always dreamed of but never thought a woman like Daphne would like.

He shoved his free hand into her hair and pulled her head back so he could kiss her throat. "So you love being fucked like this?"

"Yes!"

"Good girl." He plunged harder and deeper. Squeezed her tits again and again. Tugged on her nipple, rubbed it between thumb and forefinger, while his cock thrust relentlessly. In and out. Faster and faster.

Sweat was building on his body, and every time they slammed together, back to front, sounds of passion filled the bedroom. He was glad that Enya was gone, because there was no way he could remain quiet tonight.

He turned Daphne's face to him and kissed her, thrusting his tongue into her mouth the same way he plunged his cock into her pussy. Relentless. Demanding. Passionate. When he ripped his lips from hers to take a breath, she moaned.

"Oh, Pearce, I'm so close."

"I don't want you to come yet," he said. "I'm not done with you. I'm not done fucking you."

He continued driving his cock into her, now letting go of her breast and grabbing her hip for better leverage. But he needed more. This wasn't enough anymore.

He withdrew and flipped Daphne onto her stomach. A second later, he was behind her, pulled her hips up, and spread her legs wider. He got onto his knees and plunged his cock into her, holding on tightly to her hips so she couldn't slip away.

"Oh God! That's it! Pearce, that's..." The rest of her sentence died.

He realized immediately why: Daphne was climaxing. He felt the waves of her orgasm crash against his cock, her interior muscles squeezing him in concert with her spasms. There was no escape for him. He let go of the last vestiges of his control. His cock exploded from the tip, filling the condom with his seed. His entire body spasmed; heat shot through him; waves of pleasure crashed over him and buried him. His body was shaking. If he had to walk right now, he knew he couldn't. His legs wouldn't work. It was a miracle he didn't collapse immediately.

He managed to pull himself from her and flop next to her as she did the same, her head buried in the pillow. Somehow he managed to rid himself of the condom, but it was too much of an effort to snatch the duvet to cover them both. So they just lay there, breathing hard and utterly satisfied.

Their breaths were the only sounds in the room until Daphne finally lifted her head and turned it to him.

"You're so not the shy computer geek," she said.

"Guess my cover is blown." He chuckled. "You still like me?"

She smiled then winked. "Actually, I like you even more now."

His heart did a somersault. He would prove his colleagues wrong: his actions would change the future and save his life, because the way Daphne looked at him right now told him that she wouldn't hurt him, let alone kill him.

16

———

Daphne looked over Pearce's shoulder, marveling at the ease with which he circumvented the telephone company's security system to access their server. It was late morning, and they'd both showered and gotten dressed by the time the computer had finally given off a soft ping, indicating that it was time to get to work. Enya was gone. Pearce had mentioned that she'd probably stayed overnight at her boyfriend's place to give them privacy in the two-bedroom apartment, where the walls seemed paper-thin.

Daphne felt a twinge of guilt about the night before. She'd enjoyed herself with Pearce while her brother was locked up somewhere, suffering. But she was also realistic. She'd done exactly what the kidnappers had wanted—well, up until the moment she'd triggered the silent alarm—and after confessing to Pearce what trouble she was in. Then they'd worked on a plan to find Tim. The fact that the server of the phone company had been down wasn't her fault. What should she have done? Twiddled her thumbs? No, Pearce and her having sex hadn't delayed the search for the kidnappers one second. Therefore, she shouldn't feel guilty about it. Right.

Daphne put her hand on Pearce's shoulder. "I'm amazed at how good you are. I thought I was good, but wow, I can still learn something from you."

He briefly put his hand on hers and squeezed it. "You learn a lot when you've been at it for as long as I have."

"No wonder you're working for a defense contractor. With your skills."

He whirled his head toward her. "Defense contractor?"

"Yeah, Enya mentioned it." Seeing his surprised look, she put her hand over her mouth. "Oh, she was probably not supposed to tell me that. Sorry, but I asked her, and she swore me to secrecy."

"It's all right," he said, and turned his attention back to the computer. "I should have told you myself. I'm sorry if you feel that I'm not telling you a lot about myself. I'm just not used to sharing things with others." He shrugged. "You know, shy computer geek and all."

She put her arms around him from behind, hugging him tightly. "Right. I think we established last night that you're not shy." And that, in fact, he was very adventurous. As well as sexy, passionate, and insatiable.

Pearce squeezed her forearm. "You're not shy either." His eyes were reflected back at her in the monitor. "I enjoyed that. I hope that won't be the last time you let me ravish you like that."

Daphne chuckled. "Ravish? I believe that word belongs in a historical romance novel."

"I wouldn't know." He pressed a kiss to the back of her hand. "All I know is that you just avoided giving me an answer."

She turned into him and brought her face to his. When she pressed her lips to his and kissed him, he immediately pulled her onto his lap and kissed her back. It was hard to break the kiss, but eventually she did.

"Did that answer your question?" she asked with a smirk.

He mock-grimaced. "I wish you'd at least give me a sign, some sort of indication whether I have a chance, rather than keeping me guessing."

She playfully slapped him on the arm and rose from his lap. "Men! They don't see what's right in front of them."

Pearce chuckled and resumed his work on the keyboard. "Okay, the information is downloading," he said after a few minutes. "It'll give us the cell towers the calls were bouncing off. And once I merge it with a little program I wrote, it'll calculate the likelihood of a more specific location."

Slowly, Daphne scanned the rows of data on the screen. The column entitled *Locations* contained GPS information rather than addresses. She pointed to them. "Can you plot those on a map?"

"Yep, no problem. Just let me log off before they know what's happening." Pearce waited for the entire list to download, then severed the connection to the server.

Daphne watched him work his magic with a few clicks of the mouse and several lines of code. Then a map popped up, and red dots with little flags attached to them appeared on it. The map was of Baltimore.

"They're keeping him in the city," Daphne concluded from the information in front of her eyes.

"Looks like it. Your brother's cell phone hasn't been out of the city since he was taken. That's good. It'll narrow down our search." He zoomed in and clicked on one of the dots to get more information. "Let's start eliminating some of the locations. Do you know where this is?"

Daphne leaned in and read the street name. "I'm pretty sure that's the bar where he hangs out with his buddies."

"Looks like he, or his cell phone, was there three days ago." He clicked on it twice, then changed the color of the dot to green. "It's unlikely that we'll find his kidnapper or Tim himself there. They'd be avoiding any places where Tim is known. And in particular places that you know of and would go looking for him."

"I agree." She pointed to another dot. "Can you zoom in on this one? I think that's his apartment." Pearce followed her request. She nodded. "Yes, that's the street he lives on. It's a duplex. When was he there last?"

Pearce clicked on it. "Hmm. Yesterday." He turned to face her. "Didn't you say you got the first call from the kidnapper two days ago?"

"Yes, it must have been around eleven in the morning."

"Well, it looks like the kidnapper went back to your brother's place the day after he took Tim. Could he have been looking for something in the apartment?"

"I don't know. It's odd. But it's possible. I mean, when he showed me my brother on the video, he was tied up, so it's possible he left him alone, or with an accomplice, to go to Tim's apartment."

"Okay, we can certainly check there if they left any clues. I assume you have a spare key?"

Daphne nodded. "How about the call Guido made two days ago, the one I got around eleven a.m.? Can you see where it came from? Shouldn't that have come from the place they're holding my brother? Especially since they sent me a video from there."

"Very likely, though there's always a chance that they prerecorded the video at another location. Give me a moment." Pearce clicked on the few remaining dots until he found the one that showed the approximate time and date of the call the kidnapper had made to Daphne's cell. "Here's the cell tower the call bounced off." He clicked on a small icon, and a program began to run in a narrow window. Moments later, several dots around the cell tower location popped up. They were overlaid with percentages.

"That's the likelihood with which the call came from any of these buildings here," Pearce explained, then pointed to one dot. "This is our best bet. It looks like an apartment building." He changed the map to satellite view and zoomed in even closer. "Let me check something." He changed windows and typed an address into the search engine. The hits came back immediately, and Pearce clicked on the top link. "Yep, an apartment building with around forty flats." He looked at her. "It won't be easy to figure out which apartment the call was made from, but I think we should start there."

"I agree."

He grabbed his phone and hit a number. "Just a sec, yeah?" A moment later, he said into the phone, "Hey, Enya. We've got an address we're gonna check out. The first call the kidnappers made to Daphne was made from there. But it's an apartment building." He read out the address. "You think you can help us?"

There was a short pause, then Pearce nodded. "Okay, that's what I had in mind too. I'll text you Tim's photo in a second. Daphne and I will head there now. Is the car in the garage? Thanks, appreciate it."

He disconnected the phone and rose, typing something on the message system. Daphne watched him attach a photo of Tim, one she'd had on her own phone, and send it.

When he looked up and met her eyes, he pointed to the message he'd just sent. "I hope you don't mind, but when I had your phone to plant the trace, I sent myself a photo of Tim so that I could recognize him. I hope that's all right."

"Of course," she said. "I should have thought of that."

"No problem."

"So, what now?"

"Enya will meet us at the apartment building as soon as she can."

"I feel bad dragging her into this," Daphne said. "It's bad enough that I had to ask you for help, but Enya... What if she gets hurt?"

Pearce smiled. "Trust me, Enya is one tough cookie. She might not look it, but she's an expert in several martial arts disciplines. She could toss me on my back and disable me before I could even introduce myself. Don't worry about her. If she didn't want to help, she would say so. She doesn't mince words."

"If you're sure."

"I am."

After shutting down the computer and slipping into their jackets, they left the apartment. Pearce led her down to the garage, where he unlocked a swanky BMW and motioned her to get in. The engine hummed a few seconds later, and Daphne clicked the seatbelt.

"You asked Enya if the car is in the garage. Is this hers?"

He maneuvered out of the tight parking spot. "Company car. We share it." As he drove out of the garage, he pointed to the car's navigation system. "Can you please program in the address?"

"Sure." She typed in the street name and number of the apartment building, while Pearce merged into light pre-lunch traffic. After she'd activated the GPS system, she said, "We should be there in about half an hour."

Unease suddenly slithered down her spine. She turned to Pearce, who looked cool and collected. "What are we gonna do when we find where they're holding him? I mean, we're not armed; we don't know how many there are. We can't just march in and demand they let him go." Clearly, she hadn't thought this through at all.

Pearce put his hand on hers and squeezed it. "One thing at a time."

"Maybe we should call the police now."

"Daphne, you didn't call the police because you were worried that they're watching you and might hurt your brother. What's changed?"

Daphne sighed. "You're right. I'm sorry. I'm just nervous. I might be a convicted felon, but I never did anything violent. I don't even know how to use a gun."

"You won't need to use one. Just trust me. We'll get your brother out safely."

She wished she had Pearce's confidence, and could only hope that he could back it up with action.

17

Pearce took his time driving to the apartment building. He needed to give Enya sufficient time to scope out the building to get a clue from which unit the kidnapper had called. She'd told him over the phone that she planned to enter each apartment invisibly and do a very quick check. Even if it took her only one minute to go through each unit, it would take her more than half an hour to inspect the entire building, including the basement if there was one.

A block away from the property, Pearce pulled into a parking spot along the curb and switched off the engine. Then he turned to Daphne, who already had her hand on the door handle.

"Wait."

She looked at him.

"Ground rules first: you stay behind me at all times, and if I tell you to do something, you'll do it without protest. Agreed?" His first priority was keeping Daphne safe, his second extracting her brother—if he was indeed inside this building—without bloodshed.

"I understand."

Pearce rolled his eyes. He wasn't born yesterday. "I didn't ask whether you understood. I asked whether you agreed."

"Fine. I'll do what you say." She opened the door. "Has anybody ever told you that you're bossy?"

She got out of the car, and Pearce did the same, then looked across the car's roof to where Daphne stood waiting for him on the sidewalk. "Last night you liked bossy."

She blushed at that, but didn't retort. He sidled up to her and took her arm, ushering her along. "Just stay close, okay?" he said in a softer voice. "I don't want you to get hurt, and we don't know yet what we're walking into."

He hoped he'd have better intel as soon as Enya was done with searching the building. Under other circumstances he would have done it himself, but with Daphne in tow, he couldn't very well make himself invisible and walk through walls. And leaving her behind in the safehouse hadn't been an option either: Daphne would have never agreed to let him go alone. He knew her well enough by now. So he hadn't even tried to persuade her to stay at the house.

Now all he had to do was stall until Enya joined them.

Arrived at the building, he looked at the names on the doorbells, then turned to Daphne. "Have a look through these names. Do any of them sound familiar?"

She gave him an odd look. "Are you saying I might know the kidnapper?"

He didn't think so, but he needed to buy time without looking like he was twiddling his thumbs. "I just want to cover all our bases."

He pointed to the doorbells again, and Daphne came closer and scanned them. She lifted her head and shook it. "Nope. Don't recognize any of them."

"Okay. How about the neighborhood? Has your brother ever mentioned it?"

"If he has, then I don't remember it. Though it's not too far from where he lives, maybe ten minutes by car." She looked to the door. "So, how are we gonna get in and figure out where the kidnapper called from?"

Pearce smiled. "Easy. Let's ring a few doorbells." He pressed several random doorbells, then waited.

A few seconds later, a voice came through the crackling intercom. "Yes?"

"Delivery," Pearce said.

A door buzzer sounded, and Pearce pushed the door open. "Ladies first."

Daphne walked inside ahead of him. He followed and pulled the door shut behind him, then heard footsteps from the stairs.

"Act normal," he whispered to Daphne, and took her hand.

The moment they turned the corner to where the stairway was located, they came to an abrupt halt. Enya was coming down the stairs.

"Hey, guys," she said. "I already looked around." She made eye contact with Pearce, and he understood. She'd swept the building invisibly.

"Did you find my brother?" Daphne asked.

Enya nodded.

"Oh my God! I can't believe it. How?"

Enya shrugged. "I just knocked on a few doors, said I lived in one of the apartments, and asked if I could borrow some tape to hang up a poster."

The explanation sounded believable. Pearce was glad that Enya had thought of something good to maintain their cover. Daphne couldn't find out that he and Enya had skills that defied nature.

"And you saw him? Is he all right? Is he hurt?" Daphne glanced up toward the top of the stairs.

"He seemed fine." Enya turned to Pearce. "Didn't you say that he was tied up in the video that the kidnapper sent?"

"That's right."

"Well, he's not tied up right now."

"Are they watching him with guns?" Daphne asked.

"They?" Enya shook her head. "There's only one other guy in the apartment from what I could see."

"And did he have a gun?"

"I couldn't see any. I think it'll be easy to sweep in and grab the kidnapper. Let's go."

Enya walked ahead. Pearce took Daphne's hand and squeezed it reassuringly. Whatever they were confronted with, he would handle it for her. As they followed Enya up two flights of stairs, he turned to Daphne. "Remember to stay behind me. Just in case the kidnapper is armed after all." Not that he believed that Enya had made a mistake.

They reached the third floor. Enya pointed to the right. There was a sign for apartments 3A to 3E. A similar sign indicating apartments 3F to 3J pointed to the left. Enya continued walking. Pearce was close behind her. She stopped in front of apartment 3C and motioned to it.

"Door's unlocked," she said in a low voice.

Daphne put her hand on Enya's arm. "Why would they leave it unlocked?"

"I made sure of it. Before the guy closed it, I put tape over the bolt, so it can't lock. He didn't notice."

Enya had thought of everything. Knowing that they couldn't just walk through the door in Daphne's presence, or their secret would be out, she'd made sure there was another way to access the apartment without alerting the people inside.

"Enya and I will go in," Pearce said, looking at Daphne. "You'll stay here until I give you the all-clear. Should the kidnapper manage to get past us and run out, I want you to get out of his way. Don't try to stop him. Understood?"

Daphne tipped her chin up. "I have to go in with you. He's my brother. I can't have you and Enya take all the risk."

"We know what we're doing," Pearce insisted.

"But how? You're computer programmers, just like I am."

Pearce sighed and quickly searched his brain for a plausible explanation. "But we work for a defense contractor, and they provide all their employees with extra training in case of hostage situations and such." It was total bullshit, but Daphne didn't know that. "We know what to do in situations like this. Please trust me."

Slowly, Daphne nodded. "Okay, fine. But be careful. Both of you."

Pearce nodded and exchanged a look with Enya. They'd done this kind of thing plenty of times before. Pearce tested the doorknob. It turned. He pushed the door in slowly and, without making a noise, peered inside. When he saw nobody in the short hallway, he slid inside and waved Enya to follow him.

The television was on in the living room. Pearce listened.

"...call her to set up the handover," a man said. The voice didn't come from the TV, but from a person in the living room.

Pearce inched forward, getting closer to the door, which was half open, and picked up a scent. He sniffed. Fresh pizza. He moved closer and could see a man on the couch bending forward to take a slice of pizza from the oversized box.

"Yeah, after we finish the pizza," a different man answered, his voice coming from the right.

Pearce looked at Enya, who was now next to him, and made a sign for the number two. Were there two kidnappers and not just one, as Enya had assumed? She shrugged, then made a motion that she would take whoever was to the right, while Pearce would overwhelm the one on the left.

With a nod to her, Pearce pushed the door open and charged in, barreling toward the man on the couch who was about to bite into his pizza. He dropped it on his lap, where it landed upside down. Before he could even get up, Pearce was already on him, yanking him off the couch and slamming him onto the coffee table, his face landing in the pizza. The jerk yelled out, but his words were swallowed up by pizza sauce and extra cheese.

"What the fuck!" the other guy yelled, and Pearce whipped his head to see how Enya was doing.

She wasn't pinning the second man down, nor did she have him in a chokehold. She simply held him back. Pearce realized why: the second man wasn't a kidnapper. He was Daphne's brother.

"Tim?" Holding the kidnapper down with a knee in his back, Pearce motioned to Daphne's brother. "Are you all right? Are you hurt?"

Tim shook his head, clearly confused and upset. "What the fuck do you guys want? Let go of my friend! You're hurting him!"

Pearce exchanged a look with Enya, whose forehead furrowed.

"Friend?" Enya asked, and tugged on Tim's shoulder.

Tim stared at her, then ripped himself free. Enya let it happen. "Who are you guys?"

"We're—"

"Tim! You're okay! Thank God!" Daphne charged into the room and ran to Tim, wrapping her arms around him. "Oh my God, I was so worried." Tears streamed down her cheeks.

"Daphne?" Tim pulled away from her, then glanced at Pearce and Enya. Then his eyes darted to the man whose face Pearce was still pressing into the hot pizza, the man Tim had called a friend.

Pearce quickly looked around. No signs of weapons or restraints. Tim wasn't here against his will. It all clicked now. His eyes landed on Tim again—whose face showed no bruises, when in the video it had looked like somebody had played soccer with his head. "You little shit!"

Tim's reaction, the look of guilt on his face, the look of being caught, said it all. He opened his mouth, but nothing came out.

Daphne stared at Pearce. "What?"

Pearce shook his head and motioned to Tim. "Why don't you tell your sister? Or do you really want me to explain to her what happened here, because you're too much of a coward?"

"Pearce, why are you talking to my brother like that?"

Pearce took his knee off his captive and pulled him up by his hair. The asshole squealed, but didn't fight him. "And whom do we have here? Why don't you introduce us to your friend, Tim? You are friends, aren't you?"

Daphne stared at her brother. "What is this?" Despite the question, it appeared that she was already putting two and two together. She pointed to the stranger. "Is this your friend?"

Tim dropped his head and nodded.

"I couldn't hear you!" Daphne said.

As if he'd been whipped, he lifted his head. "That's Kevin."

Still holding Kevin by his hair, Pearce said, "Why don't you say hi, Kevin? Or do you only talk on the phone when you pretend to be Guido, the strongman?"

It was obvious that Kevin wanted to bury his head in the sand, but Pearce wouldn't allow it.

Daphne took a step toward her brother. "You made all this up? You faked a kidnapping to have me break into a house and steal for you? What the actual fuck!" She pulled her arm back and smacked her brother in the face so hard that his head whipped to the side and he lost his balance and crashed against the armchair, where he landed rather softly.

But Daphne wasn't done. "You piece of shit! I worried about you! I thought they'd cut your finger off!" She slammed her fist in his chest, while Tim held his arms up defensively. "I nearly got caught by the police! You no-good jerk! How could you?"

When Daphne readied her fist again, Pearce gave Enya a sign. Enya snatched Daphne's arm and pulled her back.

"Don't. He's not worth it," Enya said gently.

Daphne stepped back and took a deep breath.

"I'm sorry, Daph," Tim said in a rather meek voice. "But I needed the money."

Daphne whipped her head back to him, her eyes full of fury. "You needed the money? Oh, let me punch you once more for that."

Pearce let go of Kevin, who was no danger to anybody, and grabbed Daphne before she could beat up her brother even more. "Enya is right. He's not worth it." He pulled Daphne into his arms and rubbed her back. After a while, she nodded, then freed herself from his embrace and turned back to her brother.

"What was it this time? Gambling? Laziness? Or some harebrained business idea, huh?" she asked, glaring at him.

"It was Kevin's idea!" Tim said, and pointed at his friend. "He knew about the safe in the house. He'd worked there on some carpentry job. He knew about the alarm system."

"Fuck, Tim!" Kevin said.

Daphne pivoted and glared at Kevin. "Oh, by the way, about the alarm system..." She went right up in his face, but Kevin didn't dare make a move. He was actually afraid of Daphne, a woman several inches shorter and many pounds lighter than he. "There was a second alarm system, you idiot! You nearly got me arrested!" She pushed him back, and he landed on the couch.

"I wouldn't have done it," Kevin said, and pointed back at Tim, "if Tim hadn't known that guy who hawks expensive stuff. But he said that guy could sell anything for good money. And the stuff in the safe, it's worth a shitload. And Tim owed money to him from some other deal, so he needed to get him something."

Pearce let out an exasperated breath. "Enough!" All eyes shot to him. "You're both guilty! And if it wouldn't implicate your sister, I'd drag both your sorry asses to the police and let you rot there. But I won't, because Daphne doesn't deserve this. She's gone through enough." He glared at both men. "So listen carefully. If you ever plan anything like this again and even attempt to draw Daphne into it and use her, then I'll be personally skinning you both alive. Is that clear?"

Tim and Kevin gaped at him, Tim's face drained of blood, Kevin's just as white under the layer of tomato sauce.

"I need an answer. Let me give you a hint: there's only one right answer."

Both blurted out, "Yes."

Pearce motioned to Enya, letting her know that they were done here. Then he took Daphne's arm. "Let's go. I'll take you home."

Without a word, Daphne turned around and marched out of the apartment. Pearce followed her, Enya on his heels. She shut the door behind them. In the hallway, Pearce turned to her. "Thanks for the help."

Enya sighed. "Sure. What now?"

"I'll take Daphne home."

"Will you be in the office later?" Enya asked, and he knew she wanted to know if he was returning to the compound.

He nodded. He'd done what he needed to do. Daphne's brother

was safe—had been safe all along. But Tim now knew that he'd be in trouble if he ever again tried to involve Daphne in any of his criminal activities. Daphne was on the right path again. Pearce was convinced that the event that had sent Daphne on the path to kill him had now been averted. He had helped Daphne out of a jam, and she was thankful. She had no reason to kill him now. No reason at all.

18

———

Zoltan stuffed the padded envelope into the inside pocket of his coat. This time he was prepared to track Vasili down if the unscrupulous human decided to play games. He was done with bowing to the conman's terms when it came to what Vasili offered him for purchase. It was time to sniff out the man's sources and deal with them directly. What did Zoltan need a middleman for when he could deal with the original procurer himself? It would also mean that fewer people knew what Zoltan was looking for. Besides, he didn't like Vasili. The idiot thought himself superior, and nobody was superior to Zoltan. He was the Great One, the King of the Underworld, and soon the ruler of the human world too. And whoever stood in his way would be crushed.

But for this afternoon, he would play along with Vasili's game one last time.

His colored contact lenses hiding his green eyes, Zoltan left his condo and waited for the elevator. When it dinged and the doors opened, he stepped inside and realized that he wasn't alone. A well-dressed woman in her forties stood in one corner.

He met her eyes and said politely, "Good day."

She gave him a quick smile then averted her eyes, but Zoltan didn't miss the blush that colored her cheeks. Yes, she liked the way he looked. And he wouldn't be averse to a quick fuck, but two things stopped him. The first was his rule never to get involved with a woman who lived in the same building, in case he had to dispose of her at some point. The second was that he had an important meeting with Vasili. Knowing the way the shyster operated, he'd quickly find another taker for his stolen goods if Zoltan didn't show. It was something he couldn't risk.

Swallowing his lusty feelings, Zoltan turned his back on the woman and stared at the doors while the elevator descended. When the elevator dinged to announce their arrival, Zoltan stepped aside politely and let the woman pass ahead of him. She whispered a thank you that sounded more like an invitation to her bedroom than a display of good manners. But he didn't react. Couldn't.

Well, maybe after his meeting, after he'd accomplished what he needed to do, he could pick up a woman to quench his thirst for some horizontal action. Despite the fact that he fucked demon females on a regular basis, he'd grown tired of their barely disguised agendas. They let him fuck them because they wanted to sit on the throne beside him, whereas a human female didn't even know how powerful he was. They wanted him because of his charm and good looks. And somehow that was more palatable to him. And when he had them in his bed, he felt a kind of satisfaction he rarely achieved with a demon. Even though the thought of another woman, one neither demon nor human, always intruded when he climaxed. But he couldn't have her. At least not yet. For now, he'd make do with human substitutes, petite women with long blond hair, pouting lips, and slender legs. But enough of the daydreaming.

His hands buried deep in the pockets of his coat, Zoltan left the swanky condo building and started walking. Even though it was early afternoon, storm clouds darkened the sky and prevented the sun from illuminating the streets. It felt as if the city could sense the ruler of the demons walking among the imposing buildings, as if the city had eyes and ears and knew something was brewing.

Zoltan turned into the narrow one-way street where Vasili's meeting spot was. He swiftly walked along the sidewalk, then he heard a sound on the other side of the street. He spun his head in that direction and dove for the dagger in his boot. The movement saved his life. A weapon whizzed past above him, narrowly avoiding his head, and clattered to the ground, the sound of metal on stone echoing against the buildings. Had he been upright, it would have found its target.

Zoltan gripped his dagger and lunged across the deserted street, chasing the shadow he'd caught in the corner of his eye. He saw it disappear into a building slated for demolition and dove after him. Nobody attacked the Great One and got away with it.

Inside the dilapidated building it was dark, the windows boarded up. But Zoltan was at home in the dark. He heard the rapid footfalls of the person fleeing from him, trying to traverse the building to find an exit leading to the street behind, but he wouldn't get far. Quiet like a mouse, Zoltan cut off the assassin's escape route. Loud breathing gave the bastard away. When he emerged from behind a column, Zoltan pounced and tackled him. They fell to the dusty stone floor, wrestling. But Zoltan was stronger. He landed a punch in the aggressor's face, making the man's head whip to the side. When he prepared for a counterpunch and glared at Zoltan, one thing was immediately clear: the man was a demon. One of his contact lenses had fallen out and revealed a demon-green eye.

"Fuck!" The revelation gave the demon time to land a blow to Zoltan's temple, but he absorbed the pain easily and pinned the demon down.

Fear in his eyes, one beaming green, one a dull brown, the demon began to whimper. "No, please have mercy, oh Great One!"

"Mercy?" Zoltan would have laughed had the situation not been so dire. One of his own demons, though he didn't know him personally, had tried to assassinate him. "I'll show you mercy." He glared at the demon and bared his teeth.

"No, no, please. I was forced. I had to do it. Or he would have killed me."

Zoltan narrowed his eyes. "You're saying you're only a tool?" He spat in the demon's face. "Coward!" How he despised weak men.

"No, please, you have to believe me. He's planning a coup."

So, there was somebody vying for his throne, and he wouldn't even do it the honorable way by proving to the underlings that Zoltan wasn't capable of defeating the Stealth Guardians, but by simply trying to have him assassinated.

"Who? Who's that vile coward?"

The demon opened his mouth. There was a whizzing sound, and Zoltan recognized it immediately as a dagger flying through the air. He let go of the would-be assassin and dove the other way, sliding behind a thick column.

"He's here, oh God!" the demon on the floor said. "He's—"

His sentence was cut short. Zoltan didn't have to look any closer to know the fate of the demon.

Silence followed the second dagger. Zoltan didn't dare breathe, only listened, but no matter how hard he concentrated, he couldn't hear in which direction the traitor had disappeared. Most likely he'd already opened a vortex outside the building and escaped back into the Underworld.

Fuck!

When it was clear that he was the only man alive in the dark building, Zoltan came out from behind the column and dusted himself off. He confirmed that the demon was indeed dead and collected any trinkets or weapons that might connect him to the Underworld. He dragged the demon to a hole that appeared to be an unused elevator shaft and tossed him in. He wasn't concerned about the body being discovered. He had more important things to do. And finding the traitor was only one of the things on his list.

Before he emerged from the building, Zoltan looked up and down the street. But there was nobody in sight. He sent a quick text to Vasili, telling him that there was police activity around the area and changed the meeting place to a different location. Vasili replied in the affirmative.

Zoltan was extra cautious when he made his way to the new meeting place. He turned often, doubled back several times, but nobody was following him. For today, he was safe.

Vasili was only five minutes late, but for once, Zoltan didn't mind. It gave him enough time to make sure the new meeting place, at the back entrance of a club, was secure, and they wouldn't be observed.

"Do you have pictures?" Zoltan asked impatiently the moment Vasili joined him.

The Russian reached into his inside pocket, and Zoltan, still on edge about the earlier attack, went on high alert. But Vasili pulled nothing more dangerous than a few photos out of his jacket.

"Those are the items I found," he said, and turned the photos so Zoltan could see them. "One of them, I believe, is exactly what you're looking for."

Zoltan ripped the photos from Vasili's hand. The first grainy picture showed what was clearly an Egyptian artifact, a bracelet of some sort. The next was a dagger with a swastika emblazoned on its handle. Zoltan grunted impatiently, then took a look at the third picture. His heart began to pound. He was absolutely certain that he recognized the weapon in the picture. He'd stared at a drawing of it for months, searched for it just as long, put out his feelers to every art dealer, reputable and disreputable, every private collector, every museum. And finally, Vasili had found it.

"Looks good," Zoltan said casually, hoping his voice didn't betray his excitement. "I'll take this one. When can you deliver?"

"Very soon," Vasili said, then reached for the photos and put them back into his pocket. "I'm meeting with my supplier tonight. There's just one thing."

Of course there was. But Zoltan was prepared. "Yes?"

"I'll need a down payment. Just to make sure you don't back out later."

Zoltan forced a smile. "Of course." Clearly, Vasili didn't have the cash he was supposed to pay his so-called supplier. "How much?"

"Half of what we agreed."

So that was the markup, then. Vasili paid his thieves—because that was all his suppliers were—half or less than half of what he charged Zoltan. Just as well that he was planning to cut out the middleman.

"Fine." Zoltan reached into his inside pocket and pulled out the envelope he'd prepared. He handed it to Vasili. "Count it."

Vasili opened the envelope and started leafing through the bills, just as Zoltan had expected. It made it easy to slip a tiny tracker no larger than a battery for an earpiece into Vasili's jacket pocket.

"It all looks in order," Vasili said. "I'll call you when I have the item and will arrange a meeting place."

"What time?"

"Expect me to call around eight."

Zoltan nodded. Vasili turned and started walking away, but looked over his shoulder, suspicious as ever. Zoltan waved, then pivoted and walked in the other direction, knowing that Vasili would look back several times more to make sure that Zoltan wasn't following him.

At the street corner, Zoltan turned left, then stopped halfway down the block. He pulled his cell phone from his pocket and opened an app he'd installed earlier in the day. It showed a map of Baltimore. A small dot blinked as it moved farther and farther away from Zoltan's location. It was his insurance that Vasili would deliver—one way or another—the dagger depicted on the third photo. It would quite literally open a portal to the hidden compounds of the Stealth Guardians, making them vulnerable to a demon attack.

Victory was so close that he could taste it.

19

———

Pearce entered the compound and went in search for Winter. He found her in the great room, where she was drinking tea and reading. She wasn't alone. In the adjacent kitchen, Leila was preparing a snack for the twins, who were playing chase.

"Hey," Leila said. "The guys were looking for you."

Winter looked up from her book. "Enya got back a little while ago."

Which meant that she'd probably filled his brethren in about what had transpired earlier today. "They can wait." He walked toward Winter. "I wanted to ask you for a favor."

Winter closed her book and laid it next to her on the couch. "I have the feeling this involves my gift."

"You truly are a psychic," Pearce joked.

"And you're very transparent. You want me to force a vision."

Pearce sat down on the couch and turned to her. "I think after what happened today and last night, I believe I eliminated the event that will drive Daphne to kill me. I think I changed the future. But I need certainty."

"We all want certainty," Winter said, and sighed. "But there's no such thing. And you know as well as I do that I can't force a vision. I've gotten better at it in the last few months, but it's not an exact science. I still haven't learned to truly control and channel them. They may come or they may not. If I could control them, then I would have solved a lot of mysteries by now."

Pearce lifted his hand. "Please, hear me out. By preventing Daphne from breaking into that safe last night and saving her from being arrested, I changed her path in life. She owes me big time." Though he'd never want anything for it. Knowing she was safe was good enough. "She has no reason to kill me. Whatever the reason was before, she would never do it now. She's grateful for my help." Besides, they had chemistry. That couldn't be ignored. Most people were driven by emotions, and from what he knew about Daphne by now, she was no exception. Whatever she did, her heart was in it.

"Yeah, Enya mentioned something about you two helping Daphne rescue her brother, and that it was some kind of scam her brother was pulling. Total shitbag, that guy."

He had to agree. How could a man put his own sister through so much pain and agony, not to mention the danger she'd been in? "Despicable. But the details aren't important right now. What matters is that I helped her get out of a jam, no matter who ultimately caused it." Though if Tim were his brother, he'd get a more serious beating than the one Daphne had doled out.

"Just try it, Winter," Leila said from the kitchen. "Or you'll never get him off your back. He's like a dog with a bone."

Winter exchanged a look with Leila. "You're right about that. In the end, they're all the same, your mate and mine, and the rest of this motley crew. When they want something, they won't stop until they get it."

Pearce rolled his eyes. "I'm nothing like Logan or Aiden. Or any of the others."

"Right," Leila said, sarcasm dripping from her voice.

"Nothing like them at all," Winter added, just as disingenuously.

Realizing that he wasn't getting anywhere with Winter if he didn't agree with her, he finally said, "Fine, so I'm a little like Logan and Aiden. Happy now?"

Winter chuckled. "One nil for Winter." Then she stretched out her hand. "Do you have anything that belongs to Daphne?"

Pearce had prepared for this moment and reached into his jacket pocket. He pulled out a scarf he'd clandestinely taken from Daphne's apartment when he'd dropped her off there an hour earlier. She'd asked him if he wanted to stay, but he'd declined and told her he'd call her later. She'd given him the kind of look a woman gave a man when she knew he wouldn't follow through. But she'd said nothing. And he hadn't been able to promise her anything else. Nor could he, until he knew whether his actions had produced the right outcome. Only then, he could take the next step.

Winter took the scarf, closed her eyes, and concentrated. Her breaths were even, her face relaxed. Pearce waited and tried not to show his impatience. He needed to know, needed to confirm that what he'd done had changed the outcome of Winter's original vision. Because if it had, then he had options.

For a few minutes, all he could hear were the twins, Julia and Xander, playing in the kitchen, the clatter of utensils, and Leila opening and closing the refrigerator as she was preparing food.

When Winter opened her eyes a few minutes later, Pearce already knew the answer to his question.

Winter shook her head. "I'm sorry. I'm not getting anything."

Desperate for any sort of confirmation, he asked, "Is it possible that you don't have a vision because she won't kill me? I mean, you can't see an event that's not gonna happen anymore, right?"

Winter shrugged. "I don't know. Just because I don't get a vision, doesn't mean the threat is gone. You should still take precautions. Like staying away from her."

"Stay away from her?" When the words were repeated in his own voice, he realized that he'd never planned to stay away from Daphne after this. Even though he'd tossed Daphne a casual "I'll call you later" that she'd interpreted as a kiss goodbye, he now knew that a goodbye was the last thing he wanted.

They'd been good together. They had things in common, not just when it came to computers. They'd been more than just compatible in bed. They'd set the sheets on fire. He couldn't throw that away because a vision confirming that she wouldn't kill him wasn't forthcoming.

"Yes, that would be the safest," Winter said, cutting through his thoughts.

"Winter is right," Hamish said from the door.

Pearce whipped his head in Hamish's direction. He hadn't heard him or the other Stealth Guardians enter, probably because they hadn't opened the door, but walked through it.

Behind Hamish stood Logan and Enya.

"I filled them in," Enya said.

Pearce shrugged. He'd expected as much. "Then you all know that I eliminated the threat Daphne represented."

"If you really believed that," Hamish said, "you wouldn't have asked Winter to force a vision." He motioned to the scarf in Winter's hand. "You're still worried. As are we."

Sure, there was still a risk. But Pearce's entire life was paved with risk. "There's nothing to worry about. She's not a threat."

"Because you're sleeping with her?" Logan asked in a sharp tone.

Pearce sucked in a breath and glared at Enya.

She raised her hands. "I didn't say a fucking word."

"So it's true," Logan continued. "I hope you're taking precautions."

"What the fuck!" Pearce said. "Yeah, if you must know, I'm using condoms so she won't get suspicious."

Logan shook his head. "I'm not talking about condoms. I'm talking about you keeping your wits about you. About always knowing where your weapon is. Making sure she can't get it. Idiot!"

"Asshole!" Pearce cursed.

"Stop it, both of you," Hamish interrupted. "There's no need to call each other names. Listen, Pearce, we just wanna make sure you're careful. At least until Winter can confirm that the threat is over."

Pearce ran a hand through his hair. "And what if Winter never has another vision about this? Do you really expect me to stay away from Daphne for good?"

Silence followed his words. Surprised silence. All eyes were on him. Even the twins had stopped playing and were quiet now.

He'd said too much. He should have kept his thoughts to himself.

"Is it *rasen*?" Hamish asked.

Was it rasen, the craziness that overcame a Stealth Guardian when he entered mating season, the time when a guardian turned around two hundred years old, and the urge to find a mate for life was the strongest?

"I don't know." And he wasn't in the mood to discuss it. "Excuse me. I'm sure work's piling up in the command center."

He rushed out of the great room into the corridor, not bothering to use the door. His heart was pounding, his breaths irregular, his palms sweating. Fuck, was he having a panic attack, or was it true? Was he feeling the effects of rasen? Was it hitting him broadside without warning?

Rasen was like puberty, only a hundredfold more intense. It was the time in a guardian's life when he was ready to mate, when his hormones yearned for that special connection with another person, when he was ready to procreate. Sure, even before rasen, Stealth Guardians had sex, and plenty of it if they had the opportunity, but nothing was serious. Most didn't form long-term relationships in those decades and hopped from partner to partner, from playmate to playmate. Few felt the need for permanent attachment. Only when rasen hit them, that need surfaced, and the race to find a mate began.

Had it begun for him? He was the right age, but somehow he'd always thought it would bypass him, overlook him. As if he could hide behind his computer screen and nature would not notice him. But it appeared nature had other plans.

Shit! Shit! Shit!

He rushed into the command center and almost collided with Ryder, who was on his way out. The vampire hybrid, who was in his mid-twenties, was originally from San Francisco, where he'd grown up among an extended family of vampires and witches who all worked for Scanguards, a security company founded and run by Samson, a vampire who was older than Pearce. The Stealth Guardians had formed an alliance with Scanguards. They came to each other's aid when necessary, and as a token of their friendship and trust, Scanguards had sent two of their hybrid vampires—half human, half vampire—to Baltimore to help out with sniffing out demons. In exchange, the young vampire hybrids received training from the Stealth Guardians.

"Hey, finally back, huh?" Ryder said cheerfully. "Anything new? I heard you helped out with solving a kidnapping."

From the computer console, Grayson, the second vampire hybrid, turned to them. "Yeah, Enya was telling us. Sounded like a doozy. The guy wasn't even armed."

"And it wasn't a real kidnapping, either," Pearce added. "But we couldn't know that."

Grayson lifted his hands. "Didn't mean to imply that you didn't do any real work." He pasted a charming grin on his face, confirming once more why women of all ages fell for him. He had charisma in abundance, just like his powerful father, Samson. "But you should've called us. We're always good for beating up some idiot who's playing with his sister's feelings."

Pearce lifted an eyebrow. Grayson wasn't normally so conciliatory. In general, he was more combative. Was the congeniality and friendship that ruled among the warriors in the Baltimore compound finally rubbing off on him?

"Appreciate it," Pearce said. "Next time, then. For now, it's all in the bag."

However, not everything was truly resolved when it came to Daphne's brother and his idiot friend Kevin. There was something

Tim had mentioned that bothered Pearce. He motioned to Ryder. "Hey, Ryder, are you busy right now?"

"I was just gonna go grab some food and hang out, so, no, I'm not busy. Why?"

"I've got a little job for you."

Ryder grinned. "Cool. I've been cooped up here all week. I'd love to get out and do something."

"Excellent."

20

———

Daphne was still fuming about the stunt her brother had pulled. Tim had had the gall to call her shortly after Pearce brought her home. But she'd been in no mood to talk to him other than to tell him to piss off. How could he have done this to her? Used her like this? And he hadn't only dragged her into his illegal scheme, he'd caused Pearce and Enya to get involved too. What if something had gone wrong?

Daphne had changed into a comfortable hippy skirt she liked wearing around the house and a matching embroidered blouse. Her legs crossed, she sat on the couch, unable to think straight. The only good thing was that it was Saturday and a long weekend. She didn't have to work on Monday. And she would need the time off just to calm herself down and feel normal again.

And then there was one other issue: Pearce. What was he thinking of her now? She'd dragged him into this mess, and in the end, it had turned out that her brother and his friend were the criminals. How did that reflect on her? Besides, Pearce had witnessed her punch her brother, and what guy wanted to be with a woman who displayed such violence? She'd been so infuriated that she'd needed to pummel her idiotic sibling, and had Enya not stopped her, she would have done much worse. She'd felt justified, too, because of the emotional pain and stress Tim's scheme had caused her. Not to mention the potential risk to her own freedom.

Just thinking of it made her heart race and her palms perspire. So much could have gone wrong.

The sound of the doorbell startled her and made her jump up from the couch. If this was Tim, she'd toss him out on his ass. Her jaw clenched, she marched to the door and ripped it open.

"You—"

She stopped herself. It wasn't Tim who stood in the dark hallway. It was Pearce, standing in front of her door, his hands by his sides, a hesitant smile on his face.

"I guess I'm not the person you were expecting. Am I coming at a bad time?"

She let out a relieved breath. "I thought it might be Tim. He's been calling me to apologize, but I don't want to talk to him. I thought... Never mind." She smiled and stepped aside. "Come in."

Pearce entered and shut the door behind him. "I know I said I'd call..."

She nodded. "You did, but..." If she was honest, she hadn't thought he would. Which made it even more surprising that he was here, in the flesh.

"I had to take care of a few things back at the office," he started. "But it's all settled. I've got time now."

"I feel like such a fool," she blurted. "I should have suspected that it was all a setup. I'm so sorry. My brother—"

Pearce put a finger to her lips to stop her flood of words. "It's not your fault. It all looked genuine, even to me and to Enya. A little amateurish, but still genuine. Nobody blames you."

She shook her head and felt tears shoot to her eyes. "But I know my brother. I know what he's capable of. I should have guessed."

Pearce brushed his knuckles over her cheek. "You're not responsible for his actions." Then he chuckled softly. "And you clearly don't approve of them. That punch you landed in his face was a pretty clear message to your brother."

She wanted to sink into a hole, feeling ashamed for her behavior. "It's not something I wanted you to see."

At that, Pearce laughed.

"What?" she asked.

Still chuckling, he said, "I like a woman who isn't afraid of punching a guy when it's necessary. And believe me, it was necessary."

Daphne stared at him in surprise. He wasn't appalled that she'd used physical force against her brother?

"Did I say something wrong?" Pearce asked.

She shook her head. "Pearce?"

"Yes?"

"Why are you here?"

"You want me to leave?"

"That's not what I said. Why did you come back? You've seen what kind of a mess my life is... And the stuff I dragged you and Enya into... Why would anybody want to come back at all?"

"Maybe I'm a glutton for women with messy lives."

"You can do so much better. I mean, look at you: you have a great job with a defense contractor, you're handsome, articulate, brave..."

"Don't forget good in bed," he added.

When she caught his smirk, she punched him in the arm. "You're not taking this seriously."

"But I am," he protested, and pulled her into his arms. His gaze was intense, his voice beseeching. "I'm taking this very seriously. You and I, that's serious. That is, if you want it to be." He put one hand on her nape and caressed her neck with his thumb.

The tender touch made it hard for her to think.

"But... but why?"

"Why don't I show you rather than tell you, huh?"

He dipped his head to hers, until his lips were hovering less than an inch above hers.

"You do have a way with words," she murmured.

"I'm even better in non-verbal communication. Want me to show you?"

She put one hand on his shoulder and slid the other to his waist.

"I think you already showed me once or twice."

"Clearly, you need a refresher."

"So you'd accept all those crazy things I might drag you into, just for the sex?"

He pulled his head back a little and looked at her the way a schoolmaster would. "It's not just for the sex, though I must admit, sex with you is mind-blowing. I also like—"

"Mind-blowing?" Was that really what he thought sleeping with her was like? No man she'd slept with had ever made a comment like that.

"Well, okay, maybe mind-blowing is the wrong adjective." One of Pearce's hands slipped down to her ass. "Perhaps 'out-of-this-world amazing' is a better description." He squeezed her backside and yanked her against his groin.

A gasp escaped her. She could feel the hard ridge of his erection rubbing against her.

A cheeky grin formed on Pearce's mouth. "Maybe now is a good time for me to confess something."

"What do you have to confess?"

"I'm not shy, babe, just choosy."

Before she could say anything else, Pearce's lips were on hers. He kissed her with the confidence of a man who knew he wouldn't be rejected and the skill of a lover who'd perfected the game of seduction.

She had no choice but to let herself go and follow his lead. It was so easy to follow where he was taking her, to a place where all worries disappeared, all troubles vanished. She felt lighter now, less worried, less angry. And she felt her body fill with happiness, with joy and pleasure. With desire and, suddenly, with need. The need to feel this man, to touch his skin, to feel him inside her.

Everything from the night before came back to her now. His passionate kiss reminded her of how he'd kissed her the night before, how he'd worshipped her body and given her pleasure. His scent conjured up memories of their lovemaking, of his relentless thrusts, the thrill of realizing how much he wanted her, how eagerly he drove into her. And how willing she was to give him anything he wanted, fulfill any fantasy he had.

When he ripped his lips from hers to press passionate kisses to her neck, she moaned. "Last night, when you took me from behind..."

He lifted his head. His eyes were filled with lust. "Yes?" He gyrated his hips, rubbing his cock against her.

"I've never felt so wanted. The way you took me... the way your cock filled me..." She'd just discovered how much she liked talking dirty to him. And how much Pearce seemed to enjoy it.

Something akin to a growl came from him. "Keep talking like that, babe, and we're gonna do it right here." He pushed her against the wall and pinned her there. "I was gonna be a gentleman and take you out for dinner first, before I fuck you all night, but now you've made me all hot and hard, and I don't think any decent restaurant will welcome me right now."

He looked down at himself, and she followed his look to where a big bulge tented his pants. Unable to resist the temptation, she freed one hand, laid it over his erection, and squeezed.

Pearce closed his eyes and moaned. "Are you trying to provoke me?"

"Is it working?"

One side of his mouth lifted in a lopsided grin. "You're the better judge of that, seeing that you're holding the evidence in your hand."

"I am, aren't I?" It felt good to tease him. He didn't seem to mind. There were so many sides to Pearce, and she couldn't wait to explore them all. "Then maybe we should make good use of it."

"Right here?"

"Right here."

His eyes sparkled with lust and passion, and he reached for her blouse, ready to pull it over her head, but his cell phone rang. He hesitated for a moment, and she thought he would ignore it. But then he took a step back and reached for it.

He looked at the display. "Sorry, I've gotta take this." He hit answer. "Yes?"

His tone was cool and collected now, not even hinting at his arousal.

"Where?" he asked. "Be right there... No, don't interfere, unless it's a matter of life and death. Give me eight minutes." He disconnected the call and shoved the phone back into his jacket pocket.

When he met her gaze, Daphne already sensed that something was wrong. "What?"

"Your brother. He's in trouble. I'll take care of it." He already turned to the door, ready to leave—without her.

"I'm coming with you." She snatched her jacket and her keys.

"Out of the question. It's too dangerous."

"He's my brother. I need to know what's going on. You can't just shut me out."

"Apparently not," he ground out. "Fine, come. But you'll be staying in the car."

She found it wiser not to contradict him right now. Whether she would follow his orders was another question.

"Where are we going?" she asked as they rushed out of her apartment and down the stairs.

"Your brother's place."

Moments later, they jumped into Pearce's car and drove off. Pearce didn't bother entering Tim's address into his car's navigation system, yet he seemed to have no trouble finding the fastest route to the small duplex where Tim lived on the first floor.

Daphne pulled her jacket tighter around her torso, suddenly shivering a little. Too many questions bounced around in her head. Who had Pearce talked to? How did he know that Tim was in trouble?

"How do you know Tim's address?"

Pearce cast her a quick sideways look. "You told me."

"I didn't." She was sure of that.

"On the map, remember? When we checked his cell phone records to see where he'd been. You pointed out his place on the map."

Slowly, she nodded. She remembered that, but she also knew that she'd not mentioned the exact street address, and the dot on the map had encompassed an entire block. However, she didn't point this out. Maybe she was just still too wound up from the events earlier in the day and was being suspicious about everything, even when there was nothing to be suspicious about.

Pearce's estimate of how long it would take them to reach Tim's place was correct. They pulled up in front of the duplex, and Pearce killed the engine, then turned to her.

"Stay in the car. I'll come and get you when everything is clear." He didn't wait for her to communicate her compliance, just jumped out of the car and hurried toward the entrance.

21

Pearce ran up to the house. The door that led into the building was ajar. Ryder had made sure of it. Pearce slipped into the dark foyer, where Ryder was waiting, and pulled the door shut behind him. A flight of stairs led to the upper unit, and a door to the right led to the ground-floor unit.

"What are we dealing with?" Pearce asked.

Ryder motioned to the door of the lower unit. "Tim got home a short while ago, and two guys were already waiting for him. I saw them through the window when Tim switched on the light, but one of them closed the curtains."

"What are you hearing?" A vampire's hearing was supersensitive, so Ryder would hear more sounds than Pearce could pick up from inside the apartment.

"They're putting the screws on him. I heard a few sentence fragments, something about stolen goods, where the loot was, and that he's got a buyer lined up or something, but they're keeping their voices down." He gestured to the upstairs unit. "Probably because the neighbors could be home. They don't want witnesses."

"Must be the guy who Tim was supposed to do the break-in for." He knew Ryder would understand, because Pearce had explained why he wanted Tim followed. He'd expected there to be trouble once it was clear that Tim hadn't succeeded.

"Makes sense. He's probably a fence for stolen goods."

"Anything else I should know?"

"They looked pretty mean. Big guys. Humans. So, nothing we can't handle between the two of us." Ryder grinned, always ready for a brawl with a bunch of bad guys.

"I'll go in first and unlock the door for you. Follow me, but stay quiet so they won't hear us coming."

"You're the boss."

Even though he wasn't armed tonight, because he'd planned on spending the night with Daphne and didn't want her accidentally finding a medieval dagger on him when he undressed, Pearce wasn't worried about entering the apartment to confront two humans. He was stronger than them. Besides, he had Ryder as backup.

Silently, Pearce passed through the door. He found himself in a short hallway with one door to his left and one to his right. Both were closed. Ahead of him was a door with frosted glass. Behind it, there was light. Pearce quickly reached back to the door and opened it for Ryder, so he could enter. Unfortunately, his skill of passing through solid objects like walls and doors couldn't be transferred to any other creature. It was unique to Stealth Guardians, and only a Stealth Guardian's body could survive the dematerialization and subsequent rematerialization of his cells.

Pearce nodded to Ryder, and they approached the glass door. Pearce made a motion for Ryder to wait, then made himself invisible and stepped through the door. He stood in the living room. Here, Daphne's brother sat, bloodied and beaten in an armchair, while one of the guys held a knife to his throat, and the other pointed a gun at him. The TV was on, probably to drown out any sounds of agony.

Having assessed the situation, Pearce stepped back through the glass door and told Ryder, "You're right, two guys, one with a knife at Tim's throat, the other with a gun pointed at him. Tim's barely conscious."

"Which one do you want to take?" Ryder asked, utterly unconcerned about fighting two armed men.

"I'll take the one with the knife. But we're going in invisibly." It wasn't a problem for Pearce to make Ryder invisible with his mind, but there was still a risk, since Ryder had to open the door to enter the room. "I'll go in. Give me three seconds to get in position, then enter and go for the guy with the gun."

Ryder nodded. "You've got it."

Pearce stepped through the door again and, as quietly as possible, approached the man with the knife, ready to snatch his hand and wrestle him away. Just as he was in position, the door creaked loudly and opened inward.

The two assailants snapped their heads toward it, but they couldn't see what Pearce saw: Ryder was entering the room, heading for the man with the gun.

"What the fuck?" The man stared into the dark hallway and moved toward it. "Who's there?"

Ryder came closer, but had to alter his approach so he wouldn't be running straight into the man. The sound of glass crunching under a boot cut through the silence. Ryder had stepped on some shards.

Shit!

The assailant with the gun pivoted and, shaking in panic now, pulled the trigger. It hit Ryder, wrenching a groan from him. But Pearce couldn't look at where the bullet had caught Ryder, because he had to take care of the man with the knife. He gripped the man's wrist and pulled him away from Tim with such force that the thug stumbled. Startled gasps and frightened shrieks came from the heavyset assailant. Pearce wrestled the knife from his hand and tossed it in the farthest corner of the room, then kicked the bastard in the hollow of his knees and forced him to the ground. He landed like a felled tree. Pearce jumped on him and pinned him down, then chanced a look at Ryder.

Bleeding from the shoulder, he was fighting the guy with the gun. He was still invisible, giving him the advantage, even though he was only fighting with half his strength. The human had no chance, even though he was still holding the gun, but he couldn't aim it at anybody, because Ryder was pinning his hand to the wall. However, knowing that even a bullet fired through the wood ceiling could possibly injure a neighbor, Pearce knew he had to intervene.

He dealt his opponent a knock to the head so he passed out, then jumped up and rushed to Ryder's aid. Within seconds he'd grabbed the gun from the man's hand, put the safety back on, and put the weapon in the back of his pants. Then he snatched the assailant and knocked him out too.

"Thanks," Ryder said.

Only now, Pearce made them both visible again. "What a mess. How's the shoulder?"

Ryder shrugged. "It'll heal in no time. All I need is a little human blood."

Pearce motioned to the two unconscious men on the floor. "Take your pick. I'll check on Tim. He doesn't look too good."

While Ryder bent over the man who'd shot him, and drove his fangs in the guy, Pearce approached Tim. He appeared to be unconscious. Pearce put his hand under Tim's chin to lift his head.

"Don't touch him!"

Pearce spun around and saw Daphne stand in the open door, her eyes darting between him and Ryder, who'd also jumped up, his fangs dripping with blood.

"Fuck!" Pearce and Ryder cursed simultaneously.

"Step away from my brother!" Daphne ordered them, walking farther into the room, her hands shaking, her eyes shock-widened.

Pearce lifted his hands, then took a few steps closer to Ryder, away from Tim. "You should have stayed in the car," he said calmly, mostly to distract her from what had happened here, but in his gut, he already knew that she'd seen too much. Her expression of horror and disgust said it all. The little trust she'd had in him had been wiped out by whatever she'd witnessed. Just how long had she been standing there?

He could only guess that it was long enough to realize that neither he nor Ryder were human.

Knowing it was time for damage control, Pearce cast Ryder a sideways glance. The young hybrid had retracted his fangs, but his lips were smeared with blood. "Call backup."

"Already did after I called you," Ryder replied. "Enya and Grayson will be here shortly."

"Good."

Pearce caught a movement in the corner of his eye and spun around, but it was too late. Daphne shrieked. The man Pearce had knocked out earlier had snatched Daphne from behind and was holding a knife to her throat.

Pearce instinctively made a step toward them, but a warning growl made him freeze.

"One false move, and the bitch dies." To underscore his threat, the thug pressed the knife harder to her throat, making her gasp.

Pearce saw the cold fear in Daphne's eyes and wished he could undo it all. He should have smashed the guy's head in when he'd had the chance.

"You hurt her, you die," Pearce said with a calm that belied the storm inside him.

The assailant looked to where the second guy lay on the floor. "Vasili? Are you all right?"

The man was still out cold and didn't answer.

"You killed him?"

"He's alive," Ryder replied.

"And what the fuck are you?" The thug motioned toward Ryder, while still holding Daphne in a tight grip.

"You wouldn't believe me if I told you," Ryder answered casually. Then he looked at Pearce. The question was implied.

Pearce nodded. Then he locked eyes with Daphne. "Trust me, Daphne."

In the next second, he made himself invisible. It was the only way to eliminate the assailant without risking Daphne's life. That he'd have a lot of explaining to do afterward didn't matter right now.

In his invisible state, Pearce rushed toward the attacker, snatched his wrist, and twisted it away from Daphne's neck. He kept twisting until the knife clattered to the floor, and the thug screamed in agony. Daphne freed herself from her attacker's hold and stumbled away toward her brother, while Pearce kicked the asshole to the ground and pummeled his face until he felt a hand on his shoulder. He looked up. It was Ryder.

"Don't. I can take care of him later. In a different way. He won't know what happened."

When their eyes met, Pearce realized that in the moment of utter rage, he'd made himself visible. He turned his head and saw Daphne stand beside her unconscious brother. She'd seen the violence he was capable of.

Fuck!

Slowly he lifted himself off the badly beaten man and turned to Daphne. "He would have killed you."

22

———

Daphne stared at Pearce's bloodied knuckles, then lifted her gaze to his face. Did she see shame there? Regret? She shook her head. One thing was clear: Pearce wasn't who he said he was. When she'd heard the sound of a shot, she'd run to the front door and unlocked it with her spare key, then charged into her brother's apartment, only to come to a sudden stop in the hallway, where she saw what was happening in the living room—two strangers battling with invisible foes.

She'd been so stunned that she'd frozen there. Frozen until she'd seen Pearce and the other man appear out of thin air. But when that stranger had then bent down to sink his fangs into his defenseless opponent, and Pearce approached her brother to—presumably—do the same, adrenaline shot through her veins and gave her the strength to intervene.

"Who are you?" She motioned to Pearce and the other man—or should she say the vampire? "Invisible vampires?"

The two exchanged a look as if they needed to get their stories straight.

"Your call," the stranger, whose fangs she'd seen dripping with blood, said calmly, deferring to Pearce as if he was his leader.

Pearce ran his eyes over her. "I'll explain everything. But your brother doesn't look too good. We should check him out."

She took a step to shield her brother. "Until I know who or what you are, you're not getting near him." She pointed to the other man. "You think I didn't see him suck this Vasili guy's blood? Do you think I'm blind?"

"No, I don't think that at all. Exactly how long were you standing there, watching?"

She braced her hands on her hips. "Well, why don't you take a guess, Mr. Invisible?"

For some reason, the fear she'd felt earlier had been replaced with anger. Pearce had lied to her. About everything. About who he was, about what he did.

"Okay. So you saw everything. Then you must have also seen that we saved your brother from these two goons. Even if we used, uh... unorthodox methods."

Daphne thrust her chin up. "Who are you? Both of you."

A moan suddenly came from behind her. Tim was gaining consciousness. She whirled around and crouched down.

"Tim? Tim, are you okay?"

"It hurts so bad," he muttered through a thick lip. When he lifted his head, she doubted that he could see out of his eyes. They were swollen shut. Her heart went out to him. Even though she'd been so mad at him, she couldn't stand seeing him in pain.

"Daphne?" Tim mumbled.

She touched his hand, stroked it. "I'm here, Tim. I'll take care of you." How, she had no idea. There were two injured, unconscious men on the floor, and she didn't know if she could trust Pearce and his friend.

"Daphne," Pearce said softly, and she turned her head. "We can help him with the pain."

Hesitantly, she rose and took a step toward Pearce, but several feet still separated them. "How?"

Pearce motioned her to come closer, then pointed to Tim and then his ear and shook his head. He didn't want Tim to hear what he had to say?

Curious, she approached him. "Talk."

Pearce spoke in hushed tones. "You saw correctly. Ryder, my friend, is a vampire. But he's not violent."

She pointed to Ryder and said in equally hushed tones, "Hah! He sucked Vasili's blood!" She'd seen it with her own eyes.

"I know. But he had to. Vasili shot him, and Ryder needed to heal. But Vasili is alive. He didn't suck him dry. You have my word."

Yeah, and what was his word worth?

He seemed to guess what she was thinking. "I know you don't trust me right now. But for your brother's sake, please let Ryder give him a little bit of vampire blood. It will take away the pain and speed up the healing process. He'll be good as new in twenty-four hours."

Was he completely mad? "You want my brother to drink vampire blood? Are you fucking nuts? Don't you know anything about vampires?" Well, or about the lore, the legends, the fiction.

Pearce smirked. "Actually, given that I share a house with two vampires, I know quite a lot. And whatever you've heard, it's wrong. The blood won't turn your brother. It will heal him."

She cast a look over her shoulder and looked at the sad state Tim was in. He moaned and shifted as if he was trying to shake off the pain. Tears shot to her eyes. She wished she had another choice. But she didn't.

Turning her head back to Pearce, she said, "I hope you're not lying to me this time."

In his eyes, a flicker of shame lit up. "I'll never lie to you again, I promise. And I'll explain everything. But let's take care of your brother first."

Slowly, she nodded.

Pearce told Ryder, "Heal Tim."

"No problem."

Daphne watched Ryder walk to the armchair and crouch down. He extended his fangs. A shiver ran down Daphne's spine. As if he'd noticed it, Ryder turned his head fully to her. "Don't worry. He'll be okay." The eyes of the vampire shone red now, like beacons in the night, but in his voice was a kindness, a tenderness that calmed her against all odds.

"We're here. What's going on?" came a familiar female voice from the door.

Daphne pivoted. Enya entered with a young man on her heels. As soon as her eyes fell on Ryder, she cursed. "Ryder! Pearce, what the fuck? In front of her?" She pointed to Daphne as if accusing her of something. "Are you out of your mind?"

Pearce lifted his hand. "She knows."

"Yeah, of course she knows *now*!"

Enya pointed to Ryder, who held his wrist to Tim's mouth to let him drink his blood. Tim's eyes were closed, and Daphne hoped it meant that her brother didn't really know what was happening. Perhaps it was better this way. He'd gone through enough.

"Enya, stop. She saw me," Pearce said in a tight voice.

"Well, that's just perfect," the man next to Enya said.

Enya shook her head. "Ah, fuck!" Then she looked at Daphne. "Welcome to our world."

What exactly their world was, Daphne didn't know. A world of invisible vampires? The thought made her shudder. What had she gotten herself into?

"I wish I knew what that meant," she said to Enya.

Enya exchanged a look with Pearce. "I thought she knew."

Pearce sighed. "She saw everything, but I haven't had a chance to explain to her what it means. We need to clean this place up. You and Grayson can take care of these two thugs. Search them for any weapons, and take them away from here. Make sure they realize that if they ever contact Tim again, we'll be back. Then let them go."

"You're not killing them?" Daphne asked.

Pearce gave her a stunned look. "They are crooks, but they didn't kill anybody, even though they threatened yours and Tim's life. We don't kill indiscriminately."

The last word gave her pause. "But you do kill."

He hesitated for a moment. "Yes, but only those who're truly evil."

She didn't know what to do with this information.

"I'll explain later," Pearce promised, then looked to where her brother was slumped in the armchair. "Ryder, I want you to take Tim to the safehouse and watch over him to make sure he's healing. Call Leila, and see if she can look at him to make sure he doesn't have a concussion."

Daphne listened to his instructions. He sounded like a leader, like a man who was used to dealing with situations like this. But with every word he said, more questions formed in her mind.

"A safehouse?"

"The place we stayed at last night," Pearce said without missing a beat. "Ryder will take your brother there. It's best if he doesn't stay here for a while, until we can be sure that there aren't any other thugs coming after him."

"It wasn't your apartment," she said, then looked to Enya. "You two don't share an apartment, do you?"

"Not that one, anyway," Enya said.

Daphne was sick of the vague replies. "What does that mean?"

"I'll explain everything," Pearce said.

"Yeah? When?" Because her patience was wearing thin.

Pearce sighed. "I guess sooner rather than later." He gave Enya a look. "You guys don't need me here, do you? I'll take Daphne home."

"I don't wanna go home. I wanna know the truth. Now."

"Not here. These two goons can wake up at any moment, and the things I need to explain to you aren't meant for their ears."

She couldn't tell whether he was stalling, but she understood that Tim's assailants didn't need to hear what they had to discuss. Besides, she had a few personal questions she didn't need Enya or Grayson and Ryder to overhear either.

"Fine."

Moments later, they were in Pearce's car, driving back to her apartment.

"I didn't mean for you to find out this way," Pearce said when they were about halfway.

"What exactly did I find out tonight? What did I see? Can you explain that to me?"

"I understand that you're upset—"

She whipped her head to him. "Upset? You think I'm upset? Damn it, Pearce! I feel betrayed. I feel lied to." She started choking up. "And I don't know what to think about what I saw. Two guys fighting with air? And then you and Ryder just appeared out of nowhere. And his fangs. And the blood. My brother, beaten and bloodied. Fuck, Pearce, you have no idea what I'm feeling."

"I didn't mean to... Hell, Daphne, I never meant for you to get hurt. I wish I could have told you earlier who I am. But our kind... We have to remain hidden."

She sniffled. "Yeah, I get that. Nobody can know that vampires really exist."

"I'm not a vampire—"

"You're gonna deny it now? I saw Ryder's fangs. I saw him drinking blood, and you admitted it. You told me that vampire blood can heal my brother, and now you're just gonna claim it's not true."

Pearce shook his head. "Ryder is a vampire. I'm not."

She stared at him. "Then what—"

"We're called Stealth Guardians; we're immortal warriors. Enya and I, and a bunch of others, live in a secret compound in Baltimore. So, in a way, yeah, Enya is my roommate, and we work together."

He was an immortal, a man who didn't get sick, a man who didn't die. She wanted to say something, but he stopped her.

"Hear me out. Ryder and Grayson, who you just met, they're vampire hybrids, half vampire, half human. They live with us to help us combat evil."

She snorted at that, but didn't say anything.

"I see why that may be hard to believe, but the vampires I know are good people. Honorable men and women. They're our allies in the fight against the demons."

"Demons?" she heard herself ask.

"They are truly evil, out to destroy mankind. The mission of the Stealth Guardians is to thwart their efforts. We're tasked with protecting mankind. Our race has been around for millennia. We've developed certain skills. You saw one in action tonight. I can make myself and others invisible. I had to do it in order to save your brother, and to save you. Making myself invisible was the only way to make sure that bastard didn't hurt you." He ran a hand through his hair and cast her a long look. "Losing you would have been far worse."

When he kept staring at her, taking his eyes off the road for far too long, she glanced outside and realized that they'd stopped in front of her apartment building.

"Say something, Daphne," Pearce begged. "Please believe me when I tell you that all I did, I did to protect you."

Her head was spinning with too much information. She had to go through it bit by bit. "So you're not a shy computer geek working for a defense contractor?"

He smiled hesitantly. "Actually, I'm responsible for all IT needs at the compound. My job consists mainly of hacking into government and private systems to gain information that may help us ferret out the demons."

"Why did you follow me last night? Why did you help me evade the police?"

He put his hand on hers and squeezed it. "Can we talk upstairs? That is, if you trust me enough to invite me in."

That jolted something in her. "Does that mean you can't come in if you're not invited? I mean like a vampire?"

"That's just lore. It's not true. But I'd rather be invited in. I want you to know that I won't do anything against your wishes."

Why she believed him, she didn't know. But she knew he wasn't going to hurt her.

"Okay. Let's go inside."

23

———

Moments later, Daphne unlocked her apartment door with trembling fingers and entered. Pearce was behind her and closed the door, then flipped the deadbolt. The sound sent a shiver down her spine. Had she made a mistake allowing him in?

"You haven't answered my question," she reminded him. "Why did you follow me?" She turned to face him.

Pearce sighed. "I overheard you on the phone. I'd waited in a bistro across from your work. I wanted to fake running into you so I could ask you for a date. But when I caught up with you, you were on the phone. To Guido, or Kevin as we now know. And what I heard concerned me. So I followed you to make sure nothing happened to you."

"I didn't see you."

"Because most of the time I was invisible. It makes it easy to shadow somebody. But I wasn't doing it in a creepy stalker kind of way, believe me."

A faint smile stole onto her lips. "I get that. But why didn't you just call me for a date? You had my number."

Pearce shrugged. "Maybe I got the feeling that you might say no."

"So you'd rather get a rejection face to face, is that it?"

He chuckled softly. "I thought perhaps I could talk you into it with my charming smile."

She decided not to comment on his attempt at levity. There was nothing casual about the entire situation. She'd just found out that vampires, immortals, and demons existed. She didn't know what to think of it. Was she shocked? Yes. Scared? To a point. Could she trust Pearce? Not sure.

"What's bothering you?" he asked, looking at her as if he could see into her mind.

"Everything." She didn't even know where to begin. "Will my brother be all right?"

"Yes. Ryder will take care of him, and Leila is a very accomplished doctor."

"Is she a vampire too?"

"No. She's human. And the wife of one of the other Stealth Guardian warriors."

That stunned her. "An immortal married to a human?"

"It happens more often than you'd think. Our race is short of female offspring. We don't have a lot of women. Hence, when we mate, we may choose a human woman."

She didn't ask the question that was burning on her lips, how such a match would even work long term, given that the immortal was, well, immortal, and the human was not. Instead, she asked, "And Leila knows what her husband is?"

"Of course. She lives in the compound with him and their twins."

"Oh." She hadn't expected to hear that there would be children. Nor had she expected Pearce to volunteer information.

"Is there something else I can say or do to ease your mind? To make you trust me?"

Trust? She hesitated. Did she have reason to trust him? To her surprise, a few things came to mind immediately: he'd saved her from being caught by the police; he'd found her brother and uncovered his scam; he'd saved her brother from the two thugs; and, last but not least, he'd saved her from the assailant who'd pressed a knife to her throat. Plenty of reasons. But what were the cons? He'd lied to her about who he was. One minus against four pluses. The scale weighed heavily on the trust side. And she did trust him.

But she had questions. "As an immortal you never get sick?"

"Never."

While she had so many more questions, there was one more thing she had to see once more with her own eyes to cement this new reality in her mind. "Would you make yourself invisible right now? I need to see it, now that I'm calmer. I need to make sure I wasn't dreaming."

He nodded, and in mid-nod, he simply disappeared in front of her eyes.

"Are you still here?"

"I'm still standing at the same spot."

Daphne bridged the distance with two steps and reached out with her hands. She could feel him, his torso, his shoulders. She slid one hand farther up. His face. His lips. She felt him press a kiss to her fingertips, making her shiver. But this shiver was different from the one earlier. It had nothing to do with fear.

"Pearce," she said, and slid her hand onto his nape.

Though he was still invisible, she felt his body, felt how he pulled her to him, one hand around her waist, the other on the back of her head, cradling it carefully.

"When that guy had you in his grip, when he pressed that knife to your throat, I wanted to kill him," Pearce said.

"Because you kill evil?" she asked, though she guessed already that it wasn't the true reason.

"Because I don't want to lose you."

Hearing him speak with such emotion made tears well up in her eyes. "But you barely know me."

He suddenly became visible, and she found him gazing into her eyes. "I know all I need to know."

She felt herself leaning closer as if drawn to him by invisible strings.

Was he doing this to her? Did he have magical skills he hadn't told her about? Skills of persuasion, maybe. She had to know. "Apart from making yourself and others invisible, do you have other supernatural skills?"

"Yes."

"Are you using them on me right now?"

His forehead furrowed. "On you?"

"Yes, like using some sort of glamor to make me compliant."

At that, he suddenly chuckled. "You have a vivid imagination. I told you I'm not a vampire. I don't do mind control or anything alike."

"But you just said you had other supernatural skills."

He nodded. "Yes, one. I can walk through walls and doors—any physical object, really, other than a living being."

"Oh!" The wheels in her mind were turning. "You mean you can enter any place that's locked? Like the house I broke into, or my brother's apartment..." She locked eyes with him. "My place?"

His eyelids lowered in shame. "The night I followed you, you came back here. I watched you get ready for the burglary."

Her breath caught in her throat. "Did you watch me get changed?"

"I'm not some kind of Peeping Tom."

"Did you?"

Pearce sucked in a deep breath. "I wanted to, by God. I was craving to feast my eyes on you. But I didn't. It wouldn't have been right."

To her surprise, she believed him. Pearce was a good man. She put her hand on his cheek, and he turned his face to press a kiss into her palm.

"Thank you," she said.

"Is that a 'thank you, you may leave now'?"

She slid her hand onto his nape and pulled his head to her. "If you want to leave, I won't stop you."

～

Pearce held Daphne's gaze. He still held her close to his body, and her hand lay on his nape. It didn't look like she wanted to get rid of him anytime soon.

"I don't want to leave."

"Then don't," she murmured.

It was all the answer he needed. Without losing a second, he slanted his mouth over hers and kissed her. Her response was what he'd hoped for. Daphne welcomed him. Her body molded to his, igniting his passion for her in an instant.

Their lips fused; their tongues danced with one another. Pearce tugged on her jacket and finally managed to slide it off her shoulders. Quickly, he shucked his own jacket. Her casual blouse provided no barrier. With eager hands, he touched her breasts through the fabric and realized that again Daphne wasn't wearing a bra. A moan escaped him at that revelation, while farther south, his cock went fully erect and pressed against the zipper of his pants.

To make her aware what she was doing to him, he rubbed his groin against her stomach. Her breath hitched, and beneath his hands, he could feel her heartbeat accelerate. He ripped his mouth from hers and planted kisses on her neck.

"I want you," he murmured. "Right here, right now."

Daphne didn't answer—not with words, anyway. She let her hands do the talking and tugged on his Polo shirt, pulling it from his waistband. For a moment he had to take his hands off her breasts and raise them so she could pull the shirt over his head. But as soon as the garment fell to the floor, his hands were back. This time, he slid them underneath the blouse and touched her naked skin.

Daphne trembled, and he recognized the reaction as a sign that his touch excited her. He found her breasts, squeezed them and played with her nipples.

Moans and sighs issued from Daphne's throat, and she rested her head against the wall behind her. But her hands weren't idle. She'd found the button of his pants and flipped it open, then pulled on the zipper, but it wouldn't budge. He knew why: his cock was straining against it. Sucking in a breath, he helped her and managed to lower the zipper, and pushed his pants and boxer briefs down to mid-thigh.

Daphne reached for his cock, but before she could touch him, he snatched her blouse by the seam and pulled it over her head, exposing her gorgeous breasts to his hungry eyes. He couldn't resist the tantalizing sight of her firm, round breasts, and dipped his head to them. He sucked one nipple into his mouth and licked it with his tongue, while he squeezed both breasts with his hands. He moved his mouth to the other breast, but something distracted him: Daphne was wrapping her hand around his cock.

"Fuck!"

She pumped him, and for a moment, he let it happen. But only for a moment, because if she continued like that, he'd come far too quickly.

He pried her hand off him and met her surprised look. But before she could protest, he pulled up her skirt and pressed the hem into her hands. "Hold up your skirt for me, will you?"

She didn't protest.

Underneath the hippy skirt, she wore tiny panties. He reached for them and tried to pull them down, but somehow, he was too forceful, and the fabric ripped. The panties fell to the floor. Daphne didn't seem to care.

He slid his hand to her pussy and rubbed along the slit, making sure she was ready.

"God, you're dripping, babe," he said.

"Not my fault," she whispered on a moan.

"Oh, I take full responsibility, trust me."

He gripped her thighs and lifted her up, bracing her back against the wall. His supernatural strength aided him in holding her there suspended in the air, while he stepped into her center and brought his cock to the entrance of her body.

There, with his cock poised to penetrate her, he locked eyes with her. Then he lowered her onto his cock, thrusting into her to the hilt. Her tight muscles wrapped around him like a glove, cradling him in warmth and wetness. God, how he loved that feeling of being imprisoned like that, of feeling her muscles clamp around him to hold him there.

Daphne's breath shuddered. "Oh God, you're bigger than last night."

"You can take me," he said, pressing a kiss to her lips. "Wrap your legs around me."

She did, and locked her ankles behind his butt. Now he was free to let go of one thigh, so he could do what he needed to do. He brought his hand to where their bodies were joined and rubbed his finger over her clit.

A moan rolled over Daphne's lips.

"That's it, babe, let me make you come." He rubbed her clit in a circular motion, while he rocked his cock back and forth, only an inch at a time. She was right about his cock. He was bigger tonight, because he didn't have to hold back anymore. There would be no condoms tonight, no restraint, because she knew now that he wasn't human—though he hadn't shown that much restraint the night before, even though the condom had dampened his sensations.

"I can already feel your pussy relax."

As he began to thrust faster, Daphne's breasts bounced from left to right, up and down. Her nipples were hard points, and perspiration started to gather in the valley between them. He dipped his head to them and licked over one nipple, while farther south, he rubbed her clit faster.

A helpless yelp came from Daphne, and she suddenly spasmed. Fuck! He hadn't expected her to come so fast. But he welcomed it, because her pussy was suddenly relaxing, and with every wave, she squeezed his cock and pulled him back into her.

"Pearce, oh God," she said on a husky breath, her eyes a picture of passion and lust, her lips red and wet, her pulse thundering so violently that he could feel it.

Pearce grinned and gripped both her thighs tightly. "Now your pussy is ready for me."

He began to thrust in earnest now, moving his hips in an ever-increasing tempo. Daphne put her hands on his shoulders and gripped him tightly. A cacophony of sounds of lovemaking echoed in the foyer of her apartment, and Pearce didn't care if those sounds carried into the hallway of the building. Nor did he care that the light was on and anybody in the building across from Daphne's would have a clear view of them. All he cared about was that Daphne trusted him and felt as passionate about him as he about her. And that she showed that passion with her body.

He'd never thought he'd meet a woman who had no inhibitions, who offered herself so freely to him. But Daphne was all that. Sexy, smart, brave.

"Tell me you like being fucked like that," he demanded.

There was a flicker in her eyes, and for a second, he thought she wouldn't respond, but then she licked her lips. "I love your cock. I love how you fill me, how you thrust so deep and so hard."

His heart pounded like a jackhammer. "I love plunging into your pussy, taking you, filling you."

At that, there was a realization in her eyes. "Without any barrier..."

"Yes, skin on skin, flesh on flesh." He thrust harder, their dirty talk making him even hotter. His arousal was spiking. He wouldn't be able to hold back much longer.

Daphne dug her fingernails into his shoulders. "Nothing between us. Just you and me." She breathed raggedly. "I love how you fuck me. As if you can't get enough."

He plunged his cock deep and hard into her, practically nailing her to the wall at her back, her words almost severing the last thread of his control. "Fuck, babe, I need to get deeper. I need to take you harder. Damn it, I want you, all of you!"

On his last word, he climaxed and shot his seed deep into her.

Daphne gasped. "Don't stop."

He continued thrusting as wave after wave of his orgasm crashed over him. His pleasure was already ebbing when he suddenly felt Daphne's muscles spasm around him as she climaxed again. Her high prolonged his pleasure, making him drive back into her again and again, until he felt Daphne's spasms subside.

"Wow," she murmured, and blew out a breath.

He rested his forehead on hers. "What do you say we move this show to your bed?"

"That sounds good, but I don't think I can stand, let alone walk right now."

He chuckled contentedly. "Oh, that was the plan all along. See, if you can't walk, you can't run away from me, and I can have my way with you. All night long."

A soft laugh rolled over Daphne's lips. "Scoundrel."

Minutes later, they both lay in bed, naked and sated. Daphne was snuggled up to his side, her head on his biceps, one arm over his chest, one leg across his thighs.

"Can I ask you something?" Daphne said.

"Anything." He stroked his hand over her hair.

"I'm assuming there's a reason Stealth Guardians don't use condoms. Is it because you're immortal?"

"Like you said earlier, we don't get sick. We don't carry disease, so we can't pass it on."

"I figured that. But you do procreate—I mean, you mentioned that Leila has twins. I mean, not that it's a problem. I'm on the pill, you know, but..."

He put his hand under her chin to make her look at him. She was cute when she was nervous. "Yes, we procreate. But it's not all that easy. A male Stealth Guardian isn't born fertile. We only become fertile when we bond with a mate."

"Oh."

He put one hand on her thigh to tug her closer to him, loving the way her warm body molded to his. "You can ask me anything. I want you to know that."

He wished she would ask the one thing that he knew he needed to tell her, but didn't know how. He wanted to tell her that their initial meeting hadn't been a coincidence. After the intimacies they'd shared, didn't she deserve the truth? Maybe it was exactly what he had to do: be honest with her, tell her about the vision and hope, by doing so, he could make sure the vision would never come true.

"Thank you," she said. "So the condoms you got last night, they were just for my benefit?"

"Yeah. I couldn't tell you that I'm not human and that you won't have to worry about STDs. It was easier to use a condom and make you feel at ease."

She hugged him tightly. "Most men aren't as considerate as you. I understand why you had to lie to me. But I'm glad that you can be honest now."

God, he felt like a heel that she believed he was one hundred percent honest, when he wasn't, when he was still keeping the real reason why they'd met from her. He had to set the record straight.

"Daphne, you should know something…" He took a deep breath, but the ringing of his cell phone interrupted him. He'd placed it on the nightstand earlier, in case anybody from the compound needed to reach him with updates regarding Tim's wellbeing. He looked at the display and recognized the compound's main line.

"Sorry, it's the compound. Probably news about your brother." He pressed the answer button and held the phone to his ear. "Yeah, what's up?"

"You need to come back," Hamish said.

"Why? Is something wrong with Tim?"

Daphne shot up to sit and cast him a worried look.

"No, Tim's fine. He's healing. Ryder is with him, and Leila and Aiden just got back. But we have a situation."

Pearce looked at Daphne and said, "Tim's fine." He saw her relax. "What kind of situation?" he asked into the phone.

"We found something on one of the thugs. It's a matter of life and death. You'd better get your ass here pronto."

Hearing the seriousness in Hamish's voice, Pearce said, "On my way." He disconnected the call and jumped out of bed.

"What's wrong?" Daphne asked.

"We have a problem. Get dressed. And pack what you'll need for a night. You're coming with me." Since Hamish hadn't been more specific, the problem could mean anything, and if it was connected to Tim's assailants, then it could also be connected to Daphne. Under these circumstances, Pearce couldn't leave her unprotected.

"Where are we going?"

"To my home, the compound."

24

Zoltan had followed Vasili's signal all over town. In many instances, he'd been able to see whom he met with and what he did. But at no point had Vasili received any packages or handed over any money. When he'd entered an apartment building in the early evening hours, and remained there for two hours without moving, Zoltan had lost his patience and entered. He'd found Vasili's apartment without any problems and, after receiving no reply to his knock, used a lockpick to open the door.

Vasili wasn't home. Only his jacket was. He'd ditched it at his apartment, either because he'd noticed Zoltan following him, or simply because he wanted to wear something different to wherever he was going. In any case, the tracker was still inside the jacket's pocket, but of no use anymore. How Vasili had been able to slip past Zoltan became clear when Zoltan noticed a back entrance to the apartment building. Vasili had evaded him.

Zoltan cursed. He had no choice now but to wait for the crook. In the meantime, he searched the place. He wasn't surprised to find an array of stolen goods stacked in a closet, together with several guns, knives, and a crowbar. In an iron footlocker, which Zoltan cracked open with the crowbar, he found cash, lots of it. On top of the stack lay an envelope Zoltan recognized. It was the one he'd given to Vasili earlier.

No matter how long he searched and what he ripped to shreds, he couldn't find the dagger Vasili had promised him, which meant he was probably meeting the thief right now to obtain the item. Annoyed that Vasili had thwarted his plan to find out who the actual procurer was, Zoltan let himself fall into the armchair and waited in the dark.

It was close to midnight when he heard the sound of a key in the lock. About time!

The light came on, followed by footsteps, then the sound of a door closing. Zoltan rose from the armchair that had hidden his entire body and turned. Vasili, white as a sheet, froze instantly.

"What the fuck?" Vasili said, but the big man didn't sound as mean and forceful as usual. Something had shaken him.

"You're late." Zoltan narrowed his eyes. "Where's my stuff?"

Vasili's eyes fell on the opened closet and the footlocker with the cash in front of it. "You broke in."

"No shit, Sherlock! I asked, where's my stuff? The dagger!" Zoltan took several steps toward him, and Vasili backed away. But he had nowhere to go. The door stopped him.

"My guys, they backed out," Vasili said, and motioned to the footlocker. "Take your deposit and leave."

"I'm not leaving without what you promised me." Zoltan snatched Vasili by the lapels of his coat. "Where the fuck is my dagger?"

"I told you—"

A punch to his face stopped him from completing the sentence.

"Where is my dagger?" Zoltan repeated.

"They couldn't break in. The security system... it was too sophisticated. They chickened out," Vasili mumbled, fear now shining from his eyes. Something had spooked him, but Zoltan was pretty sure it wasn't his presence.

"Where is it?" He slammed Vasili against the door. "Where—"

"Stop, please, stop! I'll tell you. There's a safe. In the study of a mansion. Behind the painting. But the codes we had for it, they didn't work. I can't get to it. I'll hire another crew."

Vasili was almost shitting in his pants. Zoltan had never seen him like this. It didn't matter. A scared Vasili was a compliant Vasili.

"I'll do it myself. The address! Now!" Zoltan let go of him.

Vasili almost fell over his own feet when he walked toward the small desk and reached for a pen and a piece of paper. Zoltan stood over him while he wrote the address with a shaking hand. When Vasili was done, Zoltan snatched the piece of paper from him and put it in his inside pocket.

"I think it goes without saying that from now on you'll provide me with any information I seek without delay. I won't tolerate you and your games anymore. Do we understand each other?"

Trembling, Vasili nodded.

"I'm sick of you hiding your valuable contacts from me and stringing me along. And if you gave me the wrong address, I'm going to be back. And I won't be as friendly as I am now. You get that?"

Cold fear shone from Vasili's eyes. He muttered something Zoltan didn't understand, and Zoltan snatched his chin and made Vasili face him. "What did you say?"

"I'm as good as dead."

Zoltan smiled. Vasili was right about that, because one wrong move, and Zoltan would snuff out his life and have fun doing so.

25

P earce stopped in front of an empty lot toward the end of an alley. They'd parked the car two blocks away in a small parking garage and walked for only a few minutes.

"We're here," Pearce said, and glanced around.

Daphne turned toward the other side of the alley, where several one-story buildings that looked like abandoned warehouses and workshops sat in darkness.

"Which one is it?"

Pearce put his hands on her shoulders and turned her back to face the empty lot that was strewn with tumbleweeds and trash. "This one."

She shook her head and stepped back, feeling uncomfortable going any closer. As if something bad was emanating from it.

"What you feel is natural," Pearce said, and clasped her hand.

"How would you know what I feel?"

"It's the wards that surround our compound that make a human want to turn away from it. It helps us keep our location secret."

Daphne shook her head and pointed toward the empty lot. "But there's nothing here. Is it underground?"

Pearce smiled. "Come."

He stepped closer and left the cobblestone pavement of the alley, setting a foot on the abandoned lot. Then he reached out a hand and seemed to touch something. A moment later, it looked like he was gripping a handle, and despite the darkness, Daphne realized that whatever he was touching wasn't visible.

Hinges creaked, and Pearce pushed something heavy away from him. Suddenly, a faint sliver of light appeared. The sliver grew broader as Pearce continued to push. A foyer opened up in front of them, where before, there'd been nothing.

Her breath hitched, and her pulse raced.

"Quickly, go inside," Pearce demanded, and ushered her in. He followed her, and she heard the closing of a door.

Daphne whirled around. The alley was gone. In its place was a heavy oak door with iron ornaments.

"Welcome to my home."

"But... how?" She looked around. They were inside a small foyer with one other door. There was a ceiling, from which a single light hung to illuminate the place. Next to the second door was a keypad. Pearce typed in a code, and a faint beep sounded.

He pushed the second door open and looked over his shoulder. "The building is invisible to anybody but a Stealth Guardian. It ensures that we're safe from detection." He tugged at her hand and pulled her through the door into a hallway.

Flabbergasted, she let him lead her inside. The hallway was made of thick stone walls, as were the floor and the ceiling. Along the walls there were embellishments, too, carved symbols that seemed to repeat.

"Are those runes?" she asked.

"Yes, they are part of the magic that keeps this place hidden."

"This is amazing. I can't believe this exists, and nobody's ever found it."

He smiled at her. "It's been here for a very long time, long before Baltimore was built."

"But—"

Her question was interrupted by a man who charged around the corner. She'd seen him before. When the man saw them, he came to an abrupt stop.

"Hey, Grayson," Pearce said. "What's going on?"

Grayson gave her a stunned look, then asked Pearce, "You think that's wise?"

Apparently Pearce knew what Grayson was referring to, and she suspected it had something to do with her, because Pearce said tightly, "My business."

"I guess."

"So what's the big news?"

"They're waiting for you in the command center. I'll let them explain. I'm on my way to the safehouse to relieve Ryder."

"Where my brother is?" Daphne asked. "Is he okay? Is he healing?"

Grayson nodded. "Yes, ma'am. Ryder said he's already looking better." Then he walked past them toward the door that led into the lobby. "See you later."

"See you," Pearce called after him.

The moment Grayson closed the door behind him, Daphne looked at Pearce. "So, he's a vampire?"

"A hybrid vampire, just like Ryder. Both are good guys. You won't have to worry about your brother."

To her surprise, she hadn't even thought about her brother until now. Guilt rose to the surface. She was a bad sister, leaving the care for her brother to two strangers, two vampires. "Maybe I should check on Tim."

"He's probably sleeping right now. We can go see him tomorrow, okay?"

She contemplated a protest, but Pearce was probably right. There was no use in going to the safehouse now and waking Tim. He needed his sleep to heal from the wounds the two thugs had inflicted.

"Okay."

They continued walking along several long hallways, passing doors and stairs.

"How big is this place?"

"Big. Several stories, both above and below ground."

"It looks like an old castle."

"It kind of is."

"And you really live here?"

"I'll show you my private quarters later. You can shower there and get some rest, but I've gotta see the guys first to find out what's so urgent."

Footsteps suddenly came from a corridor to their left. Daphne glanced toward it and saw a woman with flaming red hair walk toward them. When their gazes met, the woman gasped and stopped in her tracks. She looked as if she'd seen a ghost.

"You," the redhead said.

"Winter," Pearce called out to her.

Slowly, she approached, her gaze not wavering, still fixed on Daphne. "You brought her."

Something in her tone of voice sounded like an accusation. Just like Grayson hadn't been pleased to find Daphne here in the compound. And one other thing was evident: Winter recognized her. How or why was unclear.

Pearce nodded. "Something is up. I couldn't leave her out there unprotected."

Winter didn't immediately answer; instead she ran her eyes over Daphne, until they fixed on the messenger bag she'd slung across her torso.

"Any weapons in there?" she asked.

"Weapons?" Daphne asked, stunned. "Just my computer and a change of clothes."

Winter looked at Pearce, but said nothing.

"She's not armed, Winter. Relax."

"It's not me I'm worried about." Then she sighed. "They're all in the command center, waiting for you. But you can't bring her."

"I know that. So, why don't you show Daphne to the kitchen and see if she wants something to eat or drink?" He turned to Daphne. "I won't be long. I'll meet you there when I'm done, and then I'll show you my private quarters."

Despite Pearce's reassuring words, Daphne felt uneasy about leaving with the redhead, who clearly didn't like her, or at the very least, didn't want her to be here. But Pearce was already walking down another corridor, and Winter stood there, waiting.

"This way."

"Thanks."

While they walked in silence, Daphne wondered how much Winter knew about her. Had Enya told her what had happened the previous night and earlier today? Perhaps that was why Winter had been so startled. It had to be the reason.

At a nondescript door, Winter stopped. She opened it and motioned Daphne to walk inside ahead of her. The room was huge: an open-plan kitchen with a massive island. Adjacent to it was a large living room with a TV mounted on one wall, and a sectional that could seat at least ten. Several armchairs completed the seating arrangement.

When Daphne entered followed by Winter, they weren't alone. Two women sat at the island, nursing a bottle of wine and chatting. They turned their heads and fell silent. To Daphne's surprise, she recognized one of the women. She looked like the mayor of Baltimore. But that wasn't possible. It couldn't be. Maybe the woman was just her doppelgänger.

"This is Daphne," Winter said, and pointed to the two women at the island. "That's Kim, and that's Tessa."

Tessa. Same first name as the mayor. It had to be her. "Tessa? As in the mayor of Baltimore?"

"That's right," the woman said.

"Wow…" Daphne was speechless.

"So you're Pearce's Daphne," Tessa said.

"We heard about you," Kim, the woman with the long black hair, added.

Apparently, Enya had told everybody about Daphne and Pearce.

Had she told them that she'd caught them having sex at the safehouse? Daphne felt heat rise to her cheeks. She wanted to sink into a hole in the ground, embarrassed. But no convenient hole was available. She would just have to pretend that she didn't know that these women knew pretty much everything about her sex life with Pearce. It wasn't something she was used to. She didn't even have a BFF with whom to share stories about her love life. And now three strangers—no, make that four with Enya—knew about her sleeping with Pearce a day after meeting him. No wonder they were scrutinizing her with eyes that seemed to escape nothing.

"Hi," she said hesitantly. "I didn't mean to intrude. I can just go to Pearce's quarters..."

"No, no, stay," Kim said. "We're just winding down after a long day. Would you like a glass of wine?"

A glass of red wine sounded relaxing. "Actually, yes, that would be nice."

Kim jumped off her barstool, opened one of the hanging cabinets, retrieved a glass, and poured the wine. "Here you go."

Daphne took the glass and sat down on one of the barstools that Tessa pointed to.

"Winter, how about you? Wine?" Kim asked.

"I'll make myself some tea." Winter started getting busy with the kettle.

"So you're Daphne," Kim said.

Before Daphne could reply and ask what she meant by that, if she even had the courage to find out, the door opened again. A woman with long, dark brown hair entered, blowing out a breath.

"Finally, the twins are asleep. Thanks for reading to them earlier, Tessa."

"Sure, you know I love them."

Only now, the woman noticed Daphne. "Oh, we have a visitor?"

"I'm Daphne. Pearce brought me—"

"Oh, you're Daphne. I see." She ran her eyes over Daphne, then came closer and stretched out her hand. "I'm Leila. I checked out your brother. He's doing fine. No concussion. And Ryder's blood is working wonders. He'll be like new tomorrow."

Daphne shook Leila's hand. "I'm so grateful to you and to Ryder. To everybody who helped." She let her gaze roam over the women and checked for their reactions. They seemed apprehensive, and Daphne couldn't shake the feeling that they were prejudiced against her. Had Enya's tale about the sexual encounter soured the women against Daphne? Did they see her as a hussy, as a woman not worthy of the affections of a Stealth Guardian?

"Well, we're always glad to help," Winter said as she poured water in her teapot and carried it to the island. "I hope you'll remember that it was Pearce who saved your life."

Daphne's chin dropped. Was that a threat of some sort? Before she could formulate a reply, Leila put a hand on her forearm. "Oh, I'm sure Daphne knows what a wonderful guy Pearce is, so don't you worry, Winter." She smiled. "Now, who wants a midnight snack? I think we still have ice cream in the freezer."

PEARCE STARED at the photo Hamish held up. He couldn't believe his own eyes. "You've got to be kidding me."

"It's the real thing. We compared the photo to the drawings and paintings in the archives," Logan confirmed.

"The source dagger..." It was undoubtedly the dagger that had vanished hundreds of years earlier, the only dagger forged in the Dark Days that had the power to create portals that could transport a Stealth Guardian from one side of the world to the other within seconds.

"And you think that our dagger is in that safe, the one Daphne was supposed to rob?"

Hamish nodded. "Grayson is on his way to speak to Tim to see what he knows, and Enya left to interrogate Vasili about it. After all, he had the picture on him. If Grayson had shown it to Enya right away when he frisked the guy, she could have gotten more information out of him right away, but Grayson didn't realize its significance."

"We should ask Daphne too," Manus suggested. "If she was tasked with breaking into the safe, she would have known what she was supposed to steal."

Pearce shook his head. "She was told to empty the safe, no matter what was inside it."

"What if she's lying?" Manus asked.

"And why would she do that?" Pearce growled.

"Why would she want to kill you?" Logan said. "There could be plenty of reasons for either. I'll accompany you to her place, and we'll ask her."

Pearce ran a hand through his hair. "That won't be necessary."

Logan went toe to toe with him. "I'm coming with you. End of discussion."

"She's not at home."

"Then where…" Then something seemed to click. "Really? Are you fucking nuts? You brought her to the compound?"

Pearce shrugged. "Hamish told me over the phone that it had to do with the thugs that attacked Tim. Naturally, I figured it meant that Daphne could be in danger. So I, uh… Well, she's here."

"Guess there's nothing we can do about that now," Aiden said. "I'm assuming she's not running around without supervision?"

"'Course not," Pearce said. "Winter is with her."

Logan's eyes narrowed. "You left her with Winter? What if she—"

"Daphne won't hurt her. If she's any danger at all, then she's a danger to me, and me alone. Winter of all people knows that. Besides, I'm pretty sure she won't harm me. The danger from Daphne is over."

"Because you slept with her?" Hamish asked.

Pearce spun his head in Hamish's direction. "Why is everybody so interested in my love life?"

"Oh, it's love now," Manus commented.

"Shut up, Manus!" Pearce pounded his fist on the desk. "Let's stop discussing my sex life, and figure out what to do about the dagger. We have to secure it. Sooner rather than later. The longer it's out there, unprotected, the more likely it is that the demons get wind of it. And with Zoltan knowing what it looks like..."

A few months earlier, Zoltan had managed to snatch a page from one of their books that depicted the source dagger and laid out its magical powers. Pearce was sure, just like his compound comrades, that Zoltan would try anything to get his hands on the dagger, because it meant he would be able to create a portal. A portal that was automatically connected to all portals within the Stealth Guardians' world. It would allow him to attack from within and annihilate them.

"That goes without saying," Aiden said.

Pearce nodded. "Then let's work on a plan. I know about the two security systems at the house. They won't be a problem, particularly since we're not opening any windows or doors. We can bypass the motion detectors, which will trigger the silent alarm, by remaining invisible. The safe is another question. I didn't get a good enough look at it to see what type it is, but maybe Daphne knows. She also had some possible combinations of codes that might work."

"And if they don't?" Manus asked.

Pearce had already thought of that too. "I have a little electronic device that might help if it's the right kind of safe. I'll bring it. And as a last option, we can always blow it open."

"Okay then," Hamish said. "Let's get ready. Manus, you're taking over the command center; Logan, you're keeping an eye on Daphne while we're gone. The hybrids won't be of much use to us tonight, since they can't get inside the house." He motioned to Manus. "Send us a message when you hear from Grayson about what he found out from Daphne's brother. And when Enya checks in, we need to know what Vasili said."

"I'm on it," Manus confirmed.

Pearce nodded. Everything was working like a well-oiled machine. And once the source dagger was in their possession, the entire Stealth Guardian race would have something to celebrate.

"Let's roll."

26

As was to be expected well after midnight, all rooms in the big mansion were dark. Zoltan closed the vortex with which he and three of his demons had arrived in the garden. Though he'd never been at this address, a satellite image of the property had helped him direct his vortex to the correct place.

Zoltan motioned his three underlings to following him quietly onto the deck, where large French doors led into the house. He peered through the glass and could make out the interior, a living room. Aware of the alarm the house was protected with, and not having found anybody on such short notice who could successfully circumvent it, he'd decided to enter the property in a way that wouldn't trigger the sensors on the doors or windows, nor alert the residents to their presence too early by the sound of breaking glass.

With a swift motion of his arm, he cast a vortex on the deck. The swirling mass of dark fog and mist was ready to receive him. Zoltan stepped into it with one foot, then cast a look over his shoulder for the three demons to follow him. Inside, he visualized a spot in the living room, and a second later, he felt a different kind of floor beneath his boots, a thick rug. He stepped clear of the vortex, his demons on his heels, and found himself in the mansion's interior. With a quick hand movement, he made the vortex shrink and disappear.

Careful not to make any noise, Zoltan walked into the hallway, and from there, found his way into the study Vasili had talked about, while the demons followed him. A loud thud made him whirl and glare at his companions. The last demon to enter the study, Simon, lowered his head in shame. The bag he carried had hit a sideboard and knocked a heavy book off it. It had landed on the wooden floor, sliding until it bumped into a chair.

Everybody froze and listened for a few seconds, but nothing happened. It appeared the residents, if they were indeed home, were deep sleepers. When Simon let out a relieved sigh, Zoltan shot him a disapproving look. The bastard would die right now if Zoltan didn't need his particular expertise. But letting him live now didn't mean he'd survive the night. Punishment was simply delayed for a while.

Quickly, so as not to lose any more time, Zoltan walked behind the desk to an abstract painting that hung on the wall there. He ran his hands around the edge of it, testing if any wires could trip another alarm, but found nothing. Satisfied, he tilted the painting away from the wall and exposed the safe. He turned and pointed to Simon, who still had the large bag slung across his torso. He approached and started unpacking the things he'd brought: everything necessary to blow open a safe.

Using explosives to open the safe hadn't been Zoltan's first choice, given that the noise would carry far. In addition, if they were unlucky and used too much explosive material, the contents of the safe could be destroyed completely. If they used too little, the safe wouldn't open. The noise was the least of his concerns. By the time somebody made it to the study, he and his underlings would already have left through the vortex. His chief concern remained the possibility of destroying the dagger inside.

Simon started assembling his supplies. Zoltan put a hand on his biceps and made him turn his face to look at him.

"If you damage what's inside," Zoltan whispered, "it'll be the last thing you do."

Fear shone from Simon's green eyes. "There will be no damage."

Zoltan let go of his arm, then took a step back and watched him work. The creaking of a door made him spin around. The beam of a flashlight hit him in the face, blinding him for a moment, before he could duck away and make out who was holding it: a human in a nightgown, most likely a woman.

"Get the bitch!" Zoltan ordered the two demons who should have stood guard at the door and window in the first place, but instead were watching their comrade tinker with the explosives.

Finally, the two idiots went into action and charged toward the intruder. A shot rang out. One of the demons stumbled and fell forward, while the other reached the woman and pounced on her. The flashlight went flying, and a struggle for the weapon in the woman's hands began—a very short struggle Zoltan's underling won without contest. The woman screamed, kicked at the demon, and tried to punch him, but he subdued her quickly, slamming her to the ground.

By the time Zoltan was by their side, his subject had the woman pinned down. Zoltan snatched the flashlight and shined it into her face. The older black woman ripped her arm free from her demon aggressor and tried to reach for the flashlight as if she wanted to use it as a weapon.

Zoltan hit her chin with it instead. "Should've stayed in bed, lady. But since you're up, you might as well give us a hand."

"Let me go!" she ground out. She made no attempt at yelling, at alerting anybody else in the house, making it obvious to Zoltan that she was the only person here.

"Later," he promised. He turned to Simon. "Hold off on it." Then he looked at the old woman again. "I need the code for the safe."

"I don't know it! And even if I did, I wouldn't give it to you!" She spat at him, her face a mask of defiance. He liked humans with guts, with courage. This one would make a good demon, but unfortunately, he didn't have the time to convince her to join his side. For all he knew, she could already have triggered an alarm or called the police from upstairs.

"The code, lady, or you'll die!" To underscore his demand, he pulled his dagger from his jacket and put the blade to her throat. "I'm not a patient man. The code!"

She swallowed hard. Then her lips moved. "I don't know it."

"Bullshit!"

"I'm only the housekeeper. I swear!"

Zoltan pressed the blade harder against her skin. "Don't lie to me!"

Tears started welling up in the woman's eyes. "I don't know it. I'm just the housekeeper."

Narrowing his eyes, Zoltan gripped one of her hands and looked at it. They weren't the hands of a woman of leisure, a woman who sat in a mansion all day, doing nothing. They were the hands of a working woman: short fingernails, no polish, an odd cut or burn here or there, just like one would expect from a woman who cleaned and cooked. The woman spoke the truth.

"Then you're no use to me." He rose and told the demon pinning her down, "Make sure she's no danger to us." He walked toward the safe again.

Behind him, the woman screamed, the sound so bloodcurdling that Zoltan whipped his head back. Her demon captor drove a dagger deep into her chest.

"Fuck!" Zoltan cursed. "I meant for you to tie and gag her, you idiot!" The woman's bravery had gained Zoltan's respect, but it was too late now. Her head rolled to the side. She was dead.

"But you said..." The demon jumped up and cast him a fearful look.

"Shut up!" Annoyed, Zoltan turned back to the explosives expert, who was showing initiative and working on affixing the plastique around the safe's edges. Zoltan watched him closely. He hoped this guy was sharper than the demon who'd just killed the old woman for no good reason. Why it upset him, Zoltan wasn't sure. He should feel no compassion for any human, but he'd seen something in this woman, a strength, a courage he admired.

"I'm ready, oh Great One," Simon finally said. "We need to get out of the room, in case..." He made a sign with both hands, indicating a big explosion.

"How're you gonna trigger it?"

The demon pointed to a timer attached to a wire that was connected to the plastique. "I'll set it to sixty seconds."

Zoltan nodded. "Do it!" Then he told the other two, "Out into the hallway. Now."

As the two demons charged out of the room, Zoltan followed. Seconds later, Simon joined them in the hallway, where they hovered to one side of a heavy armoire that would protect them in case anything went wrong.

But everything had better go exactly like he'd planned it.

27

———

Just like a few nights earlier, Pearce entered the private property in the fancy Baltimore neighborhood invisibly and by walking through the fence. Only this time, he wasn't alone. Hamish and Aiden were with him. Pearce could see them thanks to the various levels of cloaking Stealth Guardians could apply. It meant they could see each other, but nobody else could, which made it easier when working invisibly as a team.

Pearce had explained the layout of the exterior and interior of the house and laid out the plan before their departure, eliminating the need to talk. They would be in and out in no time. This time, Pearce didn't bother entering the house via the living room, which was accessible via the deck, and chose to walk directly from the garden into the study. He passed through the wall without any trouble and stepped farther into the room, before looking over his shoulder to make sure that Hamish and Aiden had followed him. They had.

Everything was dark and quiet.

Pearce pulled the sheet with possible combinations for the safe out of his inside pocket and walked farther into the room, then he suddenly stubbed his foot and stumbled. He almost fell over an obstacle on the floor, but caught himself on the backrest of a chair. It took his eyes a second or two to adjust before he recognized what he had stumbled over.

"Shit," he said, looking over his shoulder to his brethren. "A woman. Stabbed." He bent down and pressed his fingers to her neck, feeling for a pulse. "Dead. Still warm."

"Fuck!" Hamish cursed, while Aiden was hurrying toward the area where the safe was hidden.

Aiden's warning came a split-second later: "Take cover! Fire in the hole!"

Pearce dove behind the leather couch. He heard Hamish scramble for a hiding place, too, and saw a movement to his left. Before he could figure out in which direction Aiden had run, a loud explosion rocked the room. Debris and dust went flying, and pieces of metal crashed to the wooden floor. Pearce inhaled fine dust particles and coughed. Dust settled on his clothes. He started to rise.

"Aiden? Hamish?"

"I'm good," Aiden reported.

"Me too," Hamish said.

The door suddenly flung open, diverting Pearce's attention away from his brethren. Several men stormed in, their green eyes instantly identifying them as demons.

"Demons!" Pearce yelled, and reached for his dagger, then ducked to his right to attack from the flank.

When two of the creatures stormed directly toward him, he knew that the dust on his clothes was giving away his position, rendering him visible.

"They can see us!" Pearce called out to his friends, and barreled toward the bigger of the two demons, but the bastard sidestepped him and instead charged in the direction of the safe.

Hearing the battle cries of the others, Pearce knew that he had to defeat this demon first, before he could prevent the other from reaching the safe and taking its contents.

Pearce kicked his opponent's stomach and hurled him against the stone fireplace. Then he spun on his heel and raced into the opposite direction. Aiden and Hamish were each fighting a demon, trading blows and kicks, alternately getting catapulted into the air, then flinging their opponents against pieces of furniture, the floor, or the wall. The largest demon, the one who'd first charged toward Pearce—and by the looks of it, their leader—was dodging an attempt by Hamish to cut off his path. It failed when Hamish's opponent got back on his feet and tried to stab Hamish.

Pearce charged toward the safe, hoping the demon he'd tossed against the fireplace was out for a few seconds. He dove forward, jumped over the desk, and managed to grip the demon by his shoulders before the bastard could reach into the safe. Together they stumbled backward, but the demon was strong. He kicked his elbow back, hitting Pearce in his solar plexus, temporarily knocking the wind out of him. It gave the evil creature enough time to reach into the safe to get what they both wanted: the dagger.

"No!" Pearce screamed, and lunged forward again, only to see the demon's hand emerge from the safe. Empty.

Their eyes met. Demon-green eyes glared at Pearce, making him realize that the demon was as surprised as Pearce to find the safe empty.

In the split-second pause that followed, police sirens suddenly sounded. Either the demons had somehow tripped the silent alarm, or the dead resident had managed to call the police or sound the alarm before her death. In either case, in a few moments, the game would be up.

"Retreat!" the demon yelled.

Then he punched Pearce so hard that his head snapped back, tossing him on his ass before he could even comprehend what was happening. Despite being dazed from the powerful blow to his head, Pearce picked himself up to chase his attacker. It was too late. The demon had already conjured a portal.

"Aiden! Dagger!" Pearce cried out, and pointed toward the vortex. All four demons were rushing toward it, abandoning the fight.

Being a master with the dagger, Aiden understood and flicked his wrist toward the demon who was only a foot from the portal, about to step inside. When the dagger whizzed through the air, the demon's leader—and by now, Pearce suspected that it was Zoltan himself—snatched one of his underlings and used him as a shield.

Aiden's dagger hit the demon in the chest, and Zoltan pulled his dying underling with him as he disappeared in the vortex, the other two demons jumping after him.

Seeing that the demons couldn't be stopped from leaving, Pearce had one more thing he had to confirm before he could leave this house. He spun back to the safe and reached inside, but all he felt were charred papers, no weapon, no dagger. Just like the demon's hand, Pearce's emerged empty. "Fuck! We've gotta find the dagger."

"No time for that now!" Aiden said.

"At least we know the demons didn't get it either," Hamish added.

"We've gotta get out before the police come." Aiden motioned to his dusty clothes, indicating that if they stayed here, the police would see them despite their supernatural skill.

"Out, now, through the backyard," Pearce ordered them, and headed toward that wall.

He jumped through it and landed in the garden, Aiden and Hamish on his heels. Quickly, he dusted himself off as best he could, and his friends did the same. They managed to get most of the dust off their clothes, but to a policeman with a keen eye, they would still be visible.

Two police cars were already stopping in front of the house, their blue lights and sirens alerting the neighbors. Another few seconds, and they would enter the property.

"Through the neighbor's yard," Pearce said, and took the same route he and Daphne had taken the night before.

They ran for a couple of blocks, far enough away from the property, before taking a different route back to where they'd parked the car on a parallel street two blocks away from the mansion, which was now swarming with cops. Their protocol of never parking a getaway vehicle too close to a place they were breaking into had paid off again. Sometimes rules and protocols were a good thing, Pearce admitted to himself.

Now visible, Hamish jumped into the driver's seat, Aiden got in the backseat, and Pearce rode shotgun. Soon they were heading for their neighborhood.

"I think the largest of the demons was Zoltan," Pearce mused.

"Very likely," Hamish said, and looked into the rearview mirror at Aiden. "Looks like the demon we fought in that farmhouse in Sonoma, right?"

"The one who took Leila's pendant?" Aiden asked. "Yeah, could be him. Though he was clean-shaven back then. And I didn't get a very long look at him tonight."

"Long enough to aim your dagger," Pearce interjected. "Had he not used one of his men as a shield, he would have been toast. Good aim."

"Clearly not good enough. I should have anticipated him and aimed higher."

"Don't beat yourself up," Hamish said. "One demon less. Can't always get the top brass. But we'll get him one day." He cast a look at Pearce. "How did the demons know about the safe?"

Pearce grunted. "It looks like we were all working off the same wrong intel, including Zoltan. Which can only mean one thing: he had the same source we did."

"Vasili," Aiden said.

"One way to find out," Pearce said just as Hamish pulled into a small garage that housed three other cars.

Minutes later, they were back inside the compound. The others were already waiting for them in the command center, falling silent the moment Pearce, Hamish, and Aiden walked into the room.

Logan, Manus, and Enya ran their eyes over them, then looked at their hands.

"Where is it?" Logan finally asked.

Pearce shook his head. "The safe was empty."

"Shit!" Manus cursed.

"Yeah, and not only that," Pearce added, "the demons got there before us."

"They got the dagger?" Enya's eyes went wide with panic.

"No, nobody got it," Pearce said. "They killed one of the residents and blew open the safe, but they seemed to be as surprised as we that the safe was empty. The dagger wasn't in there. We were given bogus intel." He looked at Enya. "Did you talk to Vasili?"

"Oh, I didn't just talk to him. I put the screws on him. And he talked, sang like a canary. He believes that the dagger was in there. In fact, he swore that's the information he had. And it's also the info he gave to his client. Who was very keen on it. In fact, he'd searched for an item like it for a long time."

"Zoltan," Pearce guessed. "How does Vasili communicate with him?"

"Cell phone."

"Then we can get—"

"Don't bother," Enya interrupted. "Already tried to trace it. It was a burner to start with, and now it's defunct. Zoltan must have destroyed it after he left Vasili's place. We have no way of finding him that way."

Pearce let out a frustrated sigh. "Fuck! Are you sure Vasili told the truth? He's not holding anything back?"

"I was very thorough."

He knew he could trust Enya.

"Could he describe him?" Hamish interjected.

"Big guy, brown eyes, facial hair. Nothing concrete." Enya shrugged.

"Big guy with facial hair sounds right," Pearce said. "But his eyes were demon-green when we encountered him. Why would he take his lenses out while he was still in the human world? It makes no sense."

"Odd," Aiden said. "The other three demons wore no colored lenses either. Guess they didn't expect to encounter anybody."

Hamish hummed to himself. "Possible."

Pearce asked Enya, "And Vasili gave him the same information we got? That the dagger was in the safe?"

Enya nodded. "Vasili said so. There were other things, too, some old Nazi knife and an Egyptian artifact, but his client was only interested in the dagger. He said Tim and Kevin were supposed to steal everything in the safe."

Pearce remembered something. "And Grayson? Did he speak to Tim? Can Tim confirm that?"

"Grayson is still at the safehouse, but he called in. Tim was told there would be several valuable artifacts inside the safe. And to steal them all. When Grayson grilled him further, he admitted that his friend Kevin had actually seen the items once, when he'd done some carpentry work in the study, and the owner had taken the items out and photographed them. That's how Vasili got wind of them in the first place. Kevin mentioned it to Tim, and Tim said he knew somebody who could hawk items like that." She shrugged.

"And the owner put the items back in the safe?"

Enya nodded again. "That's also when Kevin peeked at the combination and wrote down what he thought the code for the safe was. And permutations thereof."

"Do we know when that happened? I mean, when the dagger was still in the safe?"

Enya pulled her cell phone from her pocket. "Let me find out from Grayson." She dialed a number and put her cell phone to her ear, while she stepped away from the group.

Manus asked, "Did you manage to kill any of the demons at the mansion?"

Pearce pointed to Aiden. "Aiden hit one in the chest. But he was just an underling. Zoltan got away."

"As usual," Hamish added. "That guy has all the luck in the world. We've been so close so many times, and he keeps slipping through our fingers."

Manus nodded, a grim expression on his face. "Just like when he came for the book..."

Though Pearce hadn't been with his brethren when they'd fought Zoltan and ripped Manus's mate from the demon's claws, he knew that having snatched a page from an important book gave Zoltan all the information he needed about the source dagger.

"Don't beat yourself up about it, Manus," Pearce said. "It wasn't your fault. Thanks to Kim, at least that's all Zoltan got. It could have been worse. He could have gotten the entire book."

Manus grunted.

Enya joined them again. "Grayson says that Kevin saw the dagger about a week ago. It was definitely in the safe then."

Pearce nodded. "Then we have to find out what happened between then and now. Where did the dagger go?"

Enya yawned. "I doubt we're gonna figure anything out right this minute. Guys, it's late. How about we get a few hours of shuteye and then get to work when our minds are fresh?"

Pearce hated the idea of delaying the search. "But the demons—"

"Enya is right," Logan said. "The demons don't know any more than we do, or they wouldn't have blown open the safe. They're not gonna figure it out any faster than we will. Let's get four hours of sleep, and then we'll regroup. Agreed?"

Slowly, everybody nodded, and Pearce had to admit that he, too, was beat and needed to rest. It was no use to rack his brain right now when he wasn't at his sharpest. In a few hours, he'd be refreshed and come up with a way of finding the dagger.

"All right, then," Pearce said.

Everybody dispersed. On the way out, he sidled up to Enya. "Is Daphne in my—"

"Yeah, she's sleeping in your quarters."

"Thanks."

He walked to his private rooms and passed through the wall that led directly into his bathroom, not wanting to make too much noise. He shucked his clothes right there, stepped under the spray of the shower for a couple of minutes just to rinse the dust of the explosion off his skin and hair, and dried off quickly.

Then he walked through the closed bathroom door into his bedroom.

Daphne was asleep. Naked, Pearce slipped under the covers and molded his body to hers, putting one arm around her.

She stirred. "Pearce?" she asked in a sleepy voice. "What happened?"

He pressed a kiss to her hair. "I'll tell you tomorrow." He rested his head next to hers and closed his eyes. "Sleep now."

28

It was still early morning, but Daphne had been up before Pearce, who'd come to bed extremely late. She'd showered and dressed before she had the nerve to wake him. He'd immediately sprung into action and been in and out of the bathroom and dressed in less than five minutes. She began to understand why he was in such a rush when he filled her in on what had happened the night before and what it meant.

To clarify she'd understood what it meant if the source dagger fell into the hands of the demons, she asked, "You're saying that this dagger, this artifact, can create portals through which you teleport through time and space?"

"Not time, just space," Pearce said. "Though it might feel like we're traveling through time, because traversing thousands of miles takes only a few seconds."

She could hardly believe it. She'd never seen a portal, never thought that teleportation would be real in her lifetime. Yet it had been real for millennia, ever since the Stealth Guardians and the demons existed.

"What a magical tool."

"Yes, it is. And it's even more valuable than that. It's the only weapon that can save a Stealth Guardian's life."

"What do you mean by that? I thought you're all immortal."

Pearce hesitated and looked as if he regretted telling her. "We are. However, there are weapons that can inflict a mortal wound." He pointed to the dagger that sat in a sheath on his hip. "This is one of them. It's ancient. No modern weapon can kill us. But the demons possess the same weapons we do. They can kill us. But the source dagger could save any warrior and reverse the mortal wound."

"Is that true, or is that just a myth that parents tell their kids?"

"Oh, it's true, though I have to admit, I've never seen it done. The dagger was lost before I was born."

Daphne sighed. "It's a shame for something so valuable to be lost to your race... And you're sure the demons didn't get the dagger last night?"

"Absolutely. Zoltan's surprise at finding the safe empty was unmistakable."

"Then somebody gave you wrong information. I can have a word with my brother, find out if he really told us everything he knows about the safe," she suggested.

"Grayson already did that last night. And before you worry about Tim, he's all right. He told Grayson that Kevin saw the dagger in the safe about a week ago. We can only assume that the owner removed it sometime between the day Kevin saw it and the break-in last night."

"You didn't have the time to search the rest of the house last night, but do you think the owner could have put it somewhere else?"

Pearce shook his head. "Nobody in their right mind would leave an artifact like that out in the open. Even if the owner didn't really know what he had, he had to have known that it was valuable. Priceless, even."

She nodded in contemplation. "Yes, priceless. Well, at least we have a starting point."

"We?" Pearce shook his head. "This is not your fight."

"Maybe not, but I can help you. It's time I paid you back for everything you've done for me and Tim."

"There's no need. Besides, if you want to pay me back later when this is over, I can think of something." He cast a look at the bed.

She rolled her eyes. "If I didn't know any better, I'd say that's all you think about in your life. But honestly, I want to help."

She put her hand on his forearm, Pearce's earlier words replaying in her head. The dagger was priceless. But Vasili had put a price on it and tried to hawk it. What about the owner? Had he, too, put a price on it?

She looked into Pearce's eyes. "I have an idea how to find the dagger."

"You do? What is it?"

Daphne crossed her arms over her chest. "You'll have to let me help, or I won't tell you."

Pearce sighed. "My colleagues won't like it. They..." He hesitated.

"They don't trust me, do they?" Before Pearce could confirm it, Daphne continued, "Their wives treated me nicely, but with kid gloves, as if I could snap at any moment. They don't trust me either."

"Don't take it personally. They don't know you how I know you. You're a stranger to them. It takes a while to—"

Daphne squeezed his arm. "I understand. That's why you'll have to tell your friends that you need my hacking skills to help you with finding where the dagger is now."

"You want me to lie to my friends?"

"It's not lying. Not really. Because I will be using my hacking skills to find the dagger. And I already know where to start." She sighed. "Please let me do this for you." Deep down, she knew Pearce didn't really need her. He would eventually come to the same conclusion she had and have the same idea of where the dagger could be. But she wanted to be part of this. She wanted to prove to herself that her skills were still sharp, and that she could do something good.

For a few long seconds, she thought that Pearce would shoot her down, but then he nodded. "Fine. But that's all you're gonna do. You'll help me find the location of the dagger. And then my colleagues and I will go and get it, and you'll remain in the safety of these walls. Agreed?"

"I understand."

Pearce chuckled unexpectedly. "I didn't ask whether you understood. I asked whether you agreed."

"You can be very pedantic sometimes," she said, and walked to the door. "Let's go. We're burning daylight."

Pearce followed her. "One day, I *will* paddle your ass."

She gripped the doorknob and looked over her shoulder. "But not today."

When they entered the command center of the compound, a large, windowless room with several desks and a large computer console, Pearce's colleagues were already assembled. They looked at her in surprise, then glared at Pearce without saying a word. But their displeasure was palpable.

Enya was the only person Daphne had met before. Grayson and Ryder weren't present, and the other four men hadn't been introduced to her.

"Maybe Daphne would be more comfortable spending some time with the women in the kitchen," one of them said.

Before Daphne could reply, Enya shook her head. "Manus, you sound like a chauvinist pig right now."

"Well, Enya," Manus replied tightly, "don't tell me you suddenly approve of strangers in the command center."

"I didn't say that. I only called you—"

"Enough of the name calling," Pearce interrupted. "The reason I brought Daphne is because she has an idea of how to find the dagger, and I'll need her IT help. So, unless one of you has a background in hacking, then Daphne will help me do what we need to do."

Pearce's forceful words shut everybody up. And he'd even made it sound like it had all been his idea to get her help.

A few grumbles went through the room.

"I guess introductions are in order," Pearce said, and pointed to the men. "These are Hamish, Manus, Aiden, and Logan. Enya you've already met. Now let's get to work." He turned to her. "Let's start with your idea."

"It's actually simple. The owner wasn't a collector of old artifacts. When I was inside the mansion, I noticed that it wasn't his style. His art is more contemporary, more modern. He didn't get the dagger or the other items in the safe for himself. He got them to trade or sell them. That's why the safe was empty. He sold the dagger sometime during the last week."

"And you get that from his décor?" Hamish asked skeptically.

Daphne shrugged. "It's a lead. You've got anything better?" When Hamish didn't answer, she continued, "I also know how to back up my theory." She pointed to the computer console and turned to Pearce. "May I?"

He walked ahead of her and took a seat at the console. "I'll log you in." Moments later, one of the screens woke, and Pearce moved to the computer next to it. "Take a seat." He cast her a conspiratorial look. "Not bad," he whispered. Louder, he asked, "Where do you wanna start?"

"Auction sites."

"EBay?" Logan asked with just as much skepticism as Hamish had displayed before.

"Yes, among others, though I don't expect the owner to have listed it on eBay. There are more suitable auction sites for artifacts," she said without looking over her shoulder, already typing a search on the computer. "Pearce, you have the photo of the dagger, right?"

Pearce nodded and pulled up an electronic file. "Drop your sites over here," he said, pointing to the window on his screen. "The screens are connected."

"Cool," Daphne said, and proceeded. She was pleased to see how much she and Pearce thought alike, how much they had in common. "These sites are the most likely. While you do the image search, I'll start on the text search."

Daphne's search produced several hits immediately. She waded through them, comparing the pictures of the auction items with the one Pearce's monitor displayed, while Pearce did the same with an image search.

"You think the demons are doing the same we are?" Daphne asked.

"Not sure," Pearce said.

Behind them, she heard footsteps. She looked over her shoulder and saw Aiden approach. "I think what Pearce is trying to say is that we're not entirely certain how sophisticated the demons have become. A lot of their methods are antiquated, downright medieval. But as they turn more humans into demons, they may well have acquired followers who have the same skills as we."

"What do you mean by turn? You mean like a vampire turns a human?" Daphne asked, her chest suddenly tightening with fear.

"Don't scare her, Aiden," Pearce said.

"She should be warned," Aiden replied.

There seemed to be a silent battle between the two men, then Pearce gave a tight nod and turned back to the monitor.

"It's not a bite or blood that turns a human into a demon. Nothing like with a vampire," Aiden started. "It's an action. A deed."

"I don't understand," Daphne said.

"If a human performs an evil act for the demons or in their name, it turns that human into a demon, green eyes, green blood, and all. It's irreversible. Once a demon, always a demon. There's no redemption."

"But why would somebody do that for the demons? I mean, they're evil creatures..."

"They're also very persuasive when they want to be. And they promise humans the things they want most, be that power, love, money, you name it, they'll figure out what you want most, and they'll use it against you. They'll trick you into performing an evil deed if they have to. Anything to strengthen their ranks. And once a human is seduced, it's hard to convince them otherwise. The temptation will always be there, and one day, they'll give into it and turn demon."

Daphne swallowed the knot that had formed in her chest. "My brother, did he do this for the demons? Was he seduced?"

Pearce swiveled in his chair. "Now see what you've done. Damn it,

Aiden!" He put his hand on Daphne's. "Your brother is okay. What he did was despicable, but he didn't do it for the demons, nor does his act rise to the level of evil that's necessary to turn a person into a demon. And both conditions have to be satisfied for that to happen."

Daphne sighed in relief. "Thank God. And he's better now, right?"

She looked toward Enya, who nodded. "He's healing fine. We're just keeping him at the safehouse until we can be sure this is all over."

"Got it!" Pearce announced.

Daphne turned back to him and stared at the screen. It showed the listing of the dagger at one of the classier online auction sites. *Sold* was written at the spot where the list price would have been during the time the auction was live.

The other Stealth Guardians gathered around the monitor. Their utterances confirmed that they recognized the dagger. It was the real thing.

"Now what?" Hamish asked. "Do we know who won the auction?"

Pearce pointed to an avatar. "Indy890."

"That's not a lot to go by," Hamish commented.

"It's enough," Daphne said, and exchanged a smirk with Pearce, who was clearly having the same idea, "when you can hack into the auction site's back office." She winked at Pearce. "Loser pays for beer and pizza."

"Get your wallet out," Pearce said, and started typing away on his computer.

"Geeks," Logan said behind them, though his words carried no malice, rather amusement.

"Don't knock 'em," Enya said. "These two geeks might actually save the world without a bloody battle for a change."

"I'm in," Pearce announced.

Daphne glanced at his screen, not at all jealous that he'd beat her to it. After all, he was older and had had more practice. She abandoned her attempt and watched him search for the transaction on the auction site's server.

"Got it." He pointed to a file on the screen. "Sold to Indy890 three days ago." He clicked on the link to see the entire transaction. "Shipped via next-day air to... an address in Miami."

"Check the tracking info," Daphne said. "Make sure it arrived. That carrier often has delays even if you pay for next-day air."

"Good thinking," Pearce said, and clicked on the tracking link. Another window popped up. Pearce scrolled through it. "There. It arrived two days ago and was handed directly to the resident."

"Who's the new owner?" Enya asked.

"A James Harcott from Miami. Address is right here." Pearce switched screens and entered the address into a map, then zoomed in. "Residential. A large single-family home." Pearce swiveled in his chair to turn to his colleagues. "We've gotta hurry. If I was able to find the location this quickly, it might not take the demons too long either."

"Agreed," Enya said. "There's a portal a ten- to fifteen-minute drive from that address. Let's go."

Daphne rose from her chair. "But how are you gonna convince the owner to hand the dagger over? I mean, he paid a shitload of money for it. He's not just gonna give it up."

Pearce got up. "Don't worry. This is not our first rodeo." He asked Enya, "FBI, Fine Arts Division?"

Enya nodded. "That's our best bet." She walked to a cupboard and opened it.

Daphne stared at the contents. The shelves were labeled with signs for FBI, CIA, NSA, and various other governmental agencies. In the plastic drawers were ID cards and badges.

"You're going to impersonate FBI agents?" Daphne asked, stunned.

"Nothing easier than that," Pearce said.

"I wanna come with you."

Simultaneously Pearce and Enya said, "No."

"You need me." When Pearce lifted an eyebrow, she added, "The FBI has no Fine Arts Division. It's called the Art Theft Program.

Besides, I know Miami like my back pocket. I lived there for two years. In case we have to make a quick escape, I'll be useful."

Pearce and Enya exchanged a long look. Then Enya shrugged. "I guess if you and Daphne pretend to be the FBI agents, I can sneak into the house in the meantime and make sure we're not running into any demons."

"Actually, taking Daphne might be a good idea," Hamish said. "You and Enya might have to make yourselves invisible, or a demon could spot you. They'll see Daphne only as a human. She can drive from the portal to Harcott's house, while you two are invisible. We don't want any demon reporting to Zoltan that Stealth Guardians have suddenly been spotted in Miami when we have no compound there. It might tip Zoltan off. Enya has to remain invisible at all times, and you should only show yourself once you've arrived at the residence. It'll limit your risk of being spotted."

While Daphne liked that Hamish supported her demand, there was something she didn't understand. "How would the demons know that Pearce and Enya are Stealth Guardians?"

"We have an aura the demons can see. It gives us away, whereas when they look at you, they'll only see a human."

"Oh."

Pearce let out a sigh. "I suppose you've got a point, Hamish. However"—he turned to Daphne—"Aren't you worried about your deal with the court? What if you get caught impersonating an FBI agent? That's a criminal offense."

Daphne shrugged. She appreciated that he was worried about her. "Sure, it is. But you'll make sure I won't get caught."

Pearce let out a breath. "If you say so." He pointed to the chair. "Take a seat, Daphne."

Two minutes later, Pearce had produced an official-looking laminated ID that he slipped into a leather holder with a metal badge and handed to her.

"Let's go."

29

The portal, as Pearce had called it, was located on one of the lower levels of the compound and at first looked like an ordinary stone wall. All Daphne could make out was the symbol of a dagger etched into the surface. There was no door, no way to access this supposed teleportation device.

"You're saying this is it?" She couldn't help but be skeptical.

Yet, both Enya and Pearce nodded earnestly.

"Just watch," Pearce said, and laid his palm over the etching.

The spot started to glow as if it was heating up. She focused her eyes to make sure she wasn't hallucinating, and then the wall was gone all of a sudden. Where the heavy stone wall had been, an opening had appeared. Behind it, there lay only darkness, and despite the light that shone into the space that seemed no larger than the average elevator, Daphne couldn't make out any instruments or panels on the inside.

Pearce took her hand. "Come."

She hesitated, suddenly not as brave as she'd been earlier. The idea of teleporting to another city far away intrigued her, but she couldn't shake the memory of an old movie she'd seen, where the process had gone horribly wrong, melding a perfectly normal man with a fly that had accidentally gotten trapped in the teleportation device with him.

"It's perfectly safe," Pearce said. "See, Enya is already inside."

Indeed, Enya looked at Daphne somewhat impatiently. "You wanted to come. Have you changed your mind?"

"No, no, I haven't," Daphne said, not wanting to act cowardly in front of the petite blonde who seemed to be a veritable wonder woman. To prove that she wasn't afraid, Daphne walked through the opening, Pearce on her heels, still holding her hand.

"You'll need to keep holding on to me," Pearce said, "or you'll be lost."

Darkness suddenly descended on them, and like magic, the opening was gone, replaced by, she assumed, the stone wall, though she couldn't see it.

"It might feel a little disorienting at first, but that's normal. Don't worry," Pearce said.

She wanted to ask what he meant by that, but didn't get a chance, because in the next instant, she felt weightless. Floating aimlessly as if in outer space. A gasp escaped her, and she felt Pearce's comforting arms around her, holding her tightly.

"It's okay," he murmured. "We're almost there."

He wasn't lying. A moment later, she felt solid ground under her feet again, and a second later, colored, subdued light streamed into the portal. She refocused her eyes and realized that a stained-glass door or window was right in front of them, blocking their exit.

"Stay here," Pearce said. "I'll check if the coast is clear." He vanished, and Daphne could only assume that he'd made himself invisible and had then stepped through the stained glass. A moment later, he reappeared as if he'd never been gone.

"It's empty. Let's go."

Pearce pushed against one side of the stained glass, and it swung outward. Daphne followed him and was stunned to see where they were.

"A church? You have a portal in a church?" She looked around. The altar was straight in front of them, and beyond it were the wooden pews with Bibles and hymn books stacked at their ends.

"We don't always get to choose where the portals are. This is one of the lost ones," Pearce explained as he ushered Daphne and Enya to follow him to the exit. "When the stone or wood the portal is carved into gets moved to another location and used to build something else, like this church, for example, the portal moves with it."

"That's amazing," Daphne said.

"It's pretty neat," Enya said. "Now, time to be invisible."

At the door, Pearce turned around. "You know what to do. I'll take your hand and guide you to where I want you to go. We'll need a car first. Ready?"

Daphne nodded, and both Pearce and Enya disappeared. She felt Pearce taking her arm, and pushed the heavy church door open to step outside into the bright light. It was close to midday, and the street that ran along the church was moderately busy. Adjacent to the church was a cemetery on one side, and a parking lot on the other.

Pearce tugged her into the direction of the parking lot.

"The silver Toyota," he whispered to her, and steered her toward it.

Nervously, Daphne cast a look around, but nobody seemed to notice her. Then she heard a clicking sound coming from the car's driver's-side door.

"Got it," Enya murmured close to her. "Get in."

Daphne opened the door and slid into the driver's seat. Moments later, she heard Enya and Pearce sitting down, one in the passenger seat next to her, the other in the backseat.

"I'll hot-wire the car," Pearce said, his voice now a little louder, since nobody could hear them inside the car.

Daphne felt his hands and arms brushing her legs as he fumbled underneath the steering wheel.

"Put your foot on the brake."

She followed his command. A couple of seconds later, the engine roared.

"We're good to go," Pearce said.

She wanted to make a comment, how impressed she was at both

Enya's and Pearce's skills at grand theft auto, but Pearce had instructed her not to talk while he and Enya were invisible, so that nobody would find it strange when they saw her lips move as if she was talking to herself.

Orienting herself quickly on her cell phone's app, she left the old Mision San Francisco Santa Clara behind her and drove toward the freeway. There was relatively little traffic as she drove across the bridge leading to Miami Beach. As soon as she reached the island Miami Beach was located on, she took the exit to the Nautilus neighborhood and turned into the street running parallel to the beach facing Miami.

"Two or three more blocks," Enya said from the backseat. "It's a beachfront property, by the looks of it."

"Pull over here for a second," Pearce said.

"Behind the moving pod?" Daphne asked.

"Yes, sorry. I keep forgetting that you can't see me."

She pulled over and stopped the car. "Now what?"

"Okay, nobody around." Suddenly Pearce appeared in the passenger seat.

Daphne gasped and pressed her hand to her chest. "Damn, you startled me. Not sure I'll ever get used to this."

Pearce grinned. "You will." Then he pointed to the street ahead. "Continue to the address. Park right in front of it. You and I will go and speak to the owner, and Enya will remain visible. Should the owner give us any trouble, Enya will go inside and find the dagger. Are we all good?"

"Works for me," Enya said.

"Okay," Daphne said, and drove another block before parking in front of the property. "How do I switch off the engine?"

Pearce bent toward her and reached underneath the steering wheel. The motor died. "Like this."

She rolled her eyes and reached for the door handle. "Let's go, Agent Glaser."

"I'm on your heels, Agent Soul."

Daphne crossed the street with Pearce by her side. "Wow, it's humid here. I should have worn something different."

"We won't be here for long."

They walked to the front door of the large two-story house with the modern façade. Pearce pressed the doorbell. Daphne reached into her jacket pocket, ready to whip out her fake FBI ID. A few seconds stretched to a minute. Pearce pressed the doorbell again, and Daphne could clearly hear the bell ringing inside the house. Yet nobody came to the door.

"You think he's not here?" Daphne asked.

"Enya can check."

"I'm going in," Enya said from Daphne's left, sending another shiver down her spine.

"You guys have to stop doing this."

PEARCE CHUCKLED. "TRUST ME—"

Before he could finish his sentence, a woman called out to them. "Can I help you?"

Pearce turned and noticed a woman in her fifties standing at the other side of the fence that separated Harcott's property from his neighbor's to the left.

"Uh, yes, ma'am." Pearce pulled his FBI ID from his pocket while approaching the fence. "Maybe you can."

Daphne walked with him, fumbling for her ID in her jacket pocket.

"We're looking for Mr. James Harcott." He flashed his ID in front of the woman's face. "I'm Special Agent Glaser from the FBI. My colleague—"

"Special Agent Soul," Daphne interrupted, and flashed her badge and ID.

"Yes, we'd like to talk to Mr. Harcott."

The woman's forehead furrowed. "Is he in trouble? Well, doesn't surprise me. All the dressing up and fighting, the weapons, and that role playing." She leaned farther over the fence. "I always knew there's something wrong with him. Spoiled rich kid. Thinks he's some kind of superhero or something. Always doing something weird. It's just not right."

"Excuse me?" What was this woman talking about? Could it be that James Harcott was a demon? Pearce exchanged a look with Daphne, who looked as baffled as he was. "Is there something we should know about Mr. Harcott?"

The neighbor drew back a little. "You're not here about that? About his fantasy stuff?"

"I'm afraid I can't tell you what we need to talk to Mr. Harcott about," Pearce said. "But it's urgent. Do you know where we can find him?"

"Well, where do you think? At one of those conventions he goes to, of course."

"Convention?" Pearce echoed.

"Yeah, where they dress up like characters from movies and graphic novels and do God knows what."

"Are you talking about a cosplay event?" Daphne interrupted.

The woman made an excited motion with her hand. "Yes, yes, that's what he called it. It's just not right. I mean, he's a grown man, for God's sake."

Pearce ignored the comment. "Do you by any chance know where this event is taking place?"

"Los Angeles," she replied. "He left early this morning. The taxi driver honked when he picked him up. Woke me up before six a.m. I was in my right mind to give him hell, but—"

"Thank you so much for your help, ma'am," Pearce said. "We'll catch up with him when he gets back."

"I thought you said it was urgent."

Pearce forced a smile onto his lips. "Thank you, ma'am. I'll just go ahead and slip my card underneath his door so he can call me."

He turned away and made sure Daphne joined him as they walked back to the entrance door of Harcott's house.

"What now?" Daphne asked.

"As soon as that nosy neighbor isn't watching us anymore, we're going around the side of the house and sneak inside from the back."

Pearce casually turned, pretending to write something on a card, while he lifted his eyes just enough to look into the neighbor's yard. The woman was now collecting her mail from a box at the sidewalk, her back to them.

"Now," Pearce said, and grabbed Daphne's arm.

Swiftly, they walked to the side of the house and turned a corner. There, lush vegetation formed a visual barrier to the street and the neighbor on the other side, but a high wooden gate prevented access to the backyard.

"Give me a sec," Pearce said, then walked through the gate, pivoted on the other side, and unlocked it for Daphne to enter. He closed the gate behind her, then looked around.

The house sat at the beach, with a direct view of Miami. But they weren't here to admire the view. Enya was already waiting for them inside the house and opened the French doors for them.

"What did the old biddy say?" Enya asked.

"Harcott traveled to a cosplay event in Los Angeles," Pearce said.

"Cosplay? You mean where some geeks dress up in costume and live out their fantasies?" Enya said with a raised eyebrow. "Now it all makes sense."

"What makes sense?" Pearce asked.

Enya motioned for them to follow her. "Let me show you."

They walked upstairs, where Enya led them into a large room with a cathedral ceiling. Pearce stopped at the entrance, and Daphne, too, rocked to a halt.

"Oh my God," Daphne said.

"No wonder his avatar on the auction site was Indy890," Pearce said. "This guy is an Indiana Jones fan."

"Fan?" Enya asked, and pointed to the room that looked like a set piece from one of the Indiana Jones movies, complete with traps, tunnels, and fake snakes. On one wall, an assortment of weapons, including knives, swords, and whips was displayed. "More like he lives in an alternate reality. I mean, look at this stuff. How old is this guy? Twelve?"

"More like thirty-two," Daphne said.

Pearce turned to her and saw her pointing at a picture of a man dressed as Indiana Jones, standing next to the actual Indiana Jones, Harrison Ford.

"As I said, a geek," Enya said.

"Don't knock it, Enya," Daphne said. "It's big business. And it's been around since the 1970s, though the term cosplay wasn't coined until around 1984, when a Japanese reporter wrote about it in a magazine. There are lots of these costume plays all around the world, and believe me, tickets are expensive and sell out months in advance. And the costumes..." Daphne let out a big breath. "Talking about authentic, a good costume costs megabucks."

Pearce cast Daphne a long look. "How come you know so much about cosplay?"

Daphne shrugged and looked at her shoes. "I might have attended one or two events."

Enya laughed. "Oh my God, did I say geek? I'm so on target with this, it's not even funny."

"Okay, okay," Pearce said, lifting his hands. "Let's get to work. We're searching for the dagger. Let's find it. It must be here somewhere."

"It won't be," Daphne said.

"What makes you think that?"

"It's part of his costume. Look at the picture. In addition to his whip and his pistol, he has a blade in his belt." She turned to the opposite wall with the display of weapons and pointed to one spot. "That blade. He didn't take it with him, but the pistol and the whip that match the one in this photo aren't on the wall."

"You think he took the source dagger he just won in the auction?" Pearce asked.

Daphne nodded. "He'll want to show his new purchase off to his friends."

"We'd better make sure," Enya said.

30

Daphne was right. A thorough search of Harcott's house had confirmed it. And another problem had cropped up: they searched all hotel reservations in the Los Angeles area, but Harcott's name didn't come up. He'd either booked his hotel under another name or was staying with friends. In either case, there was no way they could catch up with Harcott and take the dagger from him before he went to the cosplay event the next morning.

"At least we know where he's gonna be and when," Daphne said upon leaving Miami.

"Are you suggesting we attend the cosplay convention to find him?" Pearce asked.

"Yep."

"In a crowd of what? A thousand people?"

"Make that ten thousand. The L.A. cosplay event is huge."

Pearce exchanged a look with Enya. "We need more manpower."

Enya nodded. "The entire Baltimore compound. And we'd better talk to Scanguards too. We need more hybrids."

"And costumes," Daphne added.

Many hours and many phone calls later, Pearce, Enya, and Daphne arrived in Los Angeles and entered a large vampire-proof mansion owned by Scanguards, the Stealth Guardians' vampire allies. The place was tucked away in a side street in Brentwood, a fancy neighborhood not far from UCLA.

When they stepped into the large foyer, it was buzzing like a beehive. People carried overnight bags up the stairs, greeted each other, or stood in deep conversation, while a security guard with a clipboard looked at them. From his aura, Pearce recognized him as a vampire, even though he didn't know him personally. He had to be a Scanguards employee.

"Stealth Guardians," the guard said, and waved them to approach. "Name?"

"Pearce."

"We've got you in the Cloud Room on the top floor. Sign's on the door." Then he looked at Enya. "You must be Enya."

"Good guess," she replied.

The guard shrugged. "It's easy when you're only expecting one female Stealth Guardian." He looked at his clipboard. "You'll be staying in the Sunset Room on the second floor." His eyes roamed over Daphne, then they snapped back to the clipboard. He looked up and shook his head. "Sorry, must have been a mix-up, but I don't have a human listed here."

"She's with me," Pearce said. "She won't need her own room."

"All right, you're all set, then."

Enya was already turning away to greet somebody.

"Is everybody here?" Pearce asked.

The guard nodded. "You're the last to arrive." He pointed to an open door. "The meeting will start shortly. If you need a hand with your luggage, I can take care of that for you."

"We don't have any," Pearce said. They hadn't gone back to Baltimore, traveling straight from Miami.

"Oh, in that case, I'll have toiletries and other necessities sent up to your rooms."

"Thank you."

Pearce took Daphne's arm and steered her toward the open door, but a voice stopped him. "There you are."

He turned to his left and saw Gabriel approach, his hand stretched out in greeting.

Pearce grasped it and shook it. "Gabriel, I can't even tell you how grateful I am that you and your men are helping us with this on such short notice."

Gabriel smiled, and the large scar that marred the left side of his face twitched. "Samson insisted. He would have come himself, but figured Patrick would be of more use than he."

"Patrick?" Pearce turned back to Daphne. "Sorry, I should introduce you guys. Daphne, this is Gabriel, second in charge at Scanguards, our vampire allies, and Ryder's father."

"Nice to meet you," Daphne said with some hesitation, while she clearly tried to avoid looking at his scar.

"It's a pleasure, Daphne," Gabriel said.

"And Patrick is Grayson's younger brother," Pearce explained to Daphne, then asked Gabriel, "So why is he sending Patrick? I mean, no offense, he's a trained bodyguard, but—"

"I get what you're trying to say," Gabriel said, "but he's got some expertise that some of us old folks know nothing about." He smiled at Daphne. "He's a nut about cosplay. He knows everything about it. We figured he can be in charge of the costumes and getting us into the event."

"I can help him," Daphne offered. "I know a lot about cosplay too."

Gabriel nodded. "I'll introduce you to him. I think he's working the phone right now to get tickets."

"How many people are we trying to get inside?" she asked.

"Well, let's see...six Stealth Guardians, three hybrids, given that Patrick will insist on going, and four vampires—"

"Who are the vampires apart from you?" Pearce interrupted.

"Zane, Thomas, and Yvette."

"Excellent choices," Pearce said, and meant it.

"So, fourteen tickets, then," Daphne said.

"Uh, I think that's thirteen, actually," Gabriel said politely.

"Actually, fourteen," Daphne said. "I need a ticket too."

"No, you won't," Pearce replied.

"But I'm coming with—"

"There's always the chance, no matter how slim, that the demons know about Harcott and that he'll be at the cosplay event. They've never been far behind. Hell, they found the location of the dagger before we did. We have to assume that they know who's got it now. That's the whole reason we brought Scanguards in. They're equipped to help us fight the demons should we encounter them. You're not. You're staying here, in this house, protected by one of Scanguards' men. And that's that."

Apparently, Daphne didn't like his answer in the least. She braced her hands at her hips. "Then who's gonna get you tickets to get inside? Because I can tell you right now that you're not gonna get any legit tickets this late in the game."

From behind them, a male said, "I'm afraid she's right."

Pearce spun around to see a young hybrid approach. He looked very much like his father and his older brother. "Patrick."

"Hey, guys," Patrick said. "Sorry to be the bearer of bad news, but I tried all my contacts to get tickets. Even the usual hawkers have none left. Dad authorized me to offer whatever price would buy us access, but even with unlimited funds, I can't get us in. I was gonna talk to Thomas and see if he can hack into their system and generate some tickets for us that'll pass their scanner. Security is ultra-tight this year. Particularly after that kerfuffle last year."

"What kerfuffle?" Pearce asked.

Patrick gave a one-shouldered shrug. "Well, I guess if you're not following the industry, you wouldn't know. Anyway, last year a bunch of guys tried to kidnap the cast of *Game of Thrones*, and the way they got in was with fake tickets. I heard they've implemented a two-step security system this year. I'll talk to Thomas about it. He should know how to get around it. Or you could talk to him, Pearce, IT genius to IT genius."

"Sounds good," Pearce said. "Together we'll figure it out."

"By the time you get into their system—if you get in—it'll be too late," Daphne said in a calm voice.

"You underestimate my and Thomas's skills."

"I don't," Daphne said. "But I know the guy who wrote the program. Ex-hacker. Very talented. Better than you, Thomas, and me combined. There are more traps in that program than in a store selling mousetraps. It would take us days to hack into it. Days we don't have. I'm the only one who can get us the tickets. The guy owes me a favor."

It wasn't that Pearce didn't believe her words, but he didn't like the option he was presented with. "What if we encounter demons?"

"I'll still be safer being with you and your vampire friends than going to the event on my own."

The implication was clear. She would sneak into the event on her own if he didn't let her tag along. He exchanged a look with Gabriel. "We'll go in teams, one vampire or hybrid to one Stealth Guardian. I want Zane on my team." He was the strongest, the fiercest vampire Pearce had ever met. If anybody could scare Daphne into following orders, it was him. He looked at Daphne. "If you leave Zane's or my side for even a second, I will punish you. Don't make me regret this."

"Don't worry. You'll barely notice that I'm there."

"Ha!" As if.

Daphne had already pulled out her cell phone then moved to a quieter corner of the foyer. Pearce heard her talking in hushed tones.

"She's very resourceful," Gabriel said.

"So, that's her, huh?" Patrick asked. When Pearce raised an eyebrow, Patrick said, "Grayson filled me in."

"Well, you'd better keep it to yourself, or you'll have to deal with me."

The hybrid lifted his hands. "I can keep a secret."

"Hey, meeting is about to start," Enya called from the open door to what seemed to be the living room.

Daphne was already coming toward them, putting her phone back in her pocket. "He'll do it. We'll have to meet him in the morning at the VIP entrance. He'll get us the right passes then."

"Great, thanks," Pearce said, and smiled at her, even though he still didn't like that she was coming with them.

As everybody made their way toward the living room, Logan waved to him. "A quick word, Pearce." When Daphne stayed with Pearce, Logan added, "Alone."

Pearce turned to Daphne. "I'll be right in."

Once Daphne was out of earshot, Pearce joined Logan in the small alcove under the stairs. "What?"

"Winter had another vision," Logan said.

Excitement flooded Pearce.

"It's the same as four days ago. Exactly the same. Nothing has changed. Nothing at all. All the things you think you did had no effect whatsoever on the outcome of the vision. You'll still die, and the killer is still Daphne."

Pearce ran a hand through his hair, trying to think. Why had Winter's vision not changed? How could that be? "But..."

"You have to face the facts. Winter's visions are never wrong. Whatever you do, it'll always end the same way. With you being killed by Daphne."

DAPHNE HADN'T WANTED to eavesdrop. But the moment she'd entered the spacious living room where over a dozen people congregated, many of whom she didn't know, her bladder reared its head. It always happened when she was nervous. So she'd snuck out again, without being noticed, and walked to her left, seeing a door there, but it turned out that it was a coat closet, so she'd turned around and heard Logan's warning coming from somewhere underneath the stairs.

She couldn't see Pearce or Logan, which also meant they couldn't see her. For a moment she stood there, frozen, then realized that if Pearce or Logan found her here, eavesdropping, they would—given Winter's vision—assume the worst. Her heart beating into her throat, she managed to return to the living room and found a place to sit in the rear of the room, next to a woman she didn't know. She could only assume that she was one of the vampires Gabriel had mentioned.

When Pearce and Logan entered the room a few moments later, she was glad that there was no seat available close to her. Logan took a seat next to Enya, and Pearce walked to the front of the room, which was a wall of floor-to-ceiling windows, affording a beautiful view of manicured lawns and more mansions out to the ocean. But Daphne couldn't enjoy the view. Nor could she concentrate on Pearce's explanations. He was talking about teams and rules and precautions. About how to best find the dagger, about the man in whose possession it currently was, and how he would be dressed at the cosplay event. Somebody distributed pictures of James Harcott, while Pearce spoke about costumes and weapons, about the importance and urgency of this mission.

But Daphne heard only parts of it. Logan's words kept repeating in her head as if on an endless loop.

It'll always end the same way. With you being killed by Daphne.

Why hadn't Pearce told her? And Winter was the one who'd foretold this? Was that why she'd been so hostile at the compound? Because she knew that Daphne would kill one of them? But how? She had no reason to kill Pearce. And even more importantly, no desire to do such a terrible thing. In the short time she'd known Pearce, she'd come to care for him. Deeply. And to hurt him, kill him, was the farthest thought from her mind. He'd saved her and her brother. Even if she didn't care about him, she would never be so ungrateful as to hurt her rescuer.

No, she couldn't allow Pearce to believe that she was a danger to him. She had to tell him what she felt, explain to him that the vision had to be false, even if that meant she had to admit that she eavesdropped.

The discussions dragged on, teams were formed, communications equipment distributed and synched, while Patrick took down notes on clothing and shoe sizes for the costumes that were supposed to be delivered to the house sometime during the night.

"For the four vampires who will need protection from the sun," Patrick announced, "I've got some guys reworking Star Wars costumes to protect you from the sun. I'm afraid you'll all have to dress up as either a Stormtrooper or a Darth Vader. Sorry."

A few people in the room chuckled.

"But how are we gonna be able to recognize each other, if we're in the crowd? I doubt we'll be the only ones in those costumes," the woman next to Daphne asked. "I mean, if our entire body is covered, nobody will see our auras."

"I thought of that too," Patrick said, and raised his hand. "The Stormtrooper and Darth Vader costumes will have a little pink ribbon on the chest plate."

"A pink ribbon? Are you kidding me?" A tall bald man with a mean look shot up from the couch.

"Zane, pipe down!" the woman next to Daphne said. "A little pink isn't gonna kill you."

"Thanks, Yvette," Patrick said, then told Zane, "The idea is to make it look natural. The pink ribbon is a symbol for breast cancer awareness. Nobody is gonna question it. But we all will know what it means." Patrick looked on the piece of paper in his hand. "Okay, then. That's all from me. I'll set up two rooms with the costumes as soon as they get here. One for the men, one for the women. I need you all down here at four a.m. sharp to get ready."

"Thanks, Patrick," Pearce said, walking up to him. "Everybody knows what they need to do. The housekeeper tells me there's food in the kitchen for the hybrids and the guardians. The rest of you, I'm sure you've already fed before you flew down here. Let's get some shuteye."

31

———

Quietly, Pearce opened the door to the Cloud Room that had been assigned to him and stepped inside. Daphne had retired an hour earlier, and he didn't want to wake her in case she was already asleep. It turned out she wasn't, though she'd gotten out of her street clothes and was sitting on the bed, wearing a terrycloth robe.

"Hey," he said, and gave her a hesitant smile. "I thought you might be asleep already."

And hadn't he secretly hoped for exactly that? So he didn't have to have the conversation he knew he had to have? But it was time for Daphne to know the truth. He didn't want to go into the next battle carrying a lie on his shoulders. If only he knew how to tell her.

"I can't sleep." She swung her legs over the side of the bed and rose.

He walked toward her and stretched out his arms, but she didn't walk into his embrace. "You're worried about tomorrow. You should stay here."

She shook her head. "It's not that." She swallowed hard as if her throat was too dry.

He motioned to the door behind him. "If you're worried about all the vampires in the house, don't be. They're good people. They're not a danger to any of—"

"No, they're not," she interrupted, and looked him in the eye. "But you think *I* am. You think I will kill you. You believe that, don't you?"

Stunned at hearing the words come from her mouth, Pearce froze for a split-second, before his schooled hand made an automatic movement—that of pulling his dagger from its sheath at his waist.

Daphne gasped and slapped her hand over her mouth, tears already welling up in her eyes. "Oh my God, you do. You do think that I'm gonna kill you. You believe Winter's vision. You believe I'm a murderer." Sobs tore from her chest and burst over her lips, while tears ran down her cheeks in little rivulets that threatened to become rivers.

His heart broke for her, and he quickly put the dagger aside. He didn't want to upset her more than she already was. "How do you know about Winter's vision?"

"I overheard you and Logan. I didn't mean to... I just wanted to find the bathroom." She wailed again. This time the sobs ripped through her body like spasms.

He couldn't stand it any longer and pulled her into his arms. He pressed her to his chest and rubbed up and down her back, trying to calm her. Was this really the reaction of an assassin upon finding out that her intended victim knew what was going to happen? It couldn't be. What he felt from Daphne were deep emotions, terrible distress, genuine anguish.

"Please don't cry, babe," he murmured into her hair.

She lifted her head and looked at him with tear-stained, puffy eyes. "But how can you even be with me if you believe in this vision? How can you stand the sight of me? How can you sleep with me?"

"How can I not be with you? How can I not share your bed? Make love to you? How can I stop myself from being close to you?" He sighed, and for a moment, he didn't know how to continue, but he knew that if there was still a chance to change the outcome of the vision, it could only be brought about by the truth. "Winter's visions are always right, but they can change depending on the actions we take. I'd hoped that when we met, when we got to know each other, that my helping you would change the vision. That whatever makes you kill me in the future will never come to pass."

Daphne slowly pushed against him, and he released her from his embrace. "So, us meeting, it was all…"

He nodded. "A setup. I was invisible when I stole your wallet. And I made sure I stood behind you in the checkout line so I could help you out of the problem that was my doing in the first place." He looked away, not proud of his prior actions.

"And you slept with me only so you could change—"

"No!" He whipped his head back to her. "No, don't ever think that. What happened between us, the attraction, the sex, the chemistry, that's all real. I never expected that. When the others found out, they warned me. But I was in too deep already. I realized you were in trouble, and I was only too happy to help you sort out that mess with your brother, and then with his fence Vasili. Those things, yes, I did partially because I hoped to gain your goodwill so you'd never think of killing me, but primarily because I hate to see you hurt, physically or emotionally."

He caught himself reaching out to caress her cheek but pulled it back before he could make contact.

"Oh, Pearce, you should have told me." More tears started rolling down her cheeks. "I could have told you after our first night together that I would never hurt you. I hate seeing anybody in pain, even my no-good brother, but you, oh, Pearce, it would break my heart to hurt you." She shook her head and sobbed again. "Killing you would mean ripping my own heart from my chest. Don't you understand that? Can't you see that? I love you, and I'd never do anything to lose you."

Pearce's heart began to thunder in his chest. Had Daphne really just declared her love for him? He pulled her into his arms. "Oh, babe." He pressed a kiss to her lips. They were salty from her tears, but sometimes the truth didn't taste sweet. "Screw the vision, Daphne. I believe in you."

However many days, or months, or years he had left, he would spend them with Daphne. And every night they would fight the vision from coming to pass by loving each other. Because as long as Daphne loved him, she wouldn't hurt him. He believed that. He knew it was the truth.

"We'll fight the vision together," he promised.

Daphne's tears dried, and she slung her arms around him. "Yes, together. We can do it, my love, I know we can."

She started tugging on his shirt, and he helped her pull it over his head. Her hands on his chest felt good, reassuring, right. And her lips tasted of love, of affection, of trust. He drank it all in, soaked up everything she wanted to give him.

When he felt Daphne attempt to undo the button of his pants, he did it for her and pushed them down, kicked off his boots, and rid himself of his socks. Daphne was already stripping him of his boxer briefs, and before he could pull her back into his arms and press his lips to hers again, she was already kneeling in front of him and gripping his rock-hard cock.

"Fuck!" he said on a stunned gasp.

A moment later, he lost his ability to think clearly. Daphne wrapped her lips around the tip of his erection and slid down on him, taking him into her warm and wet mouth, making him sink into pure heaven. Her hand at the base of his cock, she pumped him hard, while her head bobbed up and down as she sucked him. All he could do was hold on to her shoulders for balance and let Daphne pleasure him with her mouth.

He couldn't hold back the moans that rolled over his lips, or prevent his heart from pumping more rapidly. Every cell in his body reacted to the sweet torture Daphne was inflicting on him. Maybe this was how she would kill him one day, by loving him until his heart exploded from being too full. But not tonight, because tonight he needed to show her that he felt the same for her, even if he couldn't put it in words yet. The vision was still hovering over him, still making him hold back that last little bit of himself that he hoped he could one day share with her. But tonight, he could give her something else—if not his soul, then his body.

It was difficult to pull himself out of Daphne's mouth, her warmth too irresistible to leave. But he couldn't let her continue, or he'd lose his control too quickly. When he pulled her up and pushed the bathrobe over her shoulders, revealing her nude body, his pulse thundered in his veins, and his cock twitched in anticipation of being inside her once more.

"I need you," he said gruffly, and eased her down onto the bed, before covering her with his body. He didn't have the patience for foreplay tonight, not after everything that had happened, and he sensed that Daphne, too, was impatient. He was almost rough when he pushed her thighs apart and plunged into her with one urgent thrust.

Daphne expelled a breath, gasping at the impact, but there was no going back now. He needed to ride her, needed to take her hard, needed to show her what she did to him, how hot she made him, how hungry.

Her pussy was warm and welcoming, like a glove that fit perfectly around him, squeezing him on every withdrawal, and sucking him in with every descent. Harder and harder he thrust, getting as deep as humanly possible, his cock demanding its due.

Daphne's lips were parted, her eyes focused on him, her breaths ragged. She moved with him, her heels locked around his thighs, her hands holding onto his shoulders as if she feared he'd stop if she let go.

"More!" she demanded.

He followed her wish, took her harder and faster, rammed his cock into her with such force that he surprised even himself. He'd always seen himself as a tender lover, a considerate partner who held back to give the woman in his arms the pleasure she deserved. But tonight, the woman in his arms wanted what he wanted. Wild, unbridled, passionate sex. Sex unmatched by anything else he'd ever experienced.

"Oh, babe," he said on a ragged breath. He wanted to say he was sorry for being so rough, but her eyes stopped him. In them, all he saw was lust and desire. No distress, no fear, no restraint. Daphne was made for him. And he for her.

Daphne pulled his head to hers and pressed her lips to his, kissing him with a passion that couldn't be faked, a truth that couldn't be hidden. Every cell of her body radiated love, and he soaked it up, took it in greedily, because this love was what would protect him in the days to come.

With that certainty, he let go of his control. He rode her until he could feel her interior muscles spasm around his cock, igniting his own release. Bliss flooded him, filling his cells with happiness, his mind with strength, and his heart with love.

Wave after wave crashed over him and lulled him into a state of utter satisfaction. Beneath him, Daphne's body relaxed back into the sheets as her orgasm ebbed. Without haste, he pulled out of her and rolled off in order to take his weight off her. But he didn't want to sever the connection with her, so he pulled her against his chest, tucked her sweet ass into his groin, and slid back into her warm pussy.

"Again?" she murmured sleepily.

He chuckled. "Whatever you want, babe. I'm your slave."

She pulled his arm closer around her. "I like the sound of that."

He nuzzled his face into the crook of her neck. "At your service, my mistress."

32

It was still dark when the activity at the Brentwood mansion went into overdrive. The living room had been turned into a dressing room for the men, while the smaller dining room was meant for the three women among them.

Despite his best efforts, Pearce hadn't been able to talk Daphne out of going to the cosplay convention with them. She'd insisted that she would be the only one her friend Claus would hand the tickets to, though of course, Pearce knew it was a white lie. She wanted to be there; she wanted to be part of this. He couldn't blame her. She'd come this far, helped him with countless things to get to this point, and now she wanted to see the fruits of her labor. He'd finally given up opposing her decision and watched her enter the women's dressing room with a beaming smile.

Pearce headed into the living room and closed the door behind him. Several clothing racks with costumes lined the room. To one side, Thomas and Zane, two full-blooded vampires, were squeezing into the rigid white uniforms of the Stormtroopers from the Star Wars movies, while Gabriel eyed the Darth Vader costume. He, too, had to be covered head to toe in order not to be exposed to the burning rays of the sun.

"I think it's only fitting that I'll take Darth Vader," Gabriel said to Thomas and Zane. "After all, I'm your boss."

Thomas rolled his eyes. "Just don't get too much into character. You're still one of the good guys."

Pearce moved farther into the room, where Patrick was helping Manus slip on some sort of gloves with spikes.

When Manus looked up and met Pearce's look, he grinned. "Check this out." He moved his hands, and the spikes on the back of his hands extended. They were long, sharp metal claws. "I'm Wolverine. Pretty cool, huh?"

Pearce smirked. "You don't look anything like Wolverine."

Patrick turned to him. "Wait until we're done with hair and makeup."

"Hair and makeup?" Pearce asked.

The hybrid pointed to another corner of the room, where two dressing tables with mirrors and professional lighting were set up. "I brought in a couple of makeup artists that work in the movies."

"Wow, you went all out."

"It's all about authenticity, trust me," Patrick said.

"If you say so. So, where's my costume?"

Patrick patted Manus on the shoulder. "You're done. Go and have them fit you with facial hair and..." He dropped his gaze to Manus's half-open shirt. His scars were clearly visible. "Maybe a little fake blood on the chest."

Manus walked away, and Patrick ushered Pearce to follow him to one of the costumes racks. "So, I've only got a few things left that might fit you. It's either Spider-Man or Jaime Lannister, you know, from *Game of Thrones*."

"I'm not gonna get caught dead in a tight red and blue jumpsuit."

Patrick tilted his head. "Well, it's Jaime Lannister, then. I've got you the leather outfit, rather than the armor, 'cause that's a little easier to maneuver in. Between you and me, Jaime Lannister is a better choice than Spider-Man anyway. He's hot right now. Total babe magnet."

Patrick handed him the costume.

"You told me that I'm the babe magnet," Hamish said from behind them.

Pearce looked over his shoulder to get a look at Hamish's costume. Hamish sported a bare chest with dark-stripe fake tattoos and a loincloth with an assortment of weapons, while his face had been transformed by a goatee, dark, bushy eyebrows, and a long braid. "Khal Drogo. Not bad." To Patrick, he said, "Why couldn't I get that one?"

"Because I got up earlier. Though if Tessa were here, you might have beat me to it," Hamish said, implying that Pearce was tardy because Daphne had spent the night with him. He wasn't wrong.

"I think I'm gonna rock the Jaime Lannister look," Pearce said. "I look good in leather." He pointed past Hamish, where Grayson was squeezing himself into a Superman costume. "Better than wearing tights any day!"

Hamish looked over his shoulder and chuckled. "Yeah, that's manly."

Grayson looked at them, clearly having heard the jab. "At least I'm not wearing a frilly shirt and knickerbockers like Ryder." He motioned to his friend, who was adjusting the sleeves of his historical-looking shirt.

"They're not called knickerbockers, and you know it," Ryder said without missing a beat. "They're breeches, and men in the eighteen hundreds wore them all the time. You're just jealous 'cause you can't carry off the look."

"It's barely a disguise," Grayson said, huffing.

"Okay, I'll ask," Pearce said. "Who are you supposed to be?"

Ryder gave an elaborate bow, then straightened and flashed his fangs. "The vampire Lestat."

Grayson rolled his eyes. "See, he's not even choosing a proper action figure. He's going as a vampire."

"As a very famous one, whereas you'll always be known as the man in tights."

"Man of Steel, Man of Steel. How often do I have to remind you of that?"

Pearce turned away and continued getting dressed. The costume was rather comfortable and had lots of pockets where he could stash weapons. Next to him, Logan was getting ready. His costume was rather simple, a beige outfit that made him look like he belonged into a dojo, but when he added a cape of the same color and stuck a lightsaber into his belt, Pearce recognized the costume.

"So you're going as Luke Skywalker."

Logan shrugged. "I can fight in this garb better than as a Stormtrooper, that's for sure. I just wanna get in, find the source dagger, and get out."

"My sentiments exactly."

Logan grinned. "Some people seem to take dressing up a little too seriously." He pointed to Aiden, who was getting his hair and makeup done at one of the dressing tables. Not that it was necessary. His costume already identified him as the Norse god Thor.

"You think Aiden is the only one into this?" Pearce laughed, glad that there was levity before the big storm ahead. "Check out what our little organizer Patrick reserved for himself." He pointed to a rack in the back of the room, where Patrick was slipping into a full-body costume.

"Aquaman," Logan said. "That little cheat! I asked him if he had any superheroes left, and he said that the only costume not spoken for was Luke Skywalker. He was hiding that costume so he could take it for himself, I swear."

Pearce winked at his friend. "So, you're not at all into this, right?"

Logan grunted something unintelligible. "Oh, shut up!"

"Well, at least you and Gabriel will look good together." Pearce watched as Gabriel, now in full Darth Vader garb, approached.

He stopped right in front of Logan. "I am your father," he said in true Darth Vader form.

"Shoot me now," Logan said, while Gabriel laughed, the mask muffling the sound and turning it into something sinister.

"Guess we're ready now," Pearce said, and looked around the room. There was a knock at the door. Seeing that everybody was dressed, he said, "Come in."

The first to enter was a Stormtrooper, no doubt Yvette, who, as a full-blooded vampire, had to stay out of the rays of the sun. Behind her, Enya entered. Her appearance silenced everybody. She was dressed as Khaleesi, mother of dragons, from *Game of Thrones*, her natural long blond hair hanging loose down to her waist. Her gown was blue and showed off her tiny figure. At her waist sat several weapons, and knowing Enya, she probably had more strapped to her thighs or ankles —just in case.

Hamish whistled. "Come to your Khal!"

Enya gave him the finger, and everybody in the room laughed.

"Where's—" Pearce started.

"Sorry I'm late." Daphne entered the room. Had she not spoken, he would have barely recognized her. She was dressed as Wonder Woman, complete with shield, high boots, and brass headdress that prevented the *long*, dark locks of her wig from falling into her face.

His heart stopped. Winter had described how Daphne looked like on the day she would murder him. Now he could see it for himself. This was the Daphne who would kill him.

33

Zoltan watched, from a distance of about five hundred yards, how one of his underlings was diverting a private coach by holding up a sign that read, *Entrance moved. Turn left for overflow parking.* Dutifully, the driver followed the demon's instructions and drove into the area Zoltan and his demons had prepared: an empty warehouse. Zoltan had taken care of the lonely security guard and put one of his own men into the man's uniform.

The fake security guard now stood at the entrance and waved the coach into the building. When the driver stopped and lowered his window, the demon said what Zoltan had instructed him to say in such a case: "Drive all the way in and park. There'll be a shuttle in five minutes to take your passengers to the convention."

The bus driver was gullible enough to follow the instruction. As soon as the coach was inside, Zoltan waved at two other demons who'd been waiting in the shadows and gave them the sign to push the heavy sliding gate shut behind them.

Inside, more demons were already waiting. Zoltan hurried inside via a side door and watched with satisfaction how the humans in their costumes waddled off the bus and looked around, still unaware that they had driven right into a trap. Even the fact that the men around them wore sunglasses, when inside the warehouse it was rather dark, didn't seem to raise any suspicions. At least not for the first minutes, when it was crucial that all passengers left the bus. Zoltan couldn't risk one of them staying back and alerting the authorities with a cell phone call.

Zoltan let his gaze travel over the humans. Several were dressed as large, hairy, animal-like bipedal creatures he recognized as Wookiees from the Star Wars franchise. Others wore the white uniforms of the Stormtroopers, an army of bad guys from the same movies. There was even a Darth Vader, a Spider-Man, several Klingons and Vulcans from *Star Trek*, as well as a lonely Batman.

"When's the shuttle coming? I don't wanna be late for the mock fights," a man dressed as Chewbacca said impatiently.

Zoltan approached. "Yeah, about the shuttle. There's been a change of plans." He motioned to his demons, several of whom now came out of their hiding places. They surrounded the humans. "I'm afraid we'll need your costumes. And your tickets."

Shocked gasps went through the crowd, and several curses bounced off the walls.

"You can't just take—"

A well-placed punch from Zoltan cut off the protest. The wannabe Klingon fell to the ground like a sack of potatoes.

"Any other objections?"

Their eyes filled with fear, the humans fell silent.

"Yeah. Didn't think so." To his demons, Zoltan said, "Strip them —make sure not to damage the costumes. Get the tickets, too, then gag them and tie them up."

Several of the humans put up a fight, but the moment one of Zoltan's underlings drew a dagger and flashed it, the humans became more docile than pets. Weaklings. No wonder they had to dress up and pretend to be somebody else, somebody stronger.

"The Darth Vader costume for you, oh Great One?" Wilson, a short, stocky demon, asked, offering Zoltan the costume.

He stared at it. "A bit on the nose, don't you think?" He didn't see himself as a villain. He was a hero. And a hero needed a hero's costume. He pointed to the lone Batman, who was still wearing his costume. "I'll be Batman." The mask would hide Zoltan's face from those Stealth Guardians who might recognize him. Besides, who would assume that Zoltan, the Great One, would dress up as the crime-fighting Dark Knight? The character suited him. A playboy, a philanthropist, a rich man. He could be all that.

"Good choice, oh Great One." Wilson was already marching toward the man, who quickly started taking off the costume, his hands visibly shaking, his face a mask of fear.

Zoltan chuckled to himself and started dressing in the black garb. The costume pinched a little in the crotch and around the shoulders, but luckily, the full-body suit wasn't made of hardened rubber, but of a softer, stretchable material. It would also make it easier for him to move during a fight, should it come to that.

It took all of fifteen minutes to strip all passengers of their costumes and entrance tickets and for the demons to tie them and the bus driver up and lock them in a shipping container inside the warehouse. It took another ten minutes for all demons to be dressed in those costumes that fit their body type. Luckily, the costumes of the Wookiees and Klingons were the easiest to suit the demons, though several had managed to don the uniforms of the Stormtroopers, and one had decided to be Darth Vader, another Spider-Man. The Stormtroopers and Darth Vader wouldn't have to worry about their green eyes. They were hidden behind their face masks. And the Wookiees and Klingons could get away with green eyes. People would assume they'd taken liberties with the costumes. Nobody would suspect them. Zoltan's own demon eyes were hidden behind colored lenses, which would be good for another six to eight hours. Sufficient time to find the current owner of the source dagger and take it off him.

"Ready?"

All nodded.

"Then get on the bus. We've got a cosplay convention to go to."

"Thanks so much, Claus. You have no idea how much you're helping us," Daphne said, and shook her hacker friend's hand. They were in the VIP lobby of the convention center in downtown L.A. Claus had handed them their tickets and ushered them past security with little more than a wink and a nod at the stern-looking guards.

It was loud in the lobby, the constant music and announcements from the main hall reaching into this smaller space. Daphne could only imagine how loud it had to be in the hall itself.

Claus, a tall guy with untamed blond hair that hung down to his shoulders, wore a Yoda costume, his employee badge prominently displayed on a lanyard around his neck. She'd always seen him as something like an older brother and was relieved that he had been able to help.

"Don't mention it," he said, and leaned closer. "I mean it. Don't mention it."

Daphne understood, and she had no intention of getting him in trouble. "You're the best." She hugged him quickly.

"Enjoy the event," he said, and nodded at the men and women Daphne had in tow. "All of you. Make sure you don't lose your tickets if you want to come back for the second day. I can't replace them. I mean that."

Next to her, Pearce said, "Not a problem. Thanks again. You're a lifesaver." How true Pearce's words were, Claus could never imagine.

Daphne folded out the map Claus had handed her. Each section of the exhibition hall was color-coded to make it easier for the visitors to find what they were looking for. She nodded to Pearce.

"Okay, listen up," Pearce said. "Each team takes a sector. Manus, Ryder, you guys have sector red. Hamish and Thomas, you'll do green. Aiden and Yvette, you comb through sector blue. Logan and Gabriel, you'll get sector orange. Enya, you'll take Grayson and Patrick and search sector gray. And Zane, Daphne, and I will be in sector pink."

Everybody nodded.

"I'm assuming there'll be plenty of guys dressed up as Indiana Jones. Make sure to get a good look at his face first to identify him. If necessary, just go up to him and ask him a random question. I'm sure the people here are all about connecting with one another. Use that to your advantage. Once you find him, use your communication device to call for backup. Then stall. Follow him, and if you have a good opportunity to get his dagger, take it. If not, wait for backup, and we'll create a diversion. Understood?"

"Don't worry, we got it," Grayson said. "Let's go already."

Pearce rolled his eyes. "Oh, yeah, and a special rule for Grayson. Don't be a hero."

Several of the men chuckled. Daphne had a hard time suppressing a laugh. Grayson was overeager, and she knew that such eagerness could lead to carelessness. And no matter how harmless the convention was, it gave too many people too many places to hide. If the demons had found out about James Harcott, they could easily be planning an ambush. That was why Pearce had drilled into them to remain inconspicuous and not draw attention to themselves.

"Let's roll," Pearce said.

Daphne met his eyes. "We can do this."

34

Pearce rubbed his neck. It was getting warmer and warmer in the convention hall. Despite the large air-conditioning ducts that ran along the high ceiling and blasted cool air into the space, he felt the heat under his heavy costume. He'd already shucked the cape that came with his outfit and tossed it behind a display. He didn't care if he never found it again. He could only imagine how Zane had to feel inside the Stormtrooper costume.

At least Daphne was dressed properly for the temperature in the hall. Her skimpy outfit exposed more than just a little bit of skin. Her arms were bare except for the brass-colored braces around her forearms. Her knee-high boots were sexy as hell, and her upper body was encased in a figure-hugging bustier that left little to the imagination. She was carrying a round shield, and inside it, Pearce had taped a Stealth Guardian dagger—just in case she needed to defend herself.

He trusted in her love for him that she wouldn't kill him with it, despite the fact that she looked exactly how Winter had seen her in her vision. He could have told Daphne about that particular detail, but what purpose would it have served? He'd done everything in his power to change the vision. Now it was up to higher powers to decide his fate.

His earpiece suddenly crackled. "Damn it, the connection is so bad in here," he said to Zane and Daphne.

"Depends on where in the hall you are," Zane said, his voice muffled behind the mask. "I heard Gabriel come in loud and clear earlier."

"Hey, guys, it's Manus," Pearce finally heard through the communications device.

"I can hear you now, Manus. What's up? Any sightings?"

"I'm afraid so," Manus said.

Daphne shot Pearce a concerned look. She, too, wore a communications device in her ear and was listening in on the conversation.

"What's wrong?" Pearce asked.

"Ryder and I found a body. Indiana Jones."

"Oh fuck!" Pearce cursed. "And the dagger? Is it gone?"

"Yeah, but it couldn't have been the source dagger," Manus reported. "The dead guy isn't James Harcott, although he's of similar height, same hair color, you know. But I found his driver's license. It's definitely not him."

Pearce let out a sigh of relief, even though he felt guilty doing so. An innocent had died. "How was he killed? Could it have been an accident?"

"No way. Stabbed in the heart. Probably died instantly."

"Demons?"

"That's my guess."

"Shit," Pearce said, and more curses from the rest of the team filtered through his earpiece, some louder and clearer than others.

"What now?" Daphne asked, a fearful look on her face. "Are they gonna kill every guy dressed as Indiana Jones?"

Pearce looked at her, but had no comforting words. "Listen, everybody. We've gotta step up our efforts. We've gotta find this guy before the demons do."

"We're doing what we can," Gabriel said through the earpiece.

Then something crackled again, and Gabriel said, "I can't hear myself think over that fucking music."

"You and me both, bro," Thomas replied. "We're heading for the Indiana Jones exhibit in sector green again. Maybe he's hanging out there. They're having a mock fight scheduled in a few minutes. Perhaps Harcott will be watching it. We'll report back shortly."

"Thanks, Thomas," Pearce said, and motioned to Daphne and Zane. "Okay, then, let's comb through the sector again. He has to be somewhere."

This was the third round they'd made in their assigned sector. They'd spotted everybody, from the Fantastic Four, Spider-Man, and the Incredibles, to Iron Man, a whole throng of Klingons, and various anime characters. They'd even encountered a few men dressed as Indiana Jones, but one of them had been black, and they knew Harcott was Caucasian, and the other two had been Japanese.

"Oh shit!" Zane said, and pointed to a spot in the crowd.

Pearce's gaze shot to it. "Fuck!"

There, at the edge of an exhibit displaying bobbleheads of characters from *Star Trek*, two men were fighting. One of them was Indiana Jones, the other Chewbacca.

"Mock fight?" Daphne asked.

"If it is, it looks a little too real," Zane said, already heading that way.

"Quickly," Pearce said, and rushed after him, Daphne in tow.

Spectators were already forming a ring around the two fighters. Chewbacca was armed with a knife or dagger, though Pearce couldn't get a good look at it, while Indiana Jones was trying to use his whip to fend off the creature—with little success. This Indiana Jones had no idea how to use a bullwhip.

"Shit, I can smell him," Zane said when they were only a few yards away from the two. "The Chewbacca is a demon."

"Fuck!" Pearce cursed and pulled his dagger from its sheath.

Pearce was already pushing people aside to get through the crowd, much to the chagrin of several onlookers, who cursed him out. Zane also charged through the throng to reach the demon who was trying to kill Indiana Jones in plain sight.

Pearce finally made it through the crowd and charged at Chewbacca, tackling him to the ground. When the creature fell flat on his back and stared up at him in utter surprise, his demon-green eyes blinked. Zane had smelled right: the guy was a demon.

Cheers erupted behind Pearce, then suddenly a bullwhip cracked next to his head.

"Hey, that's my fight!" It appeared Indiana Jones didn't want to stop fighting, unaware that Pearce was trying to save his life.

The second's distraction gave the demon enough time to toss Pearce off and catapult him into the display of bobbleheads.

There was clapping all around. The Wookiee had fans in the audience.

"Team Chewie!" somebody yelled from the crowd.

Pearce jumped up and lunged toward Chewbacca once more. He managed to grip the demon by the shaggy hair of his costume, and jerked him back, just as Zane jumped between the creature and Indiana Jones and plunged a dagger into the demon.

"Ohhhh!"

"Noooo!"

"Yay!"

Cries of various sentiments, from joy to disappointment, accompanied the killing of the demon. When he fell to the ground, green blood spurting from the mortal wound, people started clapping, while others booed.

"Wookiees don't have green blood," one bystander said.

"So lame," another added.

"These mock fights are totally unrealistic," a visitor in a Klingon costume huffed.

Pearce ignored the comments and turned to where he'd seen Indiana Jones last. The guy was rolling up his bullwhip and giving him an annoyed look. He wasn't Harcott. Just another innocent.

"I totally had this, dude," Indiana Jones said with an angry look at

Zane and Pearce. "You're such spoilsports." He turned away to merge into the crowd.

"Yeah, you're welcome!" Pearce called after him. "Ungrateful little shit!"

Zane put a hand on his shoulder. "Don't get upset. He's oblivious. It's better that way."

They made their way back to where Daphne was waiting for them.

"You both were amazing," she said with a proud smile. Then she motioned to where the dead Chewbacca lay. "What about the body?"

Pearce shrugged. "Nothing we can do about that. They'll eventually figure out he's really dead and not just playing dead. With some luck, it'll take a while." He wiped the sweat off his face. "I need some water."

Daphne motioned to one of the walls. "I saw some water fountains and vending machines over there earlier."

"Good, thanks." Pearce took her hand and started walking toward the area.

Zane marched next to them and, in passing, casually wiped his bloody dagger on a dark blue drape separating various exhibits.

"I hate demon blood," he said. "Tastes like warmed-up shit."

"Amen to that, bro," Pearce said. Then he pointed to the wall. "There are the water fountains."

"I'm thirsty too, but I'll get some from the vending machine," Daphne said, and turned her head to the side. Then she stopped in her tracks.

"What?" Pearce asked.

Daphne pointed to the right. "Harcott. He's going into the bathroom."

Pearce followed her outstretched finger and saw a man dressed in an Indiana Jones costume disappear in the men's room. "Are you sure it's him?"

Daphne nodded. "I saw his face. It's him."

"Let's go get him." He was already pulling Daphne with him toward the entrance of the men's room.

"I can't, Pearce. It's a men's room." She pointed to Zane. "You and Zane have to go. I'll stay here."

For a second, Pearce hesitated. But he knew she was right. He and Zane had to follow Harcott. "Stay here. Don't go anywhere."

Via his communications device, he alerted the rest of the team. "We spotted Harcott. He's in the men's room in sector pink." There was more crackling in his ear, but he couldn't worry about that now. "Zane, let's go."

35

———

Anxiously, Daphne watched Pearce and Zane disappear in the men's room. Finally, they were making progress. Now all the guys needed to do was to convince Harcott to hand over the dagger. Pearce had told her that should he refuse, they had several options, one of which was to offer him twice the money he'd paid for it at auction. The other options he hadn't elaborated on.

Still thirsty, Daphne headed for the vending machines, which were only a few feet away from the entrance to the men's room. She was already at the machine that sold water bottles when she realized that because her costume had no pockets, she wasn't carrying any money on her.

"Damn!" she said, and turned to look where the water fountain was located. She had just spotted it when she saw a man in an Indiana Jones costume come out of a door with the sign *Men* on it. She stared at his face. It was James Harcott.

Daphne looked over her shoulder to the spot where Zane and Pearce had entered the men's room. It clicked immediately. This bathroom was so large that it had two entrances. And Harcott had just slipped out from the opposite one.

"Pearce, Zane, he's out of the bathroom," Daphne said hurriedly via the communications device in her ear. There was static again, more crackling. "Damn it, can you hear me? Pearce? Harcott has left the bathroom. We're losing him."

But there was no reply. For a moment, she contemplated running into the men's bathroom, but it would mean losing sight of Harcott. And once he mingled with the crowd, she'd never find him again. No, she couldn't wait for Pearce and Zane. She had to hope that as she moved around the hall, somebody from a different team would hear her and help her chase down Harcott.

"Shit!" She hurried in the direction Harcott was heading. "I'm going after him. If anybody can hear me, I'm in sector pink, leaving the men's room behind me. I'm following Harcott."

She had to pick up the pace, because Harcott was already turning into one of the aisles lined with various booths of gadgets and memorabilia. Ahead of her, a mob was forming around a group of celebrities, and Daphne saw that the real Khal Drogo was greeting fans and joking with his costars.

At any other time, she would have joined in the fun, but there were more important things on her agenda today than meeting movie stars. She couldn't lose Harcott.

"Daphne?" A crackling voice suddenly came through her earpiece.

"This is Daphne. Who's this?" she asked.

"Enya. I'm with Grayson and Ryder. Did you say..." There was more static, then a clear word: "Harcott?"

"Yes, yes, I'm following him." She looked at the number of the nearest booth she was walking by. "Still in sector pink, just passing exhibit K1560. Did you get that?"

Drums coming from somewhere to her left drowned out Enya's response.

"Say again?"

But she couldn't hear anything, so she repeated her location, hoping that somebody had understood it, while she kept her eyes on Indiana Jones. "Heading down aisle K toward the lower numbers; should be getting close to sector gray or green. I think."

When Harcott finally veered to the left and walked into a short alleyway that appeared to be reserved for exhibitors and was off-limits to visitors, she had no choice but to follow him.

"Hey, lady, no access here," a guy looking like a security guard called out to her.

She spun around and flashed her VIP pass. "I'm with Jason Momoa's group," she lied. "He needs, uh, something from his bag." She was already continuing down the aisle, and it looked like the guy was gonna stop her, but then a clearly drunk Captain America crashed into a display and distracted the guard.

Daphne sighed in relief and continued down the aisle until it connected with the next row of exhibits. There, she stopped and let her gaze roam to the left and right. Where had Harcott gone? A movement ahead of her made her snap her eyes to it. Harcott. He stepped over a cordon and continued walking down the narrow way behind the exhibits.

"What the fuck are you doing, Harcott?" she murmured to herself, and followed him until the walkway ended. They were behind a stage. She'd seen it on the map earlier. It was located in the very center of the hall. She knew from previous cosplay conventions that the main stage was generally used for interviews with stars, mock fights, and acrobatics, as well as pyrotechnic shows. It wasn't unheard of that die-hard fans would try to sneak backstage to get up close and personal with their idols. And Harcott was no different. He knew the drill, and had figured out how to get close.

"Hey, Indy," she called out to him.

Harcott whirled his head to her. For a second, he looked stunned, then he shifted into a casual pose. "Wonder Woman. What's up?"

She walked up to him. "Just wondering. Is this the way to get backstage where the stars are hanging out?"

He shrugged. "Oh, is that what this is?"

"Oh, please, don't play innocent with me. You know we're at the north side of the main stage." She hoped her communications device would transmit her location to whoever could hear her. "You're trying to sneak back there, aren't you?" She chuckled. "Don't worry, I'm not gonna rat you out. I'm doing the same thing."

He relaxed and grinned. "Who do you wanna see most?"

"Oh, you know, I love 'em all." She glanced at his belt, where next to the whip, a fancy dagger was sheathed. Emblazoned on the handle were the same symbols as she'd seen on the daggers the Stealth Guardians wielded.

Harcott pulled the curtain apart and motioned for her to follow him. "Well, then let's not waste any time. The show is gonna start in fifteen minutes."

"Not for you, it won't."

Daphne spun to her left, where the voice had come from, and felt Harcott do the same. In the darkness of the backstage area, it took her more than a second to make out the figure that had addressed them. But finally she saw him: Batman. And at his belt sat an ancient dagger.

"Hand over the dagger, boy, and I'll let you live," Batman demanded.

Daphne snatched Harcott's arm. "Run! James, run!"

ZANE NEXT TO HIM, Pearce charged into the direction of the main stage in the hall. He'd finally picked up Daphne's communication. While in the restroom looking for Harcott, neither he nor Zane had been able to hear anything over the static in their earpieces. And a run-in with another man dressed as Indiana Jones had cost them valuable seconds.

Fear for Daphne made his heartbeat spike and his legs work harder to get to her in time. "Daphne, we're coming," he kept repeating into the microphone, but he wasn't getting a response. The last thing he'd been able to make out from her was her command for Harcott to run. It could only mean one thing. But he couldn't go down that road. No, he had to concentrate on getting to Daphne before it was too late.

"All teams to the north side of the main stage," Zane said for the second time.

Somebody whose voice Pearce didn't recognize over the loud music said, "ETA ninety seconds."

One more row of exhibits, and the alley that led alongside the back of the main stage opened up to their left. Pearce charged into it, Zane on his heels. As soon as he saw a spot where the dark blue curtains surrounding the entire stage were overlapping, he pulled them apart and slipped inside. It was darker here. Stage lights were affixed on a scaffold farther in, and ropes hung down to presumably operate the curtains and lights and move other stage equipment. Various crates and boxes were scattered around haphazardly. From the stage itself, some light filtered through to the back.

Pearce pushed another curtain aside, then shock made his blood freeze in his veins. Daphne was shielding herself and Indiana Jones with Wonder Woman's shield, while Indiana Jones lashed his bullwhip against their aggressor: Batman. Daphne's arm was bleeding from a knife wound, and her earpiece was tangled up in her hair, explaining why she hadn't answered him.

"He reeks of demon," Zane said with disgust.

Pearce was already charging toward them, Zane in step with him. They lunged over a wooden bench in their way, but a movement to Pearce's left made him snap his head toward it. Just in time, or the Klingon with the green eyes running toward him would have driven his dagger into him.

"Demons!" Pearce yelled out, having spotted a Chewbacca following the Klingon, and pivoted, gripping his dagger tighter.

"We'll be there in a sec," Gabriel's voice suddenly came through his earpiece loud and clear.

Pearce ducked to the side just as the Klingon tried to stab his dagger into Pearce's torso, and managed to kick his opponent into the side, making him lose his balance, while Zane already engaged the Chewbacca in a fight. While the Klingon gained his balance again, Pearce managed to cast a look at Daphne. She was using the shield to ward off the demon's blows, and was losing her grip. Indiana Jones did the best he could, and though his skills with the bullwhip were remarkable, they were no match for the demon's strength.

Suddenly the curtains moved, and Pearce was already sighing in relief, but more green-eyed Chewbaccas and Klingons stormed in.

"Shit! Reinforcements, damn it, where are you?" Pearce yelled into the mic, while lunging for the Klingon who stood between him and Batman.

"We're here," Enya's voice sounded in his ear.

The blue of her dress whooshed by his right, as she was barreling toward the Wookiees and Klingons that had just joined them, and jumped over a couple of crates. Superman and Aquaman, the two hybrids, whizzed by him on the other side, attacking the demons.

Pearce punched the Klingon in his way, but the bastard was strong and didn't even seem to feel the blow. Just beyond him, he saw Harcott stumble backward over a wooden crate and roll out of the protective huddle he'd formed with Daphne. Batman rushed toward him.

"Shit!" Pearce had to get to Harcott before Batman did.

Pearce kicked the Klingon again, and this time the beast swayed a little. Just then, Pearce saw Darth Vader approach from his left.

"Take care of him, Gabriel!" Pearce called out, and headed to the right, where he saw Batman reaching for Harcott's belt. "The dagger!"

Somebody pulled him back and swung him around: Darth Vader. "Gabriel? What the—"

Darth Vader stabbed his dagger into Pearce's chest. All air rushed from his lungs. With disbelief, he stared at the dark garb, then, as he slid down, he saw the chest. No pink ribbon. This wasn't Gabriel. "Fuck…"

He crashed to the floor and turned his head to where Daphne had so valiantly defended Harcott. She was still there, still holding the shield. And she stared at Batman, who was now holding the source dagger in his hand.

Pearce reached out. "Daphne, the dagger. Get the…" He couldn't finish the sentence, didn't have the strength for it. His vision became blurry, his brain fuzzy. And he was cold, so cold. He knew what it meant. Still, he tried to fight it. "The dagger, Daphne…" He needed to explain it. Needed to tell her. But his virta was slowly seeping from him like the blood that was soaking his costume.

DAPHNE WHIRLED her head to where, despite the loud music, she'd heard her name being called. Her heart stopped beating. Pearce lay bleeding from a chest wound, leaning against a small crate, his hand stretched out as if reaching for her, his face white as a sheet.

"No!" she screamed. This couldn't be happening.

The dagger, Daphne…

She could clearly hear his words repeating in her head.

She jumped up, her heart pulling her in Pearce's direction, her head steering her the other way, toward Batman, who'd overpowered Harcott. Batman's back was already to her as he was heading away from the battle, the prized source dagger in his hand.

"Fuck!" she cursed. All Stealth Guardians and vampires were engaged fighting a demon, or even two. And nobody was following Batman. She had to do something.

She was still holding her shield and was about to pull out the dagger Pearce had taped to its back when she had a better idea. She held the shield with both hands, then twisted it, dropped her left hand, and untwisted with her right, aiming for Batman's back as if she were throwing a Frisbee. A rather large Frisbee. It whizzed through the air and hit Batman squarely in the back of his knees.

He tumbled forward and hit the wooden floor of the stage with a thud. From the corner of her eye, she saw Harcott getting up.

"Your whip, James," she yelled at him, and pointed to Batman. "Use it!"

Harcott understood immediately, grabbed his whip, and ran toward Batman, snapping it as he approached to stop the demon hiding behind the mask from fleeing. Daphne barreled toward him from a forty-five-degree angle, but Spider-Man, who'd come out of nowhere, blocked her.

Something blue entered her field of vision from the left, and a split second later, Enya was tackling the demon to the ground. "Get the dagger, Daphne!" she yelled while she traded blows with Spider-Man.

Daphne jumped over a low crate in her way. Only three more yards and she reached her shield. She snatched it from the floor. Just in time, because Batman was getting to his feet again, the source dagger still in his hand and now aimed it at her.

"James! Now!" she called out, hoping Harcott's skills with the whip were as good as he'd shown earlier.

The whip cracked through the air, its tip snapping just outside her shield and wrapping around Batman's wrist, jerking it back. The motion made the demon lose the dagger. It clattered to the floor, slithering toward a Wookiee with green eyes. With Batman trying to free himself from the bullwhip around his wrist, Daphne knew she didn't have much time. She tossed her shield at Batman and dove for the dagger, sliding on the floor, her hands stretched out. Her hand found purchase around the weapon's hilt, just as a Wookiee lunged for her. She made a half turn, her dagger arm in front of her, and scrambled to jump up.

The Wookiee couldn't stop his forward motion. The impact drove the dagger into his chest. All Daphne could do was hold on to it and twist it, as the creature froze in mid-motion and stared at her in disbelief. Then she felt the warmth of his blood run over her fingers. With her free hand, she pushed against him, and the hairy creature fell backward.

The bloody dagger in her hand, she pivoted and saw a clear path to where Pearce lay wounded. She raced toward him, praying, hoping that it wasn't too late. When she reached him, the battle still raging around her, she fell to her knees.

"Pearce, oh God, please don't leave me."

His lids fluttered, and his lips moved. "Daphne..."

"I have the dagger. I have the source dagger. What do I do now? Pearce? What do I do?"

He managed to open his eyes, but she wasn't sure he could even see her. His gaze didn't meet hers. "Stab me with it..." His voice was so weak that she couldn't be sure she'd heard him right.

She wiped the dagger on his clothes, cleaning off the demon blood. "Are you sure? But you're..." She could see it: he was dying. He was taking his last breath. "Oh God."

"Do it, Daphne. Do it."

Tears clouding her vision, she gripped the dagger tightly in her right hand. It trembled. She couldn't do this, couldn't cause the man she loved even more pain.

"Do it," he mumbled.

Tears streaming down her face, she plunged the dagger into his existing wound and let out a sob. She looked at Pearce's face. His eyes had fallen shut again, and his head rolled to the side.

"No!" she screamed between sobs. "No! Pearce, no!" She reached for his cheek, bending over him, but then she felt heat emanate from his chest wound. Stunned, she drew back and saw light stream from the source dagger into Pearce's body. And slowly, as if by magic, Pearce's body expelled the dagger, pushed it out of the wound until it dropped flat onto his torso.

With a gasp, Pearce drew in a breath and opened his eyes. "Daphne."

She threw her arms around him, tears streaming down her face, but now they were tears of joy. "You're alive."

"The vision came true, but we had it all wrong." Winter's vision hadn't revealed that Daphne had stabbed him with the source dagger, the only weapon that could save a Stealth Guardian's life. "I should have known that you were meant to save me all along." He kissed her.

Applause erupted, pulling them apart. Daphne spun her head in the direction it was coming from and stared at the audience assembled in front of the main stage. At some point during the battle, somebody had lifted the curtain. How much the audience had witnessed, she didn't know.

"Shit," Pearce said.

Daphne looked around. Several of the demons were dead. Others stood there, frozen, distracted by the applause. Batman was gone. Suddenly, a demon at the edge of the stage made a movement with his hand and conjured a vortex, a swirling mass of fog and smoke, and jumped into it. The remaining demons rushed toward it, grabbing their dead cohorts on the way, and jumped after him, before the Stealth Guardians and the vampires could stop them.

More applause erupted. The audience cheered loudly, clearly impressed.

"Curtain!" somebody yelled. A moment later, the curtain closed.

Daphne let out a sigh of relief. Pearce clutched the dagger and stood up, then gave her a hand to help her up, while the rest of the gang crowded around them.

"What now?" Daphne asked, motioning in the direction of the audience. "They saw everything. You're exposed."

Manus, in his Wolverine costume, said, "We were lucky that this is a stage, and the people think this was a show."

"But we'd better get out of here now, before people catch on," Pearce said, and took Daphne's hand.

From the corner of her eye, she saw James Harcott approach. He looked a little shaken. "Hey, what was all this?"

Without flinching, Pearce turned to him and shook his hand. "Mr. Harcott, congratulations on winning the audience participation slot in our mock fight. You were outstanding!"

Harcott hesitated, then started smiling. "I was?"

"Are you kidding me?" Pearce patted him on the shoulder. "The way you cracked that bullwhip! I don't think we've ever seen an audience member with such skills." He waved to somebody behind Harcott. "Isn't that right, Thomas?"

Thomas, in his Stormtrooper costume, sidled up to Harcott. "Excellent. My word."

Harcott beamed. "Wow! I had no idea. Nobody told me this was a mock fight. I mean—"

"Well, that's the whole point," Pearce said. "Why don't you explain it all to him, Thomas? And then make sure he gets his cash prize."

Harcott pointed to the dagger in Pearce's hand. "And my dagger."

"Of course. Let me just have one of the stagehands clean it properly. Germs and all—you can't be too careful. I'll get it back to you in a minute."

Harcott nodded, and Thomas pulled him away.

"But you can't give him the dagger back," Daphne said.

"I won't. We've thought of this—that's why Manus brought a similar one from Baltimore in case we needed to do a swap."

Daphne shook her head. "You guys thought of everything." Then she looked to where Thomas and Harcott were talking. "Do you think he's gonna believe what Thomas is telling him?"

"I'm certain. And if he needs a little push, then Thomas will employ mind control to make him believe what he needs to believe, namely that he was chosen to participate in a mock fight." He smirked. "I hear it's a great honor in cosplay circles."

Daphne was about to laugh when she saw a man in a Yoda costume hurry into the backstage area.

"Claus."

He walked toward her. "What the fuck was that?"

"Would you believe me if I said that we just fought demons and saved the world?" Daphne asked.

Claus made a don't-bullshit-me face. "Daphne, this time you're really gonna get me in trouble. Are you out of your fucking mind?"

"I'm sorry," she said. "Listen, why don't you help us get out of here, and we'll be out of your hair? It won't happen again."

"And what do I tell my bosses?"

Pearce cleared his throat. "Just tell them we were the mystery guests. You know, a special performance troupe to entertain the visitors. We're really hot in Japan. Everybody knows us there. And look at you: you were able to get us for free. What a boon!"

Claus rolled his eyes. "You guys are insane." Then he motioned to the bloodstain on Pearce's chest. "Neat trick, though. Looked awfully real."

Pearce winked. "Hurt like a bitch." Then he put a hand on Claus's shoulder. "Now, would you please get us out of here before we have to sign autographs?"

Claus cast a long look at Daphne. "You owe me one for this. And don't you forget that."

"You're the best."

36

With Claus's help, they swiftly left the exhibition hall. A few hours later, the dagger was safely stashed away in the council compound. The same evening, everybody was back home. Pearce and his brethren were back in Baltimore. Once again, they'd thwarted the demons' plan. However, Zoltan had escaped. They would get him next time. For now, Pearce was happy to have escaped with his life and the knowledge that even if a vision showed one thing, it could mean the exact opposite. Daphne stabbing him had been his salvation. She wasn't his killer—she was his savior. And he would thank her for it for the rest of his life.

A towel wrapped around his waist, Pearce leaned against the doorframe and watched Daphne, wearing his bathrobe, rub her short hair dry with a towel. Instead of then combing it, she ran her fingers through the short strands and styled it into place. Her eyes met his in the mirror.

"What?" she said, and turned around.

"I love how uncomplicated you are."

She smiled in that wickedly sensual way that he'd grown to love. "Is that all you love about me?"

"It's not, and you know it. Vixen," he added.

A soft chuckle was her response, while she walked toward him.

"I also love the fact that you saved my life." He could still feel the dagger in his torso, the knowledge that he would die, and then the revelation of what the vision had tried to tell him all along.

"I really didn't have a choice, you know." She put her hand on his naked chest. "You can be quite bossy for a shy computer geek. You were quite insistent when you told me to stab you with the source dagger."

"Is that so?"

"See, I'm a very compliant, obedient woman who does what she's told." Her eyes sparkled with mischief.

"Compliant? Obedient? Since when? You didn't stay back when Enya and I entered the apartment where we found Tim. You didn't stay in the car, like I asked you to, when we saved him from Vasili. Shall I go on?"

"Just as well!" she said, running her hands over his chest. "Or I probably still wouldn't know that you're an immortal warrior." She caressed his damp skin with a tenderness he'd come to crave from her.

"I would have told you."

"When?"

He put his hand under her chin and drew her face closer. "When I was ready."

"Ready for what?"

"Ready to share my immortality with you." He brushed his lips softly over hers. "If you want it. If you want me." He moved back a few inches, giving her a chance to respond.

Her eyes were wide. "Are you asking me...?" She put her hand over her mouth, and suddenly her eyes began to water. She panted and waved her hand in front of her face as if she could stop the tears like that. "Are you saying...?"

Pearce cupped her cheek and smiled. "Of course, I am. In some civilizations, if you save a person's life, that life belongs to you. I can't give you my life, but what I can give you, what I want to give you, is my heart."

"Pearce," she murmured, her lips trembling.

She didn't need to say anything further, because he could read her answer in the way she beamed with joy, and her eyes shone with love and affection, the love she'd confessed to him the night before he'd almost died. The love she'd proven to him when she saved him.

"Then there's something else I need to explain. About immortality."

She smiled through the wet sheen on her eyes. "You don't need to explain. I already know about it."

"About what happens when we mate?"

She nodded. "The night you and the others went back to the house to break into the safe, I got to talk to Tessa and Leila while we were waiting up for you to return. I asked them how they could stand being with a man who didn't age, who wouldn't die, when they knew that they would age and eventually die. So they told me."

He was glad that she knew, that he didn't have to launch into a long explanation about what sharing his virta with her would mean. "And you're okay with that?"

"Okay?" Daphne shook her head and laughed. "About not aging anymore? About not dying?" She pulled his face closer to hers. "It would mean nothing if I couldn't spend those extra years with you. But because we'll be together, it'll mean everything. And to share the kind of bond Tessa and Leila talked about with the man I love, I can't imagine anything that would be more okay."

Pearce's heart expanded. He'd never felt such joy in his life, the joy of knowing the woman he loved with every fiber of his immortal being loved him just as deeply.

He wrapped his arm around her waist and pulled her to his chest. "Then there's one other thing..."

Expectantly, she lifted her lashes and looked into his eyes.

"Because you saved my life, I'm going to give you free rein tonight. You can demand of me what you want. I'll fulfill your every wish, every fantasy." That he would fulfill her every wish every day for the rest of their lives, he would tell her some other time far, far in the future.

Though somehow he had the feeling she already knew that he was putty in her hands.

She chuckled. "Well, let me see. You made me come with your mouth that first night. Then later, you took me when I pretended to be asleep. You really rode me hard that night."

Daphne recounting their exploits filled his cock with blood.

"And then the night when I found out your secret, you took me up against the wall. We didn't even fully undress."

"Are you trying to get me all hot and bothered?" Because it was working. His cock was hard and ready, and his heart was pounding like a jackhammer.

"Oh no," she said in the most innocent voice she'd ever used. "I'm just trying to jog my own memory."

As if! She was doing everything to turn him on, to get him so aroused that he lost his cool. "Right."

"And the night before the cosplay, when we spoke about the vision and I blurted out that I loved you, you went all primal on me."

"What guy wouldn't go all primal when the woman he loves sucks his cock as if she wanted to eat him up alive? Besides, what are you trying to do by reminding me of how I took you?"

A sinful smile curled her lips upward. "Just trying to show a pattern."

"What pattern?"

"That you, Pearce Douglas, immortal Stealth Guardian warrior, have no control when it comes to sex."

"No control? You didn't complain when I—"

She put a finger over his lips. "Oh, I'm not complaining now either. I'm simply telling you what I've observed. That's why tonight, my handsome warrior, I'll tie you to your bed and have my way with you."

He liked the sound of that, and rubbed his groin against her. "Then let's not waste any more time."

Daphne freed herself from his arms and tugged on his towel. The knot opened easily, and the fabric fell from his hips, revealing just how ready he was.

"Yeah, let's not," Daphne said, licking her lips. She pointed to the bedroom. "After you."

Pearce took his time walking to the bed, because feeling Daphne's eyes on his ass sent a jolt of lust through his body. The woman he'd chosen to be his mate made no secret about the fact that she enjoyed feasting her eyes on him. Nor had she ever shown any shyness about showing him exactly what she enjoyed, and asking for it if he didn't immediately give it to her. No, his Daphne wasn't beating about the bush when it came to sex. Everything was on the table. He'd sensed that about her from the moment they'd first made love. It had given him license to unleash the wildness inside him that nobody suspected him of possessing. And the only person who'd ever know that under his cool computer geek exterior was a hot-blooded male with an insatiable appetite was Daphne.

Moments later, he lay naked on the bed, while Daphne tied his wrists to the wooden slats of his headboard, using two scarves. Pearce pulled on the restraints. They held. For now. He'd leave her in the false belief that he couldn't escape from them. Because this was her fantasy. Her dream. To have power over him. And he couldn't imagine anybody else at whose mercy he'd rather be.

DAPHNE EXHALED SLOWLY and swept her eyes over the virile man who was hers. Her heart was beating an excited pattern against her chest as reality started to finally sink in. Until now, she hadn't dared hope for anything beyond a short, but passionate relationship. After all, the only reason Pearce had initially sought her out was to change his future. And though the vision had been accurate all along and needed no changing, Pearce was now changing *her* future, giving her more than she'd ever thought possible: immortality. She would have settled for just his love.

Standing next to the bed, she untied the belt of the bathrobe and slowly shoved the soft fabric off her shoulders and let it drop to pool around her feet.

An appreciative moan came from Pearce. She met his gaze and saw love and adoration in his eyes—and something else: lust and passion. She shifted her eyes lower to the area between his legs, where his cock made an unmistakable statement. Pearce was ready for her, and she was ready for him. She was always ready for him. A man like Pearce, seemingly shy on the outside, yet full of passion, only had to look at her, and she melted. She was aware that he knew what effect he had on her.

Daphne slid onto the bed and gently pushed Pearce's legs apart to make a space for herself. She kneeled there and put her hands on his thighs. His cock twitched instantly.

"Hmm, I'm going to enjoy this," she murmured, and leaned over his groin.

"Not as much as I," Pearce said with a husky voice.

His cock was beautiful, the veins snaking around its impressive girth like ivy climbing up a pole. She ran her fingers along the underside, caressing the sensitive skin there, skin that stretched taut over a rod as hard as iron, yet warm like a cozy fire and smooth like velvet. That she could ever be so enamored by a man's body, she'd never expected, but every time she saw Pearce naked, every time she touched him, she reveled in his physical perfection.

When she finally wrapped her hand around his erection, Pearce moaned and bucked his hips. Without hurry, she brought her mouth to the tip of his cock and pressed her rounded lips to it, before opening her mouth wider and letting him slide inside.

She descended on him, allowing her mouth to open just enough for a snug fit. When she could go no farther, she moved up again, letting his erection pop from her mouth. She blew a breath against his heated flesh, before wrapping her lips around him and taking him deep again.

A sound from the headboard alerted her to the fact that Pearce was pulling on his restraints. She cast him a glance without releasing his erection and met his fiery gaze.

"Are you trying to torture me?"

She released his cock from her mouth, but continued pumping him with her fist. "That was the plan."

"Then you're doing a great job." His jaw seemed tight when he continued, "It's not gonna stop me from coming, though, no matter how slowly you fuck me with your mouth."

She chuckled and pumped him harder. "Oh, I know that." She took him back into her mouth and continued her slow torture, while Pearce groaned and twisted underneath her. She loved this, loved how Pearce responded to her, and how he let her do what she needed to do.

When his breathing turned more ragged, she released him and crawled farther up, swinging herself over him. Still on her knees, she adjusted herself so his cock was poised at her pussy, the tip of it already touching her wet petals.

Pearce pressed his head back into the pillow, allowing his back to arch off the mattress.

"Fuck," he said. "Are you finally gonna have mercy on this shy computer geek?"

Daphne sank down on his cock, impaling herself. "Is that what you meant by mercy?" She felt him filling her, stretching her to capacity. Even though she should be used to his size by now, the first moment of penetration still took her breath away.

"That's exactly what I'm talking about. Now do me a favor and ride me." He tugged on his restraints. "Or I'll break free and ride you instead."

She had to smile at his threat, because she knew how much he enjoyed her taking the reins once in a while.

She bent over him and slanted her lips over his mouth. Pearce captured them and kissed her, demanding and passionate. His tongue played with hers, mimicking the rhythm with which Daphne rocked up and down on his erection. She moved faster with every minute, the leisurely ride from the beginning turning into a raging gallop. Until suddenly she felt Pearce's hands on her hips—he'd freed himself without her noticing.

And then something else happened. The room around her seemed to fill with fog, with a mist that engulfed them, a mist they appeared to float on. She stilled in her movements, not knowing what was happening, but Pearce continued thrusting into her.

"What is this?" she managed to ask.

Pearce chuckled and flipped her, so she was underneath him. "Guess Tessa and Leila didn't tell you everything." He plunged deep and hard. "This is our way, the Stealth Guardian way. The fog around us protects us now, hides us from everybody. It's just you and me at our most vulnerable." He slowed his movements, yet they were more intense now. She could feel every fiber of his body, every cell of her own. Pleasure filled her.

"What you're feeling is my virta, my life force. My essence."

She could feel it, feel the warmth that filled her, the pleasure that became more intense. And then she saw it. Saw the golden shimmer that bathed her skin.

"Oh my God," she murmured, and stared up into Pearce's eyes. She saw the love there, the love he felt for her and the love she felt for him. And she knew what to do. Knew it instinctively.

She pressed her hand over his heart and willed the life force he'd infused her body with to run through her arm, into her hand, into her fingers, and explode out from her fingertips. Tiny electrical charges seemed to emanate from her.

Pearce's body spasmed, and for a second, she was worried that she'd hurt him, but then he began to thrust into her with renewed vigor, with more strength, harder and faster, until wave after wave drowned her in a climax more powerful than she'd ever experienced.

In that moment, she felt him, felt his soul, his heart, felt the very essence of his being. They were connected. They were one.

"I love you," Pearce whispered, his body still shaking from his climax.

"You're mine now," she said.

"Yes." He smiled. "And you're mine." Then he chuckled. "And you're currently at my mercy."

"Am I?"

"Did Tessa and Leila tell you what happens as long as your skin shimmers golden?"

"No."

"Let me show you, then."

He moved again, his cock still big and hard. One thrust, and she climaxed again.

"Ohhhh!"

"Yes, every touch, every movement will give you another orgasm." His eyes twinkled.

"How long will I shimmer?"

"For hours." He took her lips and kissed her. And again, her body erupted.

"This is crazy..." she managed to mutter. "I can't believe this is real."

"It's as real as my love for you."

Daphne put her hand on Pearce's nape. "Your love alone would have been enough. But to add all this, immortality and unlimited orgasms... I don't know what to say." She felt her eyes getting moist.

"Then don't say anything. Just enjoy it."

And this was a demand she was only too happy to comply with.

37

———

Still reeling from his failure to obtain the Stealth Guardians' source dagger, Zoltan had been brooding in his private quarters in the Underworld for more days and nights than he cared to count. If it hadn't been for his need to feed off the fear of a human, he wouldn't have gone up top, and therefore would have never had the stroke of luck that stared him in the face now.

A Stealth Guardian.

And not just any Stealth Guardian.

A female.

The very woman he'd seen several times, the last time at the cosplay event where she'd made mincemeat out of his demons. She'd meant business. But tonight, she wasn't out on business, though she was dressed to kill.

A short leather skirt that revealed more than it concealed showed off her slender legs. Legs that were bare despite the cool temperatures at night. Her top was a tight bustier that showcased her breasts, though it was neither low-cut nor see-through. She wore her leather jacket open. Despite her entire outfit's black color, she didn't blend into the darkness of the night. Her blond hair, tonight hanging loosely down to her mid-back, made sure nobody overlooked her. She looked young, but Zoltan knew better. Stealth Guardians, like many immortals, didn't age the way humans did. So while this woman looked like jailbait, she was anything but. She was a warrior, a fighter, and a damn good one. But most of all, she was a member of the Stealth Guardian warriors assigned to Baltimore. And that particular group had caused him nothing but trouble.

Despite that, he'd lusted after this female warrior from the moment he'd first seen her. Enya. He'd fantasized about making her his personal slave once he'd defeated the Stealth Guardians and overthrown world order. Yes, his fantasies had been frequent and varied. Yet he'd never imagined that there could be another way. A better one. One by which Enya would become the key to his victory over the Stealth Guardians. And tonight, the opportunity was presenting itself. Was his luck finally turning?

Zoltan remained at the street corner where he'd first noticed her. She continued walking on the other side of the street until she reached a bar in the middle of the block. She walked inside with a confidence that made him suspect that this wasn't her first visit to this establishment. Through the glass front, he watched her sit down at the bar and talk to the bartender, who was already fixing a drink for her.

Perfect.

Zoltan was ready. His colored contact lenses concealed his demon-green eyes and turned them dark brown. He'd grown a goatee over the last few months, first because he couldn't be bothered to shave, then because he actually liked the look. He was well dressed, like a respectable businessman. It was his preferred disguise. Humans were so trusting when they met somebody who wore expensive clothes and was well groomed. Besides, he rocked this look.

Zoltan caught a glimpse of himself in the window of a store he passed. Oh yeah, he knew women liked the way he presented himself. And when he turned on his charm, they were all too eager to drop their panties. And by the looks of Enya's getup, she was out for more than just a drink. Yes, he knew exactly what a woman like that needed.

Tonight would be the beginning of the end for the Stealth Guardians.

And Enya would make it all possible.

ABOUT THE AUTHOR

Tina Folsom was born in Germany and has been living in English speaking countries since 1991. Tina has always been a bit of a globe trotter.

She lived in Munich, Lausanne, London, New York City, Los Angeles, San Francisco, and Sacramento. She has now made a beach town in Southern California her permanent home with her American husband and her dog.

She's written 50 romance novels in English most of which are translated into German, French, and Spanish.

https://tinawritesromance.com
tina@tinawritesromance.com

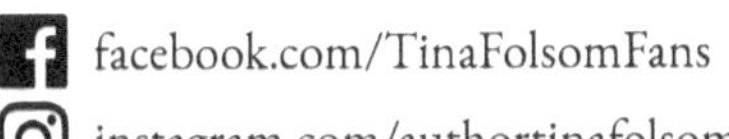

facebook.com/TinaFolsomFans
instagram.com/authortinafolsom